HOW TO GET EVEN

PIPPA ROSCOE

Boldwood

First published in Great Britain in 2025 by Boldwood Books Ltd.

Copyright © Pippa Roscoe, 2025

Cover Design by Lisa Horton

Cover Images: Lisa Horton

The moral right of Pippa Roscoe to be identified as the author of this work has been asserted in accordance with the Copyright, Designs and Patents Act 1988.

Every effort has been made to obtain the necessary permissions with reference to copyright material, both illustrative and quoted. We apologise for any omissions in this respect and will be pleased to make the appropriate acknowledgements in any future edition.

A CIP catalogue record for this book is available from the British Library.

Paperback ISBN 978-1-83633-162-9

Large Print ISBN 978-1-83633-163-6

Hardback ISBN 978-1-83633-161-2

Ebook ISBN 978-1-83633-164-3

Kindle ISBN 978-1-83633-165-0

Audio CD ISBN 978-1-83633-156-8

MP3 CD ISBN 978-1-83633-157-5

Digital audio download ISBN 978-1-83633-158-2

This book is printed on certified sustainable paper. Boldwood Books is dedicated to putting sustainability at the heart of our business. For more information please visit https://www.boldwoodbooks.com/about-us/sustainability/

Boldwood Books Ltd, 23 Bowerdean Street, London, SW6 3TN

www.boldwoodbooks.com

To Amy, Rachael, and Clare, I couldn't have written this book with any other authors. You're my ride or die, red-velvet-loving, prosecco-sipping, Delia-bonded sisters and I love you all!

SUN TZU ON THE ART OF WAR
THE OLDEST MILITARY TREATISE IN
THE WORLD
Translated from the Chinese
By LIONEL GILES, M.A. (1910)
[released as Project Gutenberg's eBook #132.]

IN THE BEGINNING...
CHICAGO, O'HARE AIRPORT, 21 DECEMBER

Bella ignored the phone that vibrated in her hand. Twice.

'Are you sure?' asked the flight attendant, blinking between her and the little old lady.

Bella looked at the large window showing a runway quickly becoming buried beneath mounds of snow from the sudden blizzard that had taken everyone by surprise.

Not that anyone should really be surprised by snow. In Chicago. Four days from Christmas.

'Ma'am? This is the last flight out of here,' she repeated, as if wanting to make absolutely sure Bella knew what she was doing. 'It could be hours before another one can leave.'

Bella heard the warning and looked into the green watery eyes of Delia, the elderly woman who was desperate to get home to hold her grandchild for the first time.

And what did Bella have waiting for her in Upstate New York?

A loving family, a huge tree with fairy lights topped with the angel her sister had made in third grade, presents, a delicious meal; all the things that almost any sane person would kill to have for Christmas.

Anyone but her.

'Absolutely. Please give Delia my seat and arrange for me to be on the next available flight,' Bella replied determinedly.

The flight attendant shook her head, but did as she was asked, while Bella fired off a text to her sister.

> I'm fine, honestly!

Please. Stop. Asking. Me. Bella silently begged.

> I'll let you know when I have flight details. Love to Mom and Dad! Xx

'Oh, thank you,' cried Delia, trembling with happiness. 'I just couldn't bear it if I'd missed her first Christmas.'

'Just promise to give that beautiful little girl a kiss from me,' Bella said with a genuine smile.

'I will! I truly will,' Delia exclaimed as the new boarding pass was printed.

The flight attendant shot Bella an unimpressed look as Delia grappled with her three bags, as if it were Bella's fault that the older woman was flouting hand baggage rules.

'Bless you, sweet child,' Delia said, nearly losing her book as she reached for the boarding pass. 'Oh here. Take this,' she said, thrusting the paperback at Bella. 'You probably need this more than I do,' she said with a saucy smile, disappearing down the gangway before the flight attendant pulled a rope across the exit.

Bella stared at the book in her hands, a lurid pink flyer peeking out from between the pages catching her eye.

Just Desserts, Opposite Gate 7

Pictures of cocktails and cakes in a pretty cartoon design called to her. She couldn't remember the last time she'd had cake. Certainly not since before the...

What did you call a wedding that didn't happen? An un-wedding? A non-wedding? Either way, before 'it', she'd been following a calorie-controlled diet to fit into the perfect wedding dress. The kind that all little girls – and a few boys too – dreamed of. The kind that her father had paid an almost eye-watering amount for.

Guilt and shame welled in her empty stomach, and suddenly, all Bella wanted was sugar. An obscene, high octane, chest exploding, fall-off-the-wagon amount of sugar. With the airport full of stranded passengers, she probably wouldn't get a seat. But maybe, just maybe, one good turn deserved another, she thought as she pulled the flyer from the page.

And then she choked on a gasp as she caught sight of the paragraph the flyer had been hiding.

Fuck me, Daddy. Please? I've been such a bad girl.

Bella slammed the book shut, looking around her to make sure that no one had seen what she had. Her cheeks flamed, hot and bright, and she used the book to fan them.

Delia!

She laughed at herself as she put the book into her purse.

Cake. Cocktails.

And then, maybe, she'd read that book.

Just Desserts loomed up ahead, bright and pink like a beacon amidst the chaos. Bella was hit with such a strong scent of caramel and chocolate that her mouth actually watered.

She scanned the café's packed tables. Each one was excessively full of people guarding them possessively, glaring at anyone who looked their way. She was about to give up when a woman with bright magenta streaks in her hair caught Bella's eye. Bella smiled back automatically, because there was something in the woman's eyes. Recognition? Expectation? Then the woman winked. Someone passed between them and the woman was gone, but there, in her place, it was – a table in the middle of the chaos shining like the Holy Grail.

Worried that it would disappear like a mirage, she hurried over and reached a chair just as another woman grabbed the one to her left, and another came careening out of nowhere, just managing to stop opposite her, before taking out a fourth woman who reached for the adjacent chair.

Bella's heart sank. If any of these women had companions, she'd have to give up her seat.

'If none of you are with anyone else, we could share?' the eclectic redhead asked in a British accent that reminded her a little of Olly.

Burying the thought beneath the relief she felt at finding a seat, Bella smiled and nodded. Introductions were made as layers of coats and scarves and bags were removed, each finally sitting down at the table with a sigh and a grateful smile.

Paige, the redhead with freckles and a gorgeous smile, was British, as was Astrid who had glossy brown hair and an aura of irrepressible energy that made Bella slightly wary. Sienna was a fellow American and had big blue eyes and golden hair that made her look like a Disney princess.

'Would you think me a terrible lush if I got a glass of prosecco?' Paige asked hesitantly.

Prosecco. It was ten in the morning and Bella would never ordinarily drink at such an hour. But suddenly she wanted to. Suddenly she wanted, more than anything, to be someone who drank when the fancy took her, ate as much cake as womanly possible. She wanted to be... a *bad* girl.

Bella cleared her throat and kicked the purse containing Delia's book further under the table.

'I'll have a glass,' she told the waitress after Sienna suggested getting a bottle. 'And some water for the table, please.' Bella wasn't quite prepared to let go of all her sensibilities in one fell swoop.

* * *

Bella squinted at the second bottle of prosecco. *When had they ordered that?* Deciding it was unimportant, she pressed her fingertip into the crumbs of her *second* red velvet cake, popped them into her mouth and savoured the mini sugar bombs exploding on her tongue as Astrid peppered Paige with questions about her Virtual Assistant business.

Astrid had her own business. Something she could be proud of. And Bella? Bella was hiding until the furore died down over the disaster of a wedding that never happened, so that she could finally assume her role at her parents' foundation.

Which was what she wanted, she reminded herself sternly.

'Is that why you're in the US? Work?' Astrid asked Paige.

'No. I was at a wedding in Chicago.'

Bella flinched.

'Oh, how lovely. How was it?' Sienna asked dreamily.

'You know. Pavlova dress.'

Bella's had been *sleek*. A twenty-thousand-dollar Vera Wang in ivory silk from the bustline down, topped by a swathe of delicate lace crossing her chest and arms.

'Drunken best man's speech.'

Bella had forbidden Olly's best man from drinking until after the ceremony.

'Smooshing cake into each other's faces. A handsy Uncle Chip.'

Bella downed the remainder of her prosecco, fearing the damp heat pressing against the backs of her eyes might actually, horrifyingly, escape. 'I'd rather not talk about weddings.' It was only the lump in her throat that stopped her from adding, *If that's okay*.

'Not a fan?' Paige asked.

'Absolutely not,' Bella confirmed.

'Don't believe in love?'

'I did,' Bella admitted. 'And then six months ago I stood up in front of 400 guests to let them know that my groom wasn't coming.'

She pressed her lips together to keep the sudden well of unruly emotions from escaping.

'Holy mother of...?' Astrid spluttered as she clutched Bella's forearm. 'You were jilted?'

'Yup. By text. The morning of.'

'By *text*?' Astrid's mouth flattened.

Bella smiled, letting the women's sympathy, their outrage, soothe the hurt caused by the wedding guests' horrified fascination.

'He's not a bad person, really, he just did a bad thing,' she admitted honestly. And he wasn't. But Olly had told her that he wanted to spend the rest of his life with her. Let her believe that, let her plan for how her life would be, *with him*. 'He was a bit of a...' She searched for the right word. 'Peter Pan. Commitment wasn't his strong suit and I made the classic mistake of thinking that it would be different with me,' she admitted with a shrug, feeling embarrassed and ashamed that she'd been so foolish.

'Doesn't excuse him leaving you at the altar,' Sienna said.

'Via *text*,' Astrid stressed, furiously.

'No, it doesn't,' Bella replied, reaching for her glass before realising it was empty and putting it back on the table.

'Well, you can string mine up,' Astrid announced. 'Unbeknownst to me he'd *already* trotted up that aisle and merrily said "I do" to someone else.'

'He turned you into the other woman?' Bella asked, outraged.

'Too right he did.'

'Are you freaking kidding me?' Sienna asked, shaking her head in disgust.

'He's an artist too. All about creating the feels in people... Chase Miller can give you "the feels" alright. The kind you want F all to do with.'

Chase Miller. Bella blinked in surprise. She'd seen one of his paintings only last month in Paris. She remembered it immediately. A huge, sprawling canvas that had stopped her in her tracks. How could such incredible talent be wasted on a man who would do such a thing? 'What is wrong with these men?' Bella demanded. 'Doesn't marriage mean anything any more?'

'I don't think men get the concept of commitment,' Sienna mused. 'Even the ones who seem to are just faking it.'

Bella leaned in, her heart going out to the sadness she felt from Sienna. 'What happened?'

'My ex kind of *discarded* me. It wasn't like some big, dramatic break up. I didn't even get the chance to throw plates. I mean, we were just kids, but we were each other's firsts, you know.' They all nodded in understanding. 'And I thought we were going to have a life together, but he hightailed it out of town without a backward glance.'

Just like Olly had done to her. Bella reached across to squeeze Sienna's hand. 'I'm so sorry,' she said. 'That's terrible.'

While the girls talked about beheading deserving men, Bella wondered whether perhaps life was better off without men altogether.

'My ex posted naked pictures and video of me on-line. He'd taken them without my knowledge or consent.'

Bella's head snapped up, Paige's words igniting a phosphorus flare deep inside her.

'Revenge porn?' hissed Sienna in disgust.

'I've never felt so *degraded*.' Paige's gaze dropped to the table, and the anger that Bella had kept at bay for months, morphed into a physical thing: a living, breathing monster that demanded payment for the hurt inflicted on Paige.

'I met Harvey at Oxford. He was studying IT and I was a third-year law student. No prestigious law firm was going to take me on after that. Hell, not even a terrible law firm would. And I couldn't bear staying on at Oxford, where everyone had seen the pictures. So I' – Paige shrugged – 'dropped out.'

Bella's heart thumped painfully. Olly might have

hurt her, but nothing, *nothing*, compared to the violation that Harvey had done to Paige. It was clear from the painful blush on Paige's freckled cheeks how much she struggled with it.

Bella clenched her hands into fists. 'What a *bastard*.'

'*Absolute* bastard,' Sienna agreed furiously.

The table fell quiet and Bella wondered if the others, like her, were imagining suitably painful punishments for Paige's evil ex.

'They shouldn't be allowed to get away with that kind of crap,' Sienna said eventually.

Astrid slapped her glass down on the table. 'Damn right they shouldn't.'

'What if we...' Sienna glanced around the circle and leaned in a little. 'Look I know this sounds crazy and I may be a little drunk...'

Bella wondered if they were *all* a little drunk.

'What if we took it upon ourselves,' Sienna continued. 'To exact some revenge.'

Bella frowned, curious despite herself. 'How do you mean?'

'I don't mean murdering them or anything,' she dismissed, which was, Bella thought, a shame in Harvey's instance. 'I mean... look, these guys have had everything go their way, right? They got to walk all over us. Or walk *out* on us. Why should they just get to live their best lives while we're picking up the remnants of ours?

'Why not have a little fun at their expense?' Sienna continued. 'Nothing serious. Stuff that would inconvenience them. That we could have a laugh over. Like signing them up to hundreds of mailing lists. Switch out their clothes for a size or two smaller. That kind of thing.'

The idea struck something in Bella, like a tuning fork finally hitting the perfect note.

For years, Bella had done everything in her power to do the right thing. *Don't cause a scene, don't make a fuss.* Hell, she even co-ordinated the unpicking of her own wedding even though she hadn't been the one to call it off. But while she was considering being a little naughty, it didn't mean she'd suddenly become reckless.

She leaned in. 'Some of those things would require us to get close,' she said, almost at a whisper. 'They'll know it was us. There's no way we'd get away with it.'

Sienna smiled triumphantly. 'That's why we pick someone else's ex.'

Oh, that was good.

'Who would you pick?'

'I'd take your cheating, married, *bastard* ex,' Bella declared, cheeks flush with an anger she'd spent far too long suppressing. Chase Miller had pulled the rug out from beneath not one but *two* women and he deserved to pay.

As the girls divvied up the rest of the ex-boyfriends, the idea gained momentum in Bella's mind.

'Look, this only works if we all agree,' Sienna said, suddenly serious. 'And nobody should feel pressured into doing it if it doesn't sit right.'

'God, fuck yes,' Astrid declared, slightly less enthusiastic than she had been before. 'The last thing I want to do is browbeat my new co-conspirators. Sorry, *besties.*'

Best friends. The phrase caught at something in Bella's chest and pulled. The truth was, she wanted to do this. Not just for herself, but for them too.

As if feeling the same, she felt Paige's gaze on hers. Paige would, if they all agreed, be tackling Olly; her job as a house-sitter making her the perfect person to invade the pristine hidey hole he'd slunk back to in Cornwall, England.

'I do love a good cream tea,' Paige said with a small smile. 'I'd be safe there?'

'Definitely,' Bella reassured her. 'For all his commitment-phobe tendencies, he's a gentleman. And I know he feels bad. Which I'm perfectly okay with exploiting to get you in there. I still have his number,' she offered.

Paige looked a little hesitant, and suddenly it felt absolutely vital that Paige say yes. That this happen. Because if it didn't then Olly'd got away scot-free and—

'Look. How about this? What if Bella texts and then we leave it up to the universe,' Sienna suggested. 'If he texts back while we're all still sitting here at this table we randomly ended up at, then it's a go. If he doesn't? We've all had a laugh and filled in a few hours. No harm no foul,' Sienna offered with a shrug.

'Ooh, I like that,' Astrid added.

'Me too,' Bella said, and she did. Because it meant that the universe had decided it. Not four women who had quite possibly consumed more alcohol than was advisable.

'Okay, yeah,' Paige said, nodding once, definitively. 'Okay.'

Bella felt everyone's eyes on her as she took out her phone.

'Olly, a friend of mine needs a place to stay in Cornwall for a bit in the New Year. She's very nice and won't bother you,' she read as she typed.

She paused. It needed something *more*.

'You have room,' she typed. 'And you owe me,' she added for good measure, before hitting send and putting the phone onto the table.

And there it sat, in the centre of their circle, everyone staring at it as if it were an unexploded bomb.

Don't answer it.

Answer it.

Her conscience wavered back and forth. A nervous silence stretched over the table until it became almost funny until the incoming text chimed and startled them all.

'Is she a Roger Prendergast groupie?' she read out loud.

Not, lovely to hear from you. How are you? How have you been? Are you okay after telling our family and friends that I couldn't bring myself to marry you?

When Paige admitted that she didn't know Olly's famous actor father, Bella typed out a single word, 'No.'

And his response was lightning fast.

'He says fine,' Bella confirmed, unable to believe how easy that was.

Because that's what it had been. Easy. And now, all of a sudden, Paige, a virtual stranger, was going down to Cornwall to stay with her ex-fiancé to wreak revenge for her. And she was going to take revenge against Astrid's married lover Chase Miller.

But as she looked around the similarly shocked faces of women who she knew with absolute conviction were no longer strangers but friends who had bonded deeply, no matter how quickly, she felt something that she hadn't felt in a very long time.

Excited.

'Okay then,' Paige said with a smile. 'Looks like I'm off to Cornwall.'

Without quite knowing how, another bottle of prosecco arrived on the table, and Astrid filled their glasses.

'To just desserts,' she announced as 'Last Christmas,' could be heard over the PA system and they all tapped their glasses together.

Paige took a hefty swallow and turned to Bella. 'Now, tell me more about this Olly.'

* * *

With the table now littered with water bottles and packets of chips, a concession to savoury carbs that they had all agreed on, Bella sat back in her chair. She was surprisingly exhausted after info-dumping an almost encyclopaedic knowledge of the man she'd been about to marry onto Paige who had just excused herself to make a phone call.

Bella was beginning to sober up and the sugar high was threatening to turn into a sugar crash. She'd thought that perhaps that might make her see sense. Might make her feel a little wary about what they had agreed. But it hadn't.

If anything, this gave her something to do over the Christmas period. Something to think about instead of her parents' awkwardly given concern. It gave her something to *plan*. And Bella was very good at plans.

She picked up her phone, pulled up Google and typed in Chase Miller.

The first few hits were various photos of him in poses that would be considered an 'artist at work'. Bella huffed out a cynical laugh. He probably had art assistants who did most of the actual painting. The next result was a picture of Chase grimly staring into the camera lens.

'That's from my profile. The one I wrote,' Astrid said, leaning over and peering at her screen. 'It's how we met,' she explained.

Bella scanned the piece. 'It's good,' she observed. 'It's really good.'

'I know,' Astrid said, with an easy, and wholly justified, confidence.

Astrid's profile was informative, easy to read, and wry. Her personality shone through but didn't dominate, giving a solid impression of her subject. It was as if Bella was reading a meeting of the minds and she could see how Astrid would have found Chase Miller fascinating.

Fascinating and dangerous.

And clearly a lying, cheating, scumbag.

As she swiped to another page, the announcement of a new gallery opening in New York caught her eye.

CHASE MILLER TO HEAD NEW YORK NAYAK GALLERY THIS SPRING.

Bella frowned. Why would someone in supposedly the height of their creative career take a job as gallery director?

What was he running from? Probably from another scandal, Bella thought. That was how these men worked, wasn't it? For all they knew, Astrid could have been just the tip of the iceberg. Well, Bella wasn't going to let that happen. He didn't get to just start all over again. None of them did.

Then she caught sight of a job posting.

Communications director for Nayak New York.

Huh.

Well. She *did* have some time to kill before she took up her role at her parents' foundation, didn't she?

She felt Astrid's gaze on her.

'What?'

'I don't know what you're planning,' Astrid said, 'but the look in your eyes says you're up to no good. And I like it.'

Bella bit the inside of her cheek but couldn't stop smiling. Astrid was right. Because Bella, the perennially good girl, was about to do some very bad things. And Chase Miller wouldn't even know what hit him.

1

All warfare is based on deception.

— *THE ART OF WAR*, SUN TZU

JUST DESSERTS WHATSAPP
GROUP. 15.05 EST.

ASTRID

Bella, you're panicking, aren't you?

SIENNA

Are you? Are you okay?

PAIGE

A little panic is understandable.

Bella bit her lip. She was very much trying *not* to panic, but as she let herself into her brand-new apartment with absolutely *huge* floor-to-ceiling windows that beckoned her towards them with a display of Central Park that most Americans would give their right arm for, it was safe to say that her current state was absolutely and undeniably one of panic.

What on earth had she got herself into?

ASTRID

Are you in yet? What's the flat like?

The serviced apartment was amazing. Bella was hardly a stranger to wealth, but this? She turned around in a circle, taking in the modern kitchen, laundry facilities and near futuristic amenities. The apartment had a voice-activated home assistant, and twenty-four-hour access to a concierge who had already let her know about a delivery waiting for her. Her family had country money, *old* money. But this? This was *city* money. Urban. Luxurious. Modern.

She placed her bag on the kitchen island and took in the minimalist design that defined elegance. A buttery soft caramel leather sofa set bracketed a fireplace, the surround a modern concrete strip against the clean white walls. A large cream sheepskin rug sat on hardwood flooring that warmed the grey tones of brushed chrome furnishings.

It should have looked cold and uninviting, but it was easy to imagine herself curled up on the sofa covered in a blanket, or bare toes curling in that sheepskin. In a daze she wandered towards the door off the living area and entered a bedroom that stopped her in her tracks.

Her phone buzzed from messages flying back and forth between the girls, but Bella barely noticed. At least half were from Astrid who was also in New York and trying to find time in a very busy schedule for them to meet up.

Here too, floor-to-ceiling windows offered a view of Manhattan that was breathtaking. Winter's dusk painted the sky in remarkable shades of pinks and early evening purples. A few stars were out already, peeking down on the snow-covered rectangle of Central Park stretched out in front of her.

Of course, the position comes with an apartment, Tejvir Nayak had informed her eagerly during their second interview over video conference. His willingness to hire her had surprised her, even though Paige – who had finessed Bella's CV with something bordering on ruthlessness – had insisted that she would be a shoe-in for it.

Having applied for the job in between Christmas and New Year she'd not expected to hear anything until mid-January at the earliest, so it had been quite the surprise to find a reply waiting in her inbox the following morning.

'He's desperate,' Astrid had announced gleefully.

'I wonder why the previous person left,' Sienna had asked.

'Does it matter?' Paige had intervened.

Not. One. Bit. Bella had decided.

Tej Nayak had been affable and laid back to a point that nearly caused Bella concern, but as the job was simply a means to an end it hardly mattered. In fact, Tej had been almost more excited about the apartment she would be staying in than the role of communications director she would be filling.

You're gonna love it. And just wait until you try the shower, her new boss had said affably, while Bella wondered if that was entirely appropriate. *It has everything you could need. And if it doesn't? Then let me know, and we'll get it for you.*

PAIGE

Have you seen him yet?

Him. Her target. Chase Miller. The cheating

scumbag who had betrayed his wife *and* an un-knowing Astrid. Bella wandered towards the incred-ible view, barely seeing the wintery magic of New York stretched out beneath her. And just like that, panic melted like ice beneath the salt of her fury.

It had been hard for her to be angry with Olly, which she knew was crazy. The girls' outrage at his behaviour had soothed a wound she'd been hiding from the world. Hidden, because Bella Carmichael didn't get angry. Didn't cause a fuss, or make a scene.

And even though Olly had stood her up in front of nearly four hundred of their closest friends and family... she *knew* he hadn't meant to. Well, no... he absolutely 100 per cent had meant to, actually. He'd done so because it was easier to leave her to clean up his mess. And he'd known she'd do it. Because that was what she did.

But she also saw how he would have struggled to tell her that he couldn't go through with it. How it all would have become too much for him. But Olly was different to Chase Miller. Because there was abso-lutely no justification for what he'd done. None whatsoever.

BELLA

I haven't met him yet. But I promise, when I do, he'll rue the day.

SIENNA

Oh, I love it when you talk posh like that.

Bella smiled, taking the affectionate teasing from Sienna exactly as it was meant.

ASTRID

Have you figured out what you're going to do to him yet?

Perhaps if she'd known Bella for longer, Astrid wouldn't have even asked the question because Bella had everything short of a PowerPoint presentation on how she was going to ruin Chase Miller. She had ordered a copy of Sun Tzu's *The Art of War*, and decided that the book of military strategies and tactics was perfect to help her get even with Astrid's ex. She'd filled an entire journal with research she'd done during the awkward Christmas she'd spent with her family and sister... and Bea's new fiancé.

Bella swallowed, hating herself for feeling mean about her sister. Bella would *never* begrudge her sister's happiness. But Bella couldn't help but remember how she and Olly had announced their engagement. How her parents had oohed and ahhed over *her* engagement ring.

Her father had seemed rather impressed by Olly, who she'd met at a charity gala for Non-Hodgkin lymphoma. She'd known of Oliver Prendergast, of course. You couldn't be female and *not* know of him. And while on the surface the son of the famed British actor had been exactly what she'd expected – 99 per cent charm – there had been something deeper that had called to her. He was educated, bright, witty. He'd made her laugh and when he'd asked for her number, she'd given it to him.

Over the next few months they'd met up when he was visiting New York, or when she was near California and they'd fallen into a long-distance relationship. And the glimpses she got of the real Olly, the one behind the mask, were enough to make her believe that they had something special.

Then his father had died and he'd seemed so lost that she'd wanted to be there for him. Bella hadn't minded making the preparations for the funeral, managing his family and bringing them all together. So then when Olly had asked her to marry him, it had felt like the natural progression of their relationship. She'd honestly thought that he was ready, wanted to spend the rest of his life with her. And she had what she'd always wanted: her person. Someone who would stand by her. Who would keep her. Who would *choose* her.

But she'd been wrong. And now her sister was embarking on the life that she'd always wanted and Bella hated how hard that was to watch. But she'd shoved her hurt behind a locked door, and taken Bea, who deserved every damn bit of happiness coming to her, into her arms and told her truthfully how happy she was for her.

Only her mother hadn't looked wholly convinced. But when she'd tried to ask Bella about it, Bella had shaken it off. Because she was fine, wasn't she?

So, it had been a blessed relief to be able to beg off the family festive joy a little and focus on exactly what would be the perfect karmic comeuppance for a man like Chase Miller. And while her family thought that she was prepping for a job interview, which she *had* been, she'd also been working out how to make a man like that hurt.

Because it wasn't through his heart. He clearly didn't have one.

No. It was his ego. His reputation. His standing in the art world.

BELLA

Oh yes, don't you worry about that.
I have a plan.

* * *

Chase Miller had a headache. One of those take-me-out-back-and-kill-me-now kinds. It had, perhaps, been stupid to try and 'smash it out at the gym', even though sometimes that did actually work. Especially when the headache was hangover-related. Which it was. But the gym had *not* worked today, he reluctantly acknowledged as he swallowed down an entire bottle of electrolyte water.

Sweat stuck his vest to his chest, and his gym shorts to his ass in a unique and distinctly uncomfortable way. He just needed to get back in to his apartment, and then he could drown under the weight of the, as promised, impressive jets of water in the en-suite shower. Man, Tej really did love talking about that shower.

And he had not lied. It was an excellent shower.

He massaged his temples as the elevator rose from the basement gym to the lobby, where the doors slid open. Eyes closed, he heard someone shuffle their way into the elevator, just as his phone began to ring because, thanks to Tej's insistence, the entire building was wired for Wi-Fi. Chase bit back a groan, accepted the call and tried to ignore the walking pile of boxes next to him.

'You are not allowed to scare this one off,' Tej announced by way of a greeting.

'This one what?' Chase growled. It was the third call he'd fielded from his old friend/new business partner that day.

'You can thank me later.'

'Thank you?'

'You're welcome,' Tej announced with glee.

'No, wait. What?' Chase asked as he dug a thumb into his throbbing temple and fielded the cell and his water bottle in the other hand. 'Who?'

'The new director of comms. She starts Monday.'

Chase let out a scoff. 'Shouldn't I have had some say in hiring?'

The mountain of boxes next to him shifted their weight from one high-heeled foot to the other.

'Yeah, well. We didn't really have time to fuck around, my friend. We're opening in just three months, and your last hire quit.'

'Before I could fire her,' Chase pointed out.

'And this one can start tomorrow. So there.'

'Name.'

'Bella Carmichael.'

Chase frowned. Why did he recognise that name? Did he? Or was he just so hungover his brain was playing tricks on him?

'She's—'

'A pampered princess socialite,' he remembered now.

The boxes shifted again.

'She has a degree in Business Management and Communication from Harvard.'

'They *all* have degrees,' Chase ground out. 'Isn't her father something big in aerodynamics?'

People like Bella Carmichael didn't have dads, like his. They had *fathers*. Mothers. *Maters and Paters*.

'How can you remember that, and not my birthday?' Tej asked defensively.

How could he not? The day he'd landed back in the States, the papers had been filled with headlines about the Redondo Runaway Groom, or something like it. The damn catchy alliteration had stuck.

Miles of column inches had been full of speculation as to why the groom had disappeared – many laying the blame at bridezilla-Bella's feet. Someone had knocked together a guestimation of how much the entire wedding had cost. It was a mind-numbing amount of money, even to Chase, who had at one point been considered to be one of the most sought-after contemporary artists around the globe. And certainly inconceivable to the son of a mechanic and a librarian.

The black-and-white pictures of the abandoned reception at the Californian vineyard had felt almost crime-scene worthy; slashes of white silk rippling in the wind from ribbons tied on the backs of empty seats, an ornate flower garland arbour where the bride and groom should have stood.

He and Annalise hadn't had anything like that. Jesus, they'd had a registry office and his best friend as a witness. At the time it had felt urgent and romantic and fucking idiot that he was, he'd thought he was the luckiest guy on the plant.

No. Chase knew exactly who the luckiest guy on the planet was. The Redondo Runaway Groom. Chase could only imagine what kind of bridezilla could scare off a fiancé on the day of their supposed wedding, despite the volume of scrutiny they were under. Clearly, the guy had made a lucky escape.

And now Chase was lumped with that very same bridezilla.

'Does she even have any experience?' Chase demanded. 'Why does she want this job, huh? So that she can swan around New York saying she works at the Nayak Gallery?'

'Dude,' Tej exhaled. 'There are genuinely worse reasons.'

'No, there aren't,' Chase bit back, knowing that it wasn't true. He wasn't quite sure why he was so adamant that he didn't want her working there.

His mind's eye flashed him a black-and-white photo of her on her supposed wedding day. The camera had caught her mid-turn, hair in some sleek updo, lace slashed across her torso, the delicate arc of a shoulder blade highlighted in shadow. Her face, pure elegance. Even in the midst of such chaos. Her grace had somehow infuriated him. Because surely, she couldn't have remained so calm if she had even an ounce of feeling for the person who had betrayed her?

He hadn't.

'Jesus, Tej. If she can't even hold down a groom, how is she supposed to hold down a job?'

'Okay. Enough, bro. You've got your grump on, I get that. And usually I'm amenable to that, given... you know. But now you're just being mean.'

Being scolded by Tej was like being scolded by your favourite school teacher, or your grannie. As someone who was almost singularly good-natured, it was the verbal equivalent of, 'I'm not angry, I'm just disappointed.'

What was worse was that Tej was right. Chase *was* being mean. He had absolutely no idea what kind of person Bella Carmichael was and he – of all people – wasn't in a position to make assumptions.

Chase began to mumble something about a headache, but Tej pressed on.

'She *is* qualified for the position, she *does* have experience, I *do* have faith that she is what we need, and I think that you will both work excellently together. And since she'll be living next to you, I expect you to be on your best behaviour.'

Chase's gut tightened as he side-eyed the boxes in the elevator beside him.

Shit. Fuck. *Shit.*

He glanced at the floor numbers on the elevator panel and only his floor was lit up. *His* floor.

Their floor?

Oh God, this was bad.

'Gotta go,' Chase said, swiping across the phone's screen and slipping it into the pocket of his gym shorts.

He bit his lip, mentally wincing. It was possible that the person behind the boxes, boxes usually used for moving things, like a person's life into a new apartment, *wasn't* the person he'd just been mouthing off about.

Possible. But horrifyingly unlikely.

The elevator arrived at the floor and the doors opened.

'After you,' he said, voice gravelly from the guilt lining his throat.

The boxes rippled. Was he imagining things? Christ, he hoped so.

But as the boxes passed him, he caught a glimpse of a high cheekbone and a sleek blonde chignon.

Fuuuuuck. He inwardly groaned.

He ran his hand through his hair as he followed in her wake. There was no shaking this off. *Christ,* what had he called her? A pampered princess socialite?

He kept his eyes firmly above ass level as she walked straight over to the door opposite his and put the boxes down to reach for her key.

'Do you need a hand?' he offered reflexively before wincing at the look she gave him as she straightened up.

'No,' she answered. And then, as if absolutely incapable of stopping herself, she added a 'thank you', that was as much 'fuck you' as humanly possible.

There were slight traces of red slashes across her sharp cheekbones and he could see it. Why she'd made such an impact on him.

She looked him dead in the eyes.

Complex and varied shards of grey slammed at him like an assault. The flecks of gold both hot as fire and cold as ice, reminded him of Turner's *Snow Storm*. Movement, slashes of anger, defiance, determination.

And for the first time in nearly twelve months his right hand twitched. The itch as if from a phantom limb, taking him wholly by surprise. He rubbed the back of his neck to buy some time as he gathered himself.

'Look, I'm s—'

The door slammed before he'd even finished the word.

And yes. He deserved that.

* * *

JUST DESSERTS WHATSAPP
GROUP. 21.36 EST.

BELLA

That man is a... you know what.

PAIGE

You can say it, Bella. We're all
adults here!

SIENNA

What happened?

ASTRID

My money's on Bella meeting
Chase Miller.

BELLA

The man is a menace. The worst
kind of snob. Mean and utterly
undignified.

ASTRID

Sounds like Chase Miller.

BELLA

I. Am. Going. To. Make. Him. Pay.

PAIGE

Yes you are!!

ASTRID

You go, girl! 😄

2

[She] will win who, prepared [herself], waits to take the enemy unprepared.

— *THE ART OF WAR*, SUN TZU

OPERATION TROJAN HORSE

- Lull CM into false sense of security.
- Identify key players.
- Become likeable.
- Become invaluable.

Bella had identified the location of the gallery fifteen minutes ahead of her arrival, had visited the highest rated coffee shop within a four-minute walking radius, and was now standing on West 30th, on a very cold January morning in New York, in front of what would be the Nayak Gallery.

A glass-fronted ground floor framed in thick black metal with gold edges created a stark contrast with the classic New York limestone building. Central enough for decent foot traffic, and certainly in the right district for art, the gallery was well positioned between culture and cuisine to make it an attractive prospect for visitors and that was without Nayak's name already making it worth a look.

Chase Miller as gallery director drew even more notoriety. His reputation as an artist, albeit slightly longer than a New York minute ago, was still impressive and one that some artists would be uncomfortable vying for attention with. But then again, notoriety was notoriety and in the art world, that meant money.

Her fingers gripped the stacked cardboard trays holding enough coffee cups to allow for nearly every possible permutation of coffee possible.

Chase Miller.

It had been one thing to look him up online and another all together to see him in person.

Being forced to listen to the litany of her perceived inadequacies by a man who had cheated on his wife and dragged another woman unwittingly in to the mire with him, had been nothing short of galling. By the time she had exited the elevator and reached her door, she'd been almost trembling with rage.

Until she'd put down the boxes and turned to find all six-foot-four, sweaty, toned inches of the man looking somewhat embarrassed at having been caught bad-mouthing his new direct report.

And then she'd been trembling for a whole different reason.

But her initial, and momentarily confusing, response to him had only been – she decided at some point around 2 a.m. the following morning – because she had expected Chase Miller to have devil horns and crimson skin.

So, seeing him dressed in sweaty workout gear that showed off a physique she would admit only on pain of death was nothing short of spectacular, had been simply that: the difference between expectation and reality.

Usually, Bella would urge on the side of charitable. He clearly hadn't known it was her, and she could concede that he had every right – as director – to question the qualifications, or lack thereof, of his new staff member. But Bella was done being charitable.

No, she was here to declare war on Chase Miller and his ilk. Sun Tzu-level war.

She glanced up. The number seventy-two was placed in simple, but elegant gold typography. The thick glass door, sandwiched in between two large front windows, with a thick strip of frost running across both, afforded a little privacy while creating curiosity too.

Nerves unfurled within her. What if she wasn't good at the job? What if the other staff didn't like her?

And then, a very Paige-sounding voice said, *You got the job. We didn't lie on your CV.*

Astrid mentally chimed in too. *Listen love, you handled that press storm around your wedding, you can sure as shit handle the comms for a gallery. At least until you need to that is.*

One month ago, she hadn't even known these women existed. And now she knew them well enough to hear them in her head!

But they were right. She wasn't here to do a *good* job. She was here to do a *certain* job. And that job was to secure the downfall of Chase Miller by any means necessary. And *that* Bella was certain she *could* do.

Shifting the tray of coffees to one hand, she

pressed the button with the little bell sign on the intercom.

'Hello?'

'Bella Carmichael,' she said, confidently. 'Your new communications director.'

* * *

Bella stepped out of the grey frosty cold into the warm embrace of soothing neutral tones and temperature-controlled warmth and gave in to the temptation to sigh.

The frosted windows either side of the entrance had concealed a large space that was surprisingly comforting despite its bare white walls. There were tracks along the ceiling which she presumed were for moveable walls to create smaller separate areas for a more intimate viewing and towards the back of the gallery the space opened out in an area that could be used either for group pieces or individual artwork that commanded greater focus and attention.

'Oh my God, it's really you,' a female voice exclaimed at a level of such surprise, Bella wondered whether the 'you' was actually someone else.

She turned to find a young brunette with wide brown eyes looking at her with something like awe.

Frowning, Bella resisted the urge to look behind her.

'You're so pretty!' the girl exclaimed and at this Bella's eyebrows shot upwards.

'I—'

'And I'm so sorry about your wedding!'

The rapid fire of statements caught Bella in a stunned vortex.

'Alison Burberry, you leave that poor woman alone,' a strong masculine voice ordered from the bottom of a staircase at the back of the gallery.

She watched as a tall man regally descended from the floor above. He had cheekbones half of Manhattan would die for and glowing ebony skin. The look he sent her was sceptical – but it wasn't anything she hadn't overcome before.

'Mr Bamboux,' she said, placing the name to the face from her research on the gallery. She closed the distance between them, hand outstretched. 'It's really lovely to meet you.'

'Mmm,' he replied, as if the jury was out and would remain firmly out until she proved herself worthy. Bella maintained her smile, respecting that territorial lines were being drawn.

'It's so nice to meet you,' Alison exclaimed and for a second Bella thought she might actually jump up and down. 'Me and my sister were also Alpha Phis and saw you speak at the NHL charity in Boston three years ago.'

For a moment, Bella's mind blanked. That was the night she'd met Olly and it took more effort than she'd care to admit to yank herself back from it.

Glaring at the girl, Bamboux inhaled his impatience before continuing, 'Please call me Maurice. The offices are this way,' he said, leading her towards the back of the gallery. 'There'll be time for a full tour a little later, but we have a 9.30 meeting scheduled.'

Bella checked her watch with a frown. Nine twenty-five. 'I'm sorry, I wasn't aware of the meeting,' she said, unsure how she'd missed that. She'd spent the whole of yesterday synching her phone to her Nayak email account and reading through all the messages she'd been copied in on following her hire. Worried that she'd not activated her alerts correctly, she pulled out her phone to double-check.

'That's okay. The email only came through ten minutes ago.'

Nope. Nothing.

Maurice peered over her shoulder. 'An oversight, I'm sure.'

Unconvinced, Bella followed Maurice upstairs into a surprisingly light space. More glass walls sectioned the floor into two rooms and an open kitchenette with a break-out area. The same frosted strip from outside the gallery continued in here, affording staff some privacy while also maintaining that sense of light and space.

One room contained four desks, which she presumed would be for her, Maurice, Alison and the art intern they employed when he wasn't studying at college, Ye-Joon. The opposite room, containing one large desk and a sofa sectional for guests would be Chase's office.

Maurice opened the door to their office and gestured to the only table bare of the various layers of chaos that could be seen on the other desks.

'Mine?' she asked with a smile.

He nodded and Alison rushed to her side.

'I've set you up with everything you'll need. There are binders with the current gallery schedule, prospective artists, client lists, as well as all the list of current vendors and some prospective ones.'

Alison's words rushed out and Bella affectionately surfed the tsunami of enthusiasm.

'I was going to offer to make you coffee, but...'

'I brought you all some instead,' Bella said, holding up the tray. 'Thank you though, Alison.'

'Oh, please call me Ali. Everyone else does.'

Maurice hmmed.

'Well, *almost* everyone else,' Ali confided with an eye roll.

'Perhaps we could have the coffee at the meeting,' Bella hedged, looking to Maurice who confirmed her thought with a nod. 'There are some extra shots and some hot milk, in case I got the orders wrong.'

'Kind of you,' Maurice replied in clipped tones that still conveyed his Martinique heritage.

'The last comms director would *never* have—'

'Alison Burberry,' Maurice exclaimed with such outrage Bella had to bite her lip to stop from laughing.

Alison blushed prettily but the need to gossip filled her fit to burst. Maurice's frustration was as harmless as it was affectionate – and who could blame him. Alison was like a golden retriever puppy, all happy and excitable.

She turned to see Chase stalking through the offices with a natural authority that felt like an afront to Bella. But even she couldn't deny that he commanded attention. This time, he was dressed in a long dark wool coat, collar upturned with a dark orange scarf draped around his neck. A navy blue knit jumper clung to his torso and even the frosted glass failed to mar the dark blue jeans that clung lovingly to thighs she remembered from the day before yesterday.

She could understand how Astrid had been taken in. There was no doubt about it, Chase Miller had looks. But looks were deceiving and Bella was glad that she'd been on her guard from the very beginning.

'And so it begins,' Maurice proclaimed ominously, before tapping his watch to remind them of the meeting.

And so it begins, indeed.

* * *

Chase stalked into the office at 9.29, already in a mood. He'd hoped to have seen Bella in the apartment block but she had remained elusive. And while the last place he'd ever wanted to have this conversation was in the office that they now both shared, it was all he had. He knew he needed to apologise and this time he wouldn't let her shake him off.

At least he'd done a little more research on Bella Carmichael, including reading her CV, and while it still remained to be seen whether she was, in fact, a pampered princess socialite, she certainly *was* qualified for the role. At least, more qualified than the last one.

He removed his jacket and hung it up, dropping his bag beside his desk and turning on the computer. For a moment, he saw himself from outside his body, this smart clothed stranger, settling into a near enough nine-to-five job with a pension and healthcare.

Not once in his childhood had he ever wanted this, or anything like it. It certainly wasn't what his mother had imagined for him. And somewhere deep inside was that seven-year-old boy telling him that he still didn't want it. That he shouldn't be here. He should be elbows-deep in oil paints, acrylic and terps. His fingers twitched reflexively, as if in response to the absence of a paintbrush, before he shoved that thought aside as Maurice knocked on the door to the office.

He nodded and Maurice and Ali came in and sat on the sofa, leaving the two armchairs on the other side of the coffee table free.

Chase frowned, rounding his desk. 'Is she coming?' he asked Maurice.

'Yes, but not because you invited her,' Maurice replied tartly.

Chase closed his eyes and bit back a curse. It

seemed that once again he was on the back foot with his new comms director.

Through the glass walls he saw her at the kitchenette. He braced himself for what he knew he needed to do. For what he should have done immediately after the incident in the lift.

'Give me a moment,' he tossed over his shoulder as he made his way out of his office and into the kitchen area.

She had her back to him. Cream wide-legged pants were nipped in at the waist with a gold belt. A matching cashmere polo neck jumper made her look elegant again. Gold earrings winked in the kitchen's lighting and by the time he reached her face, he realised she'd turned and caught him staring.

Shit.

Why did she make him feel like a naughty school boy?

'I owe you an apology,' he said, straight out. 'There isn't an excuse for what you overheard in the elevator. I was presumptuous and rude,' he admitted, 'and I'm sorry.'

She stared at him in a way that made him wonder if they taught classes to society women on how to make you feel inadequate. She put the lid back on one of the four take-out coffee cups in a carry tray on the counter, nodded once to acknowledge his apology and returned that startling grey gaze back on him.

The weight of that gaze was unfamiliar. Heavier than it should have been, assessing and perhaps secretive even. But then in a heartbeat everything changed.

'Of course. You couldn't have known,' she offered with a smile and a kindness that he probably didn't deserve but wanted to take with both hands.

She shrugged as if dismissing the matter and held out her hand to shake.

'I'm Bella and I'm really looking forward to working with you.'

She held his gaze as he took her hand in a shake.

'Chase Miller,' he said by way of finally introducing himself, trying to ignore the unaccountable feeling he got when they touched. 'It's nice to meet you.'

She nodded, that little curve to the edge of her lips suggesting... warmth? No, that didn't quite feel right. It was harder than that. More knowing. *Wry*.

She picked up the cardboard tray of coffees and waited for him. 'Shall we?' she asked, head gesturing to the meeting.

'Yes,' he said, nodding more firmly than necessary.

He was pretty sure that he'd escaped a little less scathed than he should be, but he'd take it. Because professionally he needed something to go his way. He'd just about managed to surf the rumours surrounding the change in direction of his career – with Tej's help at least. And he was pretty sure that once news of the sudden departure of the last comms director got out, it wouldn't help him one bit. What he needed now was smooth sailing, all the way to the opening. And whether he liked it or not, he was going to need Bella Carmichael on side to do it.

He led her back to his office and they settled in around the coffee table where Maurice and Ali were already sat, reaching for the coffee cups in front of them. Bella pushed a paper cup with a lid towards him.

'That's okay, I like my coffee a particular way,' he dismissed before she could get offended. Or *more* offended at least.

Her smile pulled at a lip a dusky shade of rose.

'I know,' she said simply and pushed the cup towards him again.

He eyed it suspiciously. He was still deeply attached to his morning coffee *and* the very specific amount of sugar required to keep him *compos mentis* at this point in the day.

He picked it up, all eyes on him, and hoped that the scent of the coffee would give him advance warning of any alien flavours, lack thereof, *or* – given the first impression he'd made on the new comms director – poison.

Smelling nothing – while noting that there were a good number of poisons that had no scent whatsoever – he clenched his jaw before taking the smallest possible sip, without being seen to be rude.

He tried to keep the pleasant surprise from his features as he welcomed the rush of coffee that was, as his father used to say, strong enough to fight back. No milk, obscene quantities of sugar and caffeine. A lot of caffeine.

'Thank you,' he said, somewhat bemused.

'You're welcome. Maurice was kind enough to advise me on your coffee preference.'

Maurice accepted the credit, but Chase's gaze returned to Bella. A distant part of his brain – the one he couldn't switch off, no matter how useless it was – categorised the parts of her features that drew his attention. She was bordering on conventionally beautiful – which for an artist was about as repellent as you could possibly get. But...

And it was the 'but' that kept him coming back. Something he couldn't quite put his finger on...

Maurice cleared his throat and Chase, realising he was staring, remembered where he was.

Shit. Get it together, dude.

Leaning back in his chair, he pulled out the pad he'd been making his notes on.

'First order of business is to welcome the new comms director. Bella Carmichael, this is Maurice Bamboux our registrar and archivist, responsible for everything that happens inside the gallery as well as the archives and catalogues. Alison Burberry, our receptionist and general gallery assistant. And later on in the week you'll meet Ye-Joon, our intern, who handles the pieces and manages the storage in the basement level below the gallery on the ground floor,' he concluded.

'Thank you,' she said with a beauty-queen-level smile. 'And thank you for giving me this opportunity. I know that my... *history*,' she said, her head cocked to one side, 'might give the impression that I... mmm, how should I put this, that I'm a bit of a spoiled socialite.'

Chase felt his cheeks flush.

'But I have every confidence that I will be an asset to the team, once I've got fully up to speed. And I can assure you that I want nothing less than a roaring success to the opening of the Nayak New York.'

Ali clapped and did a little jiggle in her seat, and Maurice scowled a little less.

She had been eloquent, humble, affable and sincere – and even managed to put him in his place without everyone knowing it. As such, Chase was pretty sure that she would do exactly what she said she would. Be an asset to the team.

So why was it that Chase felt there was something he was missing?

3

[She] will win, who knows how to handle both superior and inferior forces.

— *THE ART OF WAR*, SUN TZU

OPERATION TROJAN HORSE

- Secure access to CM's office.
- Make MB Smile. Once.
- Get A to stop smiling so much.
- Find a better coffee shop.

Bella frowned at the website's welcome page, not happy with it. The marketing company had developed some great-looking mock-ups, but the content was stilted and performative.

'Ali, who wrote the copy for the website's landing page?' she asked, without taking her eyes from her screen.

'Julia did, just before Christmas.'

Maurice was returning from lunch with an old colleague, ostensibly 'catching up', but instead actually trying to uncover the industry gossip on Nayak New York. The gallery was working with Magenta, a marketing and PR firm, but it was Bella's job to oversee both internal and external comms and until she could develop the business contacts she had to rely on a still reticent Maurice for 'on the ground' information.

She caught his gaze as he took a seat and Maurice grimaced. Clearly the gossip was not good. Bella internally groaned. She might be determined to tank their boss, but she still had a job to do in the meantime and to do it convincingly too.

'What do *you* think of the home page copy?' Bella said, swivelling in her chair to face him as he took a seat at his desk.

He sniffed. 'It's not my job to think about the copy of the website.'

Despite his words, the single raised eyebrow of

disdain had her convinced that he thought the same as she did.

The copy was awful.

Over the last four days, she'd been kept busy enough by what she was beginning to think of as her 'day job', Operation Trojan Horse had been put on the back burner. Between getting up to speed with half completed plans for the gallery opening, website copy, mailing lists, advertising slots, Magenta's marketing plans, and working with Maurice on the brochure content, she'd actually not seen much of Chase since Monday's team meeting.

But that was about to change. She gathered her tablet and made her way to Chase's office, knocking on the glass door.

He was staring at his computer.

Bella frowned. Had he not heard her? She knocked again a little louder and when there was still no response from him, she pushed open the door.

'No.'

Shock had her pulling up short. He flicked his gaze angrily to her and back to the desk.

Bella opened her mouth. 'I—'

Chase held up a hand to cut her off and she realised that he was on speaker phone.

'No, not that either. Or that,' he said, clicking through something on his computer screen.

'Chase, you have to take into consideration—'

'I don't have to take anything into consideration, Dermot. You think that you can treat me like a first-time gallery director who can't tell the difference between unsatisfying back-list paintings, rather than recent works of value. And, putting it mildly, it's offensive.'

His tousled hair hung in tufts as if he'd run his hands through it several times. Frustration rolled off him in waves, and if Bella were honest, she didn't actually mind that one bit.

'Tell Michaela to call me if she wants to talk. But I'll not deal with you again.'

And with that Chase hung up the phone.

'I wasn't sure if you—' she tried.

'I didn't tell you to come in,' he said, finally turning to face her.

No wonder the last comms director left. Chase Miller was clearly a monster to work for. What on earth had Astrid been thinking?

'You didn't tell me not to either,' she countered saltily, stepping further into his office. She was quite aware that Maurice and Ali were capable of seeing this interaction and she didn't want to have her authority questioned any more than it already was.

It only struck Bella, much later, that Chase might have been feeling exactly the same way.

'I need to talk to you about the copy being used for the website's welcome page.'

He eventually gestured for her to take a seat.

She lowered herself onto the sofa and presented him with the page pulled up on her tablet as he took a seat in the chair at her right.

Bella had marked up the copy with her concerns which he scanned with a shrug.

'I'm not sure what the problem is.'

Which was worrying enough. She bit back a sigh. She had hoped to get him on side in the first week here. Lulling him into some kind of false sense of security. That, however, was proving to be almost impossible when he was making the most basic errors.

'The copy here is clear, precise and informative.'

'Yes,' he stated.

'But it lacks *tone*.'

He was already glaring before she'd finished. 'And?'

Now it was Bella's turn to frown.

'Well, it's just that the copy you have here is' – she

searched for a word that wouldn't offend – 'a little flat.'

He simply held her gaze. Either he was being purposefully obtuse or simply didn't care.

'Chase, the copy lacks anything that would convey to a perspective client what it is they will experience here.'

'I don't want to *sell* an experience,' he said as if the word was a curse. 'The work here will speak for itself. Quality, precision and innovation are where we will attract the right clients.'

She was unable to bite back the scoff of incredulity that fell from her lips.

'Of course you want to sell an experience. Especially on the home page of your website. You can absolutely sell quality, precision and innovation – if that's what you want, but this,' she said, picking up the paper. 'No one will come for this,' she stated boldly, suddenly free from the need to 'play nice' by his wholly irrational behaviour.

'I don't want the kind of hard sell, cynical jargonistic crap that comes with art galleries,' Chase said, leaning back in his chair.

His phone vibrated on the table and he picked it up and put it in his pocket without checking the screen.

'You as an artist, or you as a director?' she said, the response slipping out quickly and deadly and landing, somewhat unintentionally, with the impact of a full punch to the jaw, from the way his eyes narrowed.

She wouldn't regret her words. As an artist, he had shunned the fame he had found. But as a gallery director, he couldn't afford to do the same. And while she was happy to help Chase fall flat on his face, she was less happy at the idea of him taking the gallery with him.

'Because as director, you should know that hard sell, jingoistic crap works. It attracts the people that enjoy that kind of stuff. And they tend to be the people with fat wallets.'

'As director, I'm saying the copy is fine,' he declared.

'And as your comms director, I'm letting you know that it's not,' she said, getting up from the sofa and leaving the office.

As she threw the folder back onto her desk and sat in her seat, she heard Maurice announce, 'Round One, Miller.'

JUST DESSERTS WHATSAPP
GROUP. 16.42 EST.

BELLA

Is it illegal to copy a set of keys for your office? Asking for a friend.

SIENNA

Depends what's written in your contract.

ASTRID

Depends if you get caught.

* * *

Chase watched Bella leave and closed his eyes in frustration. He pulled his phone out of his pocket and saw five missed calls from Tej. There wasn't really any avoiding this. He went back to his desk and pulled up the video call app.

He steeled himself and hit send.

Tej's worried face appeared before the ringing stopped.

'Are you okay?'

'Yes *Mom*,' Chase fake-whined.

'That's shit, man, I'm sorry.'

Chase shrugged his shoulder, hoping he could pass his speechlessness off as nonchalance. But it *was* shit. They had lost their feature artist, Zadzisai – a South African painter Chase had been courting for months – following the news of Julia's abrupt departure.

'Look, this didn't come from Zadzisai.'

'I know,' Chase bit out.

He knew where it had come from and why. There was an understandable amount of scepticism about his role as gallery director. General consensus seemed to be that either he would get bored and go back to being an artist, or he would fail because he didn't know what he was doing. Only a few people seemed to think that he could actually do this. Zadzisai had been one of them.

At least until Julia. Her sudden departure had run through the art world like wildfire, and Tej's chosen replacement, another complete newbie, had been the nail in the coffin.

'It's not your fault,' Tej continued, attempting to counter the inner demons haunting Chase's internal monologue.

'I know,' Chase lied. 'I've got a call in with another possible artist I'm hoping to meet with later.'

'That's great,' Tej replied, a little heavy on the enthusiasm. 'Really great. How's everything else?'

Chase looked over to where Bella stared mutinously at her computer screen.

'I just went head to head with the new comms director,' he admitted.

Tej smirked. 'And how did that go?'

'I'm impressed,' he admitted. 'She held her ground.'

Tej winced. 'She still breathing?'

'I'm not that bad.'

'You can be chilling, bro.'

'And you sound like you're still in high school, *bro*, yet you're running the US arm of a family business that would rival Rupert Maxwell.'

'What was it? The home page website copy?'

Chase nodded.

'You hate that copy. Julia wrote it,' Tej offered.

'I know. I just wanted to see what she would do.'

'That can backfire, you know. I wouldn't do it again.'

'It wouldn't *work* again; she's too clever for that,' Chase admitted. Bella had been careful but fierce, and he'd liked that.

'High praise from Chase Miller. She just earned herself a bonus.'

'No need to go overboard,' Chase muttered. He dragged his eyes away from the halo the table lamp was creating around her golden hair and focused on Tej.

'Is she aware of what people are saying?' Tej asked, referring to Bella and the bitchy gossip that sailed horribly close to Chase's first reaction to her hire.

Chase pulled a face. 'Doubt it.'

'Do you think it's worth giving her a heads up?'

'I think we were the ones that hired her to do this job. It's up to us to hold the fort until she can prove herself. Telling her now would only make her self-conscious.'

'Your call,' Tej said, leaving it with Chase.

And Chase hoped it was the right one. It was a fine line protecting her from the industry's doubts about her, but he'd put money on Bella changing their minds pretty damn quick.

'How's your mom?' he asked Tej, changing the subject.

'From anyone else I'd think that was the start of an insult, but she loves you more than me, dude.'

'What can I say? I'm charming. Mothers love me,' he said, ignoring the tightening of scar tissue across an old wound.

'Can you start on the aunties too? They're the worst ones. *Beta*, I have the perfect woman for you. *Beta*, you just have to meet her. *Beta*, she makes the most amazing insert-your-favourite-snack-here.'

Chase smiled as Tej's accent thickened with his impressions. His mother had been trying to get him to marry for the last five years and so far, Tej had done everything to avoid an engagement aside from declaring himself gay – which he couldn't do, because he couldn't lie to his mother. But ever since his thirtieth birthday last year, things had got intense.

'Just go on a few dates,' Chase tried.

'Don't take this the wrong way, but only a white guy would say something so monumentally stupid to an unwed Indian first-born son this damn close to the marriage mart.'

'Fair enough,' Chase said, raising his hands in surrender.

'Have you told the others about Zadzisai?' Tej asked.

Chase pulled a face and shook his head. 'I don't want to worry them. And Bella will really want to change the copy then.'

Tej smiled. 'I like her.'

'Mmm,' was all Chase would say in response. The jury was still out. Though she had won some points just now on the copy for the website.

'I'm due back in New York in a week or so. We'll grab some drinks.'

'It's a plan,' Chase said, leaning forward to disconnect the call, hoping that he could find a solution to the main featured artist just as easily.

* * *

Bella's eyes hurt. She wasn't exactly a stranger to staring at a computer, but at this hour the overhead light was off, leaving her at the mercy of the glare from her screen. Covertly she watched Chase shut down his computer and stand back from his desk.

She trained her eyes on the email she'd re-read a million times, not wanting to make eye contact with the arrogant, cheating, jerk as he left the building. She tried not to flinch when she heard his knuckles rap on the glass door to the office.

She peered around the screen and raised an eyebrow in question.

She thought for a second that he was repressing a smirk, but she couldn't be sure as Chase was mostly in shadow.

'Did Maurice show you how to lock up?' Chase asked.

'Reluctantly,' she admitted.

'Don't mind him. He just wants to make sure that you'll stick it out,' Chase explained. 'Call if you have any problems.'

'I won't.'

'Fair enough,' he replied, and this time she did see a smile, which just confused her even more.

She'd have thought that her clipped responses would have irritated him, or at least offended his clearly delicate sensibilities. But the about-turn from his behaviour left her reeling.

And then, he didn't even say goodbye, he just left. *Damn the man!*

Bella waited at least five minutes after he'd gone before making her move.

She had a two-pronged plan of attack. One would take almost the entire run-up to the gallery opening to achieve – that was the end of his professional career. She had to be meticulous. The second involved a series of short-term sneak attacks, intended to destabilise and disorientate.

She had chosen this two-faceted approach because to cheat on someone, to drag an innocent woman into the mess too, Chase Miller clearly didn't value his personal life. His career on the other hand... a very different matter.

But to simply sabotage someone's career wouldn't work either, because then Chase could just blame it on someone else. No, Bella's plan was much more complicated than that. She would have to undermine

Chase's belief in *himself*. She would have to make him believe that there was something wrong with *him*.

Because wasn't that the *true* just desserts? Hadn't he made Astrid question everything about their relationship and herself? Hadn't he taken his marriage vows and betrayed them, leaving his poor wife to discover his infidelity for herself when she'd turned up at the hotel room to find Astrid and Chase together?

So that was what *she* was going to do. Slowly, bit by bit, step by step, she would make him question everything. And her first idea had come courtesy of her sister's favourite childhood story: *The Twits*. Which only seemed fitting really. Given that Chase Miller was a twit of the highest degree.

Heart pounding in her chest, she crept into Chase's office, remembering how she'd explained all this to the girls on the group call they'd had last night.

'You,' Sienna had said with a wariness in her gaze that hadn't been there before, 'are actually quite a scary lady.'

'You know,' Paige said, after some consideration, 'after this, I really think you should consider government work.'

'The federal civil service?' Bella had asked.

'No. The CIA.'

'Private sector pays better though,' Astrid added. 'I'd imagine,' she clarified a little too quickly.

Bella smiled as she pulled out the chair behind the desk. She got on her hands and knees, wanting to get in and get out in the quickest time possible. She lowered the chair by one centimetre and loosened one of the wheels.

She moved the desk light back just a few inches, but that was all she would allow herself to do today. Any more and he'd just think the cleaner had moved things and that wouldn't do.

No, he needed to question it *himself*. It needed to seem so minor he could be imagining it.

Then, she carefully removed the doctored sugar sachets and placed them into the holder that Chase kept on the coffee station on top of the fridge, mixing them with the others. It had taken her nearly an hour and a half last night after finishing her call with the girls, but she had achieved perfection. And given the fact he consumed enough sugar a day to keep Krispy Kreme in business, it shouldn't take him long to hit her substitutes.

She backed out of Chase's office and went through the process of closing down the floor as Maurice had directed – in a very detailed, fifteen-minute briefing – and left the gallery humming all the way back to the apartment.

Round Two, Carmichael.

JUST DESSERTS WHATSAPP
GROUP. 18.55 EST.

BELLA

Didn't get caught! ☺

4

Whoever is first in the field and awaits the coming of the enemy, will be fresh for the fight.

— *THE ART OF WAR*, SUN TZU

Bella prised open one eye and peered blearily at a near aerial view of Central Park in surprise, having forgotten that she was no longer in her childhood bedroom at her parents' house, and craned her neck to squint at the alarm clock beside her bed.

Ugh.

Six thirty a.m.

Four hours. She'd had four hours of sleep.

She pulled a pillow across her face and groaned

into it, aware that *Good Bella* didn't do things like groan. Against the backs of her eyes, she saw slashes of paint, a large canvas, and an explosion of pigment.

Go away! she mentally yelled at Chase Miller, throwing the pillow across the room.

She'd been up late last night doing research; *know thy enemy*, Sun Tzu commanded. So, after scanning her copy of *The Art of War* for motivation, she had spent a few hours – okay, so maybe more like *four* hours – watching videos and interviews with him through different stages of his career.

Which was fascinating, because Chase the painter was very different from Chase the gallery director.

Chase the painter was dynamic. The early videos on YouTube showed a softness and a humour that she couldn't quite equate with the man in the apartment opposite her. Later videos were of 'the artist at work', promo pieces for up-and-coming exhibitions that she felt he'd tolerated more than courted. But there was one that had kept playing over and over in her mind, in her dreams and into this morning.

He'd been in his studio, a large warehouse-like space somewhere in London. The music in the background was angry, furious beats played across a hypnotic baseline. It wasn't the kind of music she listened to, but she could see the attraction.

He'd painted like he was trying to run from something, the noise so loud it could drown out the world. And for just a moment she'd found herself wondering if he'd succeeded in drowning out himself.

Because she knew that feeling. Recognised it from when she ran. The music so loud in her ears, almost to the point of pain, where she couldn't hear herself think, where all she could do was hold onto the music and keep going.

And then, flashing against the back of her eyes, there it was: Chase staring at the camera dead on, a knowing glint in his eye, bringing her out in goosebumps. She'd scanned the first few of the nearly five thousand comments left on the video and choked.

@helmart23 He can paint me any day.

@BensJammin Loving his use of acrylic and texture to define...

@HeavenlyFather You can find God in your heart, if know where to look.

@CMWIFE I know EXACTLY where he can put that paintbrush.

Which for some inexplicable reason, reminded her of the book that Delia had thrust into her hands just before she got on the last flight out of O'Hare.

Bella had fallen asleep and been dragged head-long into strange dreams about having paint thrown over her by journalists because she was marrying Tej Nayak, and being chased by a book-waving Delia, until a larger lady with magenta hair offered her safe harbour in a piece of red velvet cake.

She glared at Delia's book where it peered at her from her nightstand.

Read me.

No.

Instead, she picked up her phone and checked it for emails and sat up, seeing the one from Chase.

To: BellaCarmichael@NayakNY.com
From: ChaseMiller@NayakNY.com
Subject: Website copy

You were right. It'll need reworking.
    C

Oh, that man!

She bit back a curse and just about managed to stop herself from hurling the phone across the room in the same path as the pillow. Throwing back the covers, she stalked to the shower and hoped she could wash him out of her hair as easily as Doris Day.

By the time she was out and dry, her parents had messaged, asking how she was getting on. Bella knew that they felt bad that she'd not been able to start her job at the family's foundation because of the negative press attention following the wedding. Olly probably wasn't even aware that it had cost her that too. The best thing she could have done – and *did* do – was leave. So, she'd spent the last six months of the previous year in France with her cousin. And she told herself that it didn't hurt that her parents had been forced to send her away. Again. And she reminded herself that it wasn't their fault. Again.

Snap out of it, she commanded herself. She picked her phone back up and wavered. Astrid wasn't far away...

BELLA

Fancy brunch?

It was something she'd done every weekend with her friends in Boston, after graduating. But it was strange to think of them as friends now because with

Paige, Astrid and Sienna in her life, *they* felt like friends in a way the people she'd spent a significant part of the last five years of her life with didn't. But she'd realised, in the weeks and months following the wedding debacle and her time in France, that out of sight clearly had meant out of mind for the 'ladies that brunched'.

And if Bella was being brutally honest with herself, she could understand why. Because she'd kept herself removed from them in a way that she hadn't with Paige, Sienna and Astrid. In just little over four hours, she'd been more honest and truthful with them than she had ever been in her life. And that thought made her feel both deeply uncomfortable and deeply thankful.

ASTRID

Brunch IS fancy.

BELLA

I know a place.

ASTRID

And I would LOVE a place but my uncle's pad looks like a clothes shop exploded in it and I'm still no closer to choosing what to wear for Operation Heartbreak.

BELLA

Want a hand?

ASTRID

Please! Though give me a few
hours, no one needs to see this…
💀

Bella put her phone down feeling better… for a
moment. Yes, it was great to be meeting up with
Astrid – brilliant even – but it didn't quite fix the
squirminess she was feeling. And she knew why.
She'd thought that she'd feel just a little more satisfied by her act of revenge last night than she pres-
ently did. And, yes, she knew it was part of a longer
game, and yes, the effects of it were supposed to be
cumulative. But why was she so unsatisfied?
Shouldn't she have felt *something* about it? Success?
Satisfaction? Where was the sense of accomplishment she'd thought she'd feel?

In some distant part of her mind she thought
about Paige and Olly in Cornwall together. The pictures Paige had shared of the apocalyptic-level chaos
she'd wreaked upon Olly's pristine kitchen had been
incredible. Bella could just imagine his eye twitching
and his barely suppressed wince, even now. And

Bella couldn't help but wonder whether Paige might be feeling a little less lonely than she was.

One thing she could categorically say about Olly Prendergast was that he was no holds barred, good company. Even for people who were determined to see him at his worst. And a part of Bella missed that. The way that Olly would make her feel a little less... serious. Which was why it had hurt so much that it was exactly that seriousness he'd relied on when he'd unceremoniously dumped her in the proverbial and high-tailed it out of America.

And perhaps she was a little uncomfortable with just how much she *did* actually want Olly to get his comeuppance. Even if it was at the hands of someone else. She wandered to the kitchen and made herself a coffee.

Her phone beeped. And then beeped again. And again. And she couldn't help it, but her lip curved into a side-smile and she reached for her phone knowing that it was from the girls.

And no. They weren't *girls*, but together they were GIRLS. Friends. A group. A gang. And knowing that, took a little of the sting out of being a little lonely.

JUST DESSERTS WHATSAPP
GROUP. 07.42 EST.

PAIGE

[picture attachment]

Bella stared at the picture and was thankful she hadn't taken a sip of her coffee, because it would have certainly been promptly spat back out. All over the white sheepskin.

SIENNA

Is that Pavarotti?

ASTRID

The singer??!

BELLA

It's the hamster.

ASTRID

Is it a Richard Geer kind of hamster, or…

PAIGE

It's the 'or'!

SIENNA

😂

PAIGE

[picture attachment]

This time the photo attached was of the most glorious layered red velvet cake that looked so good, Bella's mouth watered.

PAIGE

A café in NY makes them.

B, can you find it? Please?

SIENNA

So that one day we can all meet there to celebrate the downfall of these bastards.

ASTRID

You say that like she'd not busy making 'destroy Chase Miller' plans!

PAIGE

With replacement back-up plans.

SIENNA

And a list to back up the back-up.

Maybe they did know her better than she thought, Bella decided, smiling and feeling just a little better.

* * *

Chase was still breathing hard as he exited the elevator. He swiped at a bead of sweat that ran down his temple and then nearly tripped over his own feet as he saw Bella coming towards him dressed in running gear.

Eyes up. For the love of God, eyes up.

But it was too late.

Chase knew, right then and there, that the image of Bella encased in black, figure-hugging workout gear would be indelibly printed on his brain for the rest of his life. It didn't matter that there was barely an inch of the pale skin that never failed to make him think of Dutch Golden Age painters.

There she was, looking fresh, vibrant and practically glowing, and he felt like an old, haggard, unfit, has-been. And with his reputation already hanging by a thread, he didn't need to add sexual harassment in the work place.

She acknowledged him with a tight smile as she passed.

He nodded in return, pretending that the nine-mile run hadn't nearly killed him that morning. Of course, it wouldn't have been so bad if he'd been able to run his usual five, and not been detoured after one particular part of the park had been closed. He opened his mouth to let Bella know, but what if she wasn't planning to run that way? What if she wasn't actually planning to run at all? She could be on her way to a gym. She could be on her way to pick up coffee for all he knew. Maybe that was the kind of thing socialites liked to do.

But she was more than a socialite, wasn't she? She'd certainly sounded like it when she was hauling his ass ever so politely, if not quite angrily, over the copy for the website.

He looked up to find her staring at him.

'Did you want something?' she asked, peering at him strangely.

No, *he* was the one that was behaving strangely as he realised he'd just been caught staring at her while his slugging brain clunked its way through a thought process.

Jesus, get a grip, Miller.

'Nope,' he said, the word leaving his mouth on a pop as he spun on his heel and continued down the corridor to his apartment door, resolutely refusing to look her way again. At least until the elevator dinged its departure. He banged his head against the door, once, slowly, before inserting the key and nudging the door open with his foot.

Chase still had that moment of jarring surprise not to find himself in his apartment back in Muswell Hill. The sheer difference between the very British London flat and the swanky New York apartment was as jarring as jet lag.

He missed that strange damp smell that the hallway had had. He missed the small stained-glass windows in each of the building's apartment doors. He missed the highly illegal ginger cat from one floor above, who would try to trip him by winding through his feet like it was a game. He missed the age of the building. He missed the dry sarcasm of the Brits, and the fact no one here knew what Marmite was. He missed the silly Britishisms he'd collected in his time there and he even missed the God-damned tea.

He missed a time when he didn't question things, took everything for granted, where what he'd had had been enough. Now he just seemed to be playing out someone else's life because he couldn't do what he did before.

Twelve months ago he'd have already been in his studio, knee-deep in a painting, or prep for one. He'd be covered in paint, chalk, pigment, PVA glue, and whatever else he could get his hands on to create the textures he liked exploring in his artwork. But ever since he'd accidentally walked in on his wife and his best friend – *and agent* – going at it on the sofa, his entire world had changed.

Chase threw his keys onto the breakfast bar and crossed the room to look out the window.

The betrayal had been such a shock that he'd been numb to pretty much everything and anything. At least for the first few months.

His life had become unrecognisable. He had no wife. No home. No best friend.

So, it hadn't been until somewhere around the third month that he'd realised he had a problem. A serious problem.

Creative block.

The word echoed scornfully around Chase's brain.

Such an innocuous way of describing the slow and very painful desecration of everything he'd ever known. Painful in that heart-pounding, breath-stealing, needle-poking, sharp stabbing panic kind of pain. The terror, genuine terror, that his purpose in life would forever remain just beyond reach. That he'd never find the success his mother had wanted for him.

It had been the last conversation they'd had before she died. He'd been pressed up against her thin body in the too-small hospital bed. As if he could attach himself to her, so that she couldn't leave. As if he could keep her with him.

Make something of yourself, Chase. You have too much in you. Talent, generosity heart.

I promise, Ma. I'll make it happen.

And he had. He'd thrown himself into it all.

Before he'd lost it.

Chase searched the streets below, his gaze scanning the tops of heads until he found what he was looking for. He followed the blonde cap of hair across the road and into Central Park, already regretting not having told her about the diversion.

He turned back to the apartment when Bella finally disappeared from view and made his way towards the shower, peeling off sweat-soaked gym clothes and tossing them onto the floor as he went.

But by the time he *had* realised he had a problem, Chase had wanted to find a dark hole and crawl into it. But he'd still been booked into a final show in Amsterdam that he couldn't decline, because he'd also agreed to an interview with a magazine as part of it. If he failed to turn up, he'd be in breach of contract which would cost him a shit tonne of money. Which wouldn't usually be a problem, but for the fact that the majority of his money was tied into a joint account that his wife had locked him out of.

Tej would have loaned him the money, but if there was one thing that Chase was not, it was a free-loader. Hell, he'd go back to Secaucus and go work in his dad's garage before that happened.

By that point he had been living in a Premier Inn for nearly three months, only having gone back to the flat when he'd known Annalise would be out, so he could pack a bag of clothes. He'd wanted nothing else. Nothing of her, nothing of what they were supposed to have had, no pictures, no memories, nothing. He'd left his wedding ring on the dresser where she'd see it, and an envelope with the first round of what would prove to be many rounds of legal papers from his solicitor.

Everything had hurt. His mind, his body and his soul. But he'd still got on the plane to Amsterdam with the hope that maybe, just maybe, being around creative types, being around his own art was what he'd needed to paint again.

And that was when he'd met Astrid.

Chase turned on the spray in the shower.

Astrid. Man, he'd fucked up big time with her.

She had been such a surprise to him. A genuine, honest-to-God surprise and the very fucking last thing he'd expected from his trip.

He'd been a grumpy, monosyllabic bastard, partly

because the visit to Holland hadn't been the prover-bial magic bullet and being around people admiring the art he could no longer do, expounding the virtues of technique and inspiration – all of which had frankly been a load of bollocks – had just made him angrier.

By the time Astrid sat down to interview him, he was ready to explode. And he did just that. He launched into a rather impressively disparaging diatribe against everything that was wrong with commercial art, the lack of originality, of true authenticity, of the failures of successive government funding cuts, and how social media had lobotomised a whole generation of young people into thinking that fucking NFTs were a genuine way of owning art. By the time he'd stopped to catch a breath, he'd thought she'd have bolted. But instead, she'd looked up at him like she wanted to rip his clothes off and had asked if he wanted to get out of there.

Yes. Yes, he damn well had.

But what was only supposed to be a short-term thing had rolled into an exchange of messages and happy coincidences in travel plans. They'd met sev-eral times over the next few months in different cities. Chase, happy to get as far away from the fact that he still hadn't picked up a paintbrush in months, was drowning in denial. Half-finished legal paperwork and a readily dwindling bank account didn't matter when you could lose yourself in an intelligent, beautiful woman who seemed to find you quite fascinating.

He'd been a fucking coward, that's what he'd been.

But it had come to a head when Annalise, incensed that her increasingly extreme attempts to get his attention weren't working, had managed to track him down the first time he'd tried to use his joint credit card to pay for the hotel he'd booked in Paris for him and Astrid.

He'd come out of the shower to find Annalise staring somewhat victoriously at him from the doorway beside a truly horrified Astrid.

'You're fucking married?' she'd rightfully demanded. 'You're... I...'

Chase swallowed even now at the memory. She'd *never* been lost for words. The passionate, near constant, jubilant stream of words that poured from her like no one else, had been completely stopped by his actions.

She'd tried to mask the hurt she'd felt, but it had been too late. He'd felt it. And he'd deserved to, too.

He'd behaved like a selfish bastard and there was absolutely no excusing it.

Guilt and shame twisted painfully in his gut. And while he'd genuinely believed that his marriage was over the moment that he'd walked in on his wife and his best friend, legally he'd still been married. And while he'd *also* known that Annalise had painted a less-than-true picture of the state of things when confronting Astrid, it hadn't mattered, because legally he'd still damn well been married.

His dad had brought him up better than that. Christ, his mother... he wouldn't have been able to look her in the eye.

He dropped his head to the cold shower tile. The look on Astrid's face. He'd never forget it. And he never deserved to forget it.

5

Hold out baits to entice the enemy. Feign disorder, and crush him.

— THE ART OF WAR, SUN TZU

OPERATION TROJAN HORSE

- Get CM's password.
- Kill CM.
- Re-write web copy.
- Find another new coffee place.

JUST DESSERTS WHATSAPP
GROUP. 9.56 EST.

BELLA

Is it illegal to use computer password spyware and where might one get hold of it?

SIENNA

Why do you need it?

BELLA

The less I say the better.

Every single part of Bella ached. It had been two days and she still hadn't recovered from her run in Central Park on Saturday. Which was why she'd decided that no matter what the time was she was wholly justified in eating the red velvet cake she'd bought from the bakery that offered gorgeous cakes but disgusting coffee.

As she swallowed the sweet deliciousness, she glared at Chase as he walked from his office to the kitchenette. He'd *known* about the diversion and had specifically decided not to tell her about it.

What wasn't his fault was the alcohol-fuelled headache she'd incurred while helping Astrid pick out the most suitable clothing to seduce Aiden Carter with. But as it was her muscles that hurt the most, from visiting four of the galleries she'd identified as

Nayak's closest competition for research purposes *after* the unnecessarily long run she'd taken, Bella had absolutely no qualms about holding Chase wholly responsible for her agonies.

'You're growling,' Maurice observed.

'I am not,' Bella flatly denied.

'Well, you *were*. It's only 10 a.m. on a Monday morning. Who put sand in your panties?'

'No one,' she said, shooting another glare at Chase as returned to his office.

She'd arrived early, in the hope to snoop around a bit, but Chase was already here. And because she'd already looked over the briefing document for her meeting with Magenta later that afternoon *and* prepared for the meeting with Maurice to discuss the plans for Nayak's quarterly magazine later that morning, she had turned her attention to the gallery's computer files, hoping that somewhere someone had documented each user's passwords.

Of course, if *she'd* been office manager, she would have put everyone's passwords somewhere safe, but easy to hand in case someone was taken ill, or was out of reach and the team needed access to information in their emails.

Bella assumed that if there *was* a list of passwords, it would have been given to Ali, as gallery assistant. And having read through the pack Ali put together for her, and been pleasantly surprised by the level of information and organisation, Bella knew it wouldn't simply be in a folder marked *passwords*.

She flicked from one folder to another, in the admin folder. Contact lists, addresses, copies of identification.

'If you're not in the middle of something, we could meet now?' Maurice asked, peering over the top of his computer at her.

Bella bit her lip. It was quite clear by her demeanour that she *was* in the middle of something – something that Good Bella would never be caught doing in a million years.

'Not at all, Maurice. I just need a minute,' she hedged, hoping that 'CRIMINAL' wasn't written in a painful red blush across her forehead for him to see. She clicked through another folder titled *important*, then *documents*, then *sick days*.

Maurice stood.

Bella knew she could come back to it, but she'd come so far. And, after all, Ali was an Alpha Phi who would absolutely be so organised as to keep passwords located within reach of when she would be documenting sick days.

From the corner of her eye, she saw Maurice check his watch, his right eye twitching in warning.

Bella clicked on the Excel spreadsheet, skimmed a glance over the bottom tabs.

Notes.

A shadow cast down over her keyboard.

'If now isn't a good time?'

'Not at all, Maurice. Now is perfect,' she replied with a mega-watt smile, the fizz of victory running through her veins. She grabbed her folder, mentally retracing the folder pathway.

Admin, internal, personnel, sick days, bottom tab, notes, *passwords*.

She was in. Jason Bourne, eat your heart out.

* * *

Only six hours later, she was feeling more like the villain that Bourne had just beaten the daylights out of.

Bella stared at the documents provided by Eloise, the project manager from Magenta who had been working with Julia, and couldn't work out whether Julia was a mastermind at disguising her ineptitude, or Chase Carter was bordering on criminally negligent.

It had taken every bit of Bella's self-control not to drop all sense of propriety and ask a very Astrid sounding question: *What the fuck?* That she had been driven to the point of uttering a curse in a professional setting should have been warning enough. Instead she had asked Eloise to *give her a précis of the situation as she saw it.*

And now Bella wished she hadn't.

She flicked a gaze at Maurice, wondering whether he knew or was in the dark like she had been. But discarded the thought as soon as it arose. She knew the pride he took in his work, and his integrity wouldn't have countenanced such deception.

But Bella needed a minute. Because while Bella could certainly use the information she'd gleaned to knock a chunk out of Chase Miller, it would also bring down the entire gallery. And she didn't want to do that. They were hard-working people, Maurice was clearly fiercely loyal under neath all his snark, and Ali was just joyous and Bella would hate to do anything that would dim that light.

'The generally held belief is that the last comms director quit under mysterious circumstances. That Nayak is a bored billionaire playing with Daddy's money and wouldn't know a piece of artwork from a toilet. That hiring you was a PR stunt – no offence.'

Offence had been taken.

'I'm only repeating what's being said. And rumours are that you've lost your featured artist. At this point it would be a miracle if this gallery gets to opening night at all.'

Oh yes. Bella could absolutely find the straw that would break Chase's back, but it would break hers and everyone else's too, and she didn't even have to check in with the girls to know that they had a zero *collateral damage* policy.

They had lost their featured artist and Chase had not told her, communications director! He'd let her be blindsided by an external hire and *oohhhhh* she was mad.

Oh, this man!

* * *

Bella hovered in the corridor between their offices, drumming her fingers on the folder, deciding how to play it. She took one step towards his office then stopped. Then turned to go back to her desk, anger making her forget that the entire office, *including* Chase, could see her wavering. And then finally, deciding to confront him, she turned to find Chase already holding the door open and gesturing her inside.

The bemused expression on his face just made her even more mad. And what he saw in hers was clearly enough for him to think again.

'What is it?' he asked, as if concerned.

As. If. Concerned.

Did this man even have a conscience?

She opened her mouth, but closed it to prevent the stream of hot angry fury from pouring out into the room. Years of being the good girl, the fixer, the smoother of heated emotions warred with outrage and she was caught in the vortex of that storm, help-less and immobile.

'Bella, are you okay?' Chase asked, very con-cerned this time as he guided her into a seat on the sofa.

No. She wasn't okay. She was furious with male incompetence, with their egos, with their refusal to communicate the basics, like *we've lost our featured artist*, or *I don't want to marry you*. She just couldn't keep her cool around this man and every time he did something to make her mad, it *all* came pouring out. Why? Why was it like that? Why couldn't she control herself and her emotions any more?

Shockingly on the verge of tears, Bella felt a small glass of cool water thrust into her hands.

'Drink that.'

She did as was told and the moment that the sharp hit of vodka caught the back of her throat, she promptly spat it out. All over Chase.

He leaped back with a yelp, while Bella proceeded to choke on the fumes from the sudden shocking mouthful of alcohol.

'What is *wrong* with you?' she demanded when she could finally find her breath.

'You looked like you'd had a shock,' Chase replied defensively.

'And your solution is to feed me alcohol?'

'I asked, *several times*, if you were okay and you didn't reply,' he said, brushing his shirt and tie down with a napkin.

She swallowed around a slightly raw throat – though she couldn't precisely say whether that was from the alcohol or the coughing and sank into the sofa. Where did she start? She knew where.

'Why did Julia quit?' Bella demanded.

'What?' Chase's response to the question was confusion.

'I want to know why Julia quit?' Bella asked firmly. Lack of information created a vacuum, a vacuum filled with far-reaching answers, all of which were beginning to make Bella faintly nauseous.

Chase sat in the chair opposite, peering at her until understanding dawned in his eyes. His hands fisted and flexed on his thighs.

He looked her hard in the eye.

'Whatever you're thinking, it's absolutely wrong,' he said, slashing his hand through the air.

'You don't know what I'm thinking,' Bella replied, trying to keep her cool.

'Don't ever play poker, Carmichael.'

'This isn't a time for jokes, Chase,' she said, with all the poise she didn't feel.

She could see the muscle in his jaw flickering from the pressure he'd applied to his teeth.

'Julia is in Cabo.'

'What?' Bella asked, not expecting the answer.

'She didn't even bother handing in her notice. Her father – a friend of Tej's – called me one morning to tell me Julia wasn't coming back and that he'd pick up her things just before the office closed for Christmas,' Chase declared mutinously.

'Cabo?'

'Yes, Bella, it's where...'

Spoiled socialites, Bella's mind filled in the blank left by Chase's words.

'Rich kids go to have fun,' he finished pointedly, as if Bella didn't know how to have fun.

She knew how to have fun! She *did*.

Bella sighed, smoothing the sides of her hair back as she gathered her thoughts.

'She was a silly kid with no skill and a whole lot of desperation, whose father's intervention put her in a position she wasn't ready for,' he explained. 'There's nothing more to it.'

'Okay,' she said, ordering it in her mind. 'And the featured artist?'

Air punched out of Chase's lungs. *Jesus Christ*, she was hitting him with both barrels today.

'How did you know about that?' he demanded, rising out of his chair.

She glared at him and he couldn't quite work out whether her famous poise was holding her tongue, or just because she was that angry.

'Our PR firm heard rumours. Do the team know?' she asked.

'No,' he confessed, taking a breath. 'I'd wanted to be able to present the team with a solution.'

He'd wanted so much not to fuck this up. *Dammit.* He ran a hand over his face.

'You have to tell them,' she as much as accused.

'No,' he denied. Not until he'd figured out who to replace the featured artist with.

She stared at him blankly, the look having the

same impact as a sharp inhale of frustration, which was impressive, really, when you thought about it.

'I would like you to advise me how best to do my job when you are withholding significant information from me,' she articulated with such patience that it only served to show how *impatient* she was with him.

Chase barked out a laugh.

'You know, most people would phrase that question differently,' he said.

'How so?'

'Something along the lines of... How the fuck am I supposed to do my job like this?'

He watched her closely. She all but flinched at his curse.

Jesus, they were like chalk and cheese. But that didn't mean she was wrong.

He bit his lip, failing to see her eyes flick between his mouth and his gaze and by the time he glanced back to her there was a pretty blush on her cheeks, presumably from his curse, or her question.

'Is this how you want to run a gallery?' she asked hotly. He seemed to have driven her beyond the boundaries of her usual poise, and that he felt a second's worth of pleasure from it was warning enough. But he couldn't deny that he quite liked seeing her off balance, when it was all he was most of the time. 'We're all doing separate things and no one person is talking to another. It *will* be a miracle if we make it to opening at this rate,' Bella said as if more to herself than to him. But it was her last jab that landed particularly hard. 'How can we help you if you won't let us?'

The question reverberated in Chase's mind, echoing back through the years. One that he'd said himself, to the father who had been stretched to the point of breaking. Standing in his father's garage, sucking the smell of oil and exhaust into his lungs the way most kids did with the sugar in a candy store. His father, his hero, callused hands the size of dinner plates and overalls that were never clean, utterly devastated by the loss of the wife he'd loved more than anything in this world.

All those people who'd come by after the funeral, wanting to help with food, or things around the house and his father had not let anyone help him. He'd done it all himself – the Miller way – but it had come at a cost. Unable to talk about his feelings, a distance had grown between them, and Chase had been left alone to navigate his grief. A distance that became physical when he'd left for art college in London.

Was that what he was doing now? Making the same mistake as his father?

'Can I ask, what is it you want for Nayak?' Those grey eyes, startling and surprising in such a classically beautiful face, delving where he didn't want her to go.

'Because I can't see it,' Bella said. 'Not in any of the material provided to Magenta, not in the website design, not in the artists that you *have* managed to secure. I can't see it in the layout, I can't... *see* it,' she concluded with frustration.

That she even wanted to see it was frankly a minor miracle. So far, since arriving, he'd insulted her, tested her without her knowledge, withheld information that she needed to do her job and – from the looks of the way she'd held herself walking around the office – accidentally committed bodily harm by omission.

Is this how you want to run a gallery?

Christ, no. He railed at the accusation. He'd just... he'd just wanted to prove that he *could* do it. He'd wanted to come up with the solutions. Wanted to get them out of the mess that he'd caused. Dammit.

And it *was* his fault that she couldn't see what he wanted Nayak New York to be. Tej trusted him completely. He wanted, *needed*, Bella to see what he did, what he knew Nayak could be. He might not be able to explain it, but he could *show* her.

He looked at his watch.

'What are you doing right now?'

She squinted at him. 'I'm talking to my boss,' she said slowly as if he were a child, or had had a stroke. Either one was a possibility in her eyes, he realised with a smirk.

'Funny. Okay, do you have plans after work or can you come somewhere with me?'

'Now?'

'No. Tomorrow.'

'Funny,' she shot back and him and his thought was, *There is still hope.*

He pulled out his phone and fired off a message to an old friend.

She was right. What he wanted for Nayak wasn't here. But hopefully when she saw what he wanted to show her, she'd get it.

'Grab your stuff. I want to show you something,' he said.

She hesitated.

'If you want to see what I want from Nayak, then this is it,' he said. Now or never. It seemed a tad on the dramatic side, but for some reason it felt that way.

'Okay,' she said, rising and leaving his office to get

her things. His phone pinged with a message from Mannon explaining that keys had been left with security. The simple act of trust in Mannon's reply meant a million times more now that he was starting his own gallery.

And frankly, after Annalise, he wasn't sure that he'd ever be able to trust someone like that ever again.

6

[She] will win who knows when to fight and when not to fight.

— *THE ART OF WAR*, SUN TZU

Bella followed Chase out of Nayak, wrapping a scarf around her neck to stop the bite of the wind and rubbing her hands together as Chase nodded towards downtown and set off at an unhurried pace. Their breath streamed out like jets of smoke only to be eaten away by the night.

How can I help you if you won't let me?

She'd nearly said sabotage. How can I *sabotage* you, if you won't let me?

Bella bit her lip.

'It's not far. We'll be out of the cold soon,' he said as he forged his way through harried commuters and tourists heading to their important destinations.

'That's okay, Paris was even colder just before I left,' she said, choosing to weave through them instead.

'Did you like it?' Chase asked.

She blinked. No one had asked her that. Not really. In part because they'd all known that she'd been pretty much exiled by the fallout from the aborted wedding.

'No,' she admitted with a rueful laugh. 'Not really. I mean, don't get me wrong, it's beautiful and the food is delicious,' she said. And there hadn't been a bunch of reporters hiding behind corners, waiting to judge her for eating all the sweat treats she could before exercising the calories away.

'But?'

Bella scrunched her nose.

'Why were you there then?'

'It was deemed prudent,' she admitted.

'For who?'

'Whom,' she absently corrected. 'For my family's foundation. They didn't want the negative press attention.'

She felt the heat of his gaze on her.

'They sent you away? After the...?'

His shock made her uncomfortable. It skated too close to how she'd felt. It nudged at the closed door she'd locked her hurt behind.

'But who wouldn't want six months in Paris?' she said, forcing a smile to her lips.

'Whom,' he incorrectly corrected.

'That's not the—'

She looked up to find him smiling at her, a tease glinting in his eye. He'd given her a chance to change the conversation. And she took it. But she didn't like being so easily readable to him. And she didn't like how it made something in her gut flip when he did that.

She'd had a little of that with Olly, but not like this. With Olly, he'd been obvious to the point of charming. There was a wryness to it that she had become used to. But Chase? Chase was sneaky, hoarding his charm until you least expected it, so when you were hit with it, it was sudden, unexpected, and much harder to defend against.

She looked back across the sidewalk only to find that she'd lost him. She pulled up short, catching the person coming towards her by surprise and Bella had to step nearly into the road to stop them from colliding.

She glanced back over her shoulder to find him standing by a side alley waiting for her with a smirk that made her want to growl. She didn't have this reaction to people. But there was something about Chase Miller that got her hackles up.

Standing there in his long line coat, the street light picking out the tussles of his hair and the sharpness of his cheekbones, he looked like restrained wildness.

Bella shook her head. She must have caught hypothermia. It was the only possible explanation.

Shaking herself off, she cut her way through the throng of people and met him at the mouth of an alleyway, peering down into the darkness warily.

'Don't chicken out on me now, Carmichael.'

She clenched her jaw and shot him a look. No one had ever called her Carmichael. Apart from maybe the boys' Phys Ed teacher in high school. There was something taunting about it, a challenge that she was helpless to resist.

Half way down the alley, Chase tugged her elbow and led her to a back door with the word EXIT clearly printed on the sign, and knocked.

She quietly shifted out of his grasp without his

notice and stamped some feeling back into her feet, until a large man in a security uniform pulled open the door.

Every good-girl instinct screamed in alarm. Were they doing something illegal? Surely if not, they would have just used the front entrance to wherever they were.

'Chase,' she whisper-hissed, now pulling at his elbow.

'Miller,' exclaimed the big burly man in the uniform. 'Been a while.'

Chase huffed out a laugh. 'Just a bit,' he replied as the security guard pushed the door open wide enough to let them through into a brightly lit startlingly white corridor.

'Ma'am,' the security guard said, dipping his head to her before returning his attention to Chase. 'Mannon said you'd need these.'

'Thanks, man,' Chase replied, taking the keys from the guard's palm and slapping him on the beefy side of his arm.

'Lock up when you're done and drop them off on the way back out.'

'Sure thing,' Chase said easily as Bella watched the guard lope off down the corridor all the way to the end.

She looked back to Chase who had that infuriating smirk across his face again. One she wanted to wipe off with a startling amount of violence. Still, she followed him down the corridor until Chase paused in front of one of the many doors. Chase slid a key into the lock and pushed open the heavy door into the darkness beyond.

She was curious despite herself, which was warning enough.

She cleared her throat. 'I would like to know if I'm about to be involved in a bank heist.'

He peered at her, something bright flickering in his gaze.

'Would you do that?'

'No,' she replied definitively.

'Just checking,' he teased, and pushed the door completely open, reaching around to the left to find the light switch that illuminated an absolutely huge space.

Oh.

Bella couldn't help herself. Her footsteps echoed as she walked past him into a space that was inconceivably near football-stadium large. The space seemed to be partitioned into zones that made her organisational heart near sing with joy. The flooring changed from concrete to white slats, not joined like wooden flooring, but with a line running across them. She followed the line to the deceptively simple wire racks on which hung frames of different sizes and shapes.

This was a gallery storage. And from the glimpse of the paintings she saw, a very well-known gallery.

'Chase!' she exclaimed. 'We shouldn't be in here,' she realised, the flush of wrong-doing painting her cheeks in a pink blush.

'I know a guy,' he dismissed with a shrug.

'You *know* a guy?' she demanded.

'Take a look,' Chase said, gesturing to the sliding racks. 'We have time. If memory serves, there's a Rembrandt in that one.' He pointed just over her shoulder.

Oh, the arrogance of this man! To just be able to wander through the most highly secret, inconceivably valuable, part of one of the world's most renowned art galleries. As if it were his own apartment and she could just 'take a look'.

But she wanted to!

In that moment she didn't think she'd wanted anything more in her life. She'd seen some incredible artwork at galleries around the world. But this was different. It was intimate. It wasn't *curated*.

She walked deeper into the belly of the warehouse, casting longing gazes at the racks either side of her, feeling a thrill of doing something illicit as the lighting flicked on above her.

If you want to see what I want from Nayak, then this is it.

And what *was* 'this' for Chase?

Because it wasn't about famous artists. He'd been near dismissive telling her that there was a Rembrandt on the rack. And she knew that there were hundreds more just as famous, she thought, catching a glimpse of a Hannah Höch.

She paused to take it all in.

'What is your favourite painting?' Chase asked, following her from a few feet behind, watching – *inspecting* – her reaction. She felt as if he were giving her a test and couldn't help but wonder whether he'd brought Maurice and Ali here.

But she didn't think so.

'That's a bit like asking what someone's favourite movie is,' she replied.

It's a bit like a date question, she thought and bit her lip.

He waited patiently for her answer.

It wasn't a date question, but it wasn't a harmless getting-to-know-you question either. From an artist, from Chase, it was *more*.

'*Judith Slaying Holofernes*,' she replied over her shoulder as she veered off to take a closer look at the racks. The sounds of her shoes punctuated the thick silence of the warehouse.

'One of my favourite critiques was written about that painting,' Chase said, his voice unusually thick.

'Really?' she asked, not wanting to know. Not wanting this intimacy at all. Suddenly she wanted to be back out on the street, with anonymity amongst the pedestrians and—

'"Relentlessly physical",' he quoted, pulling her reluctant attention back to him, only to find his eyes *thankfully* on a painting on the other side of the warehouse.

He seemed to be searching for something. 'There is another Gentileschi down' – he paused and pulled on the handle at the end of a rack – 'here.'

He gestured for her to take the handle as if he were offering her an apple in the garden of Eden.

Chase bit back a smile as Bella looked longingly towards the rack.

'I can't just...' She hissed out the words in a whisper, but it was clear how much she wanted to.

Christ.

That was something, right there.

Bella *tempted*.

It was like the name of a painting itself.

Her eyes lit with a desire to do something she thought naughty. Wrong. And it was probably the most beautiful thing in this entire room.

'You do that, while I just go and find...'

Something else to look at.

He turned away from her, leashing his body back under his control with a restraint that was alarmingly difficult. He tried to walk it off, thinking of anything that would dampen his suddenly raging libido. Mrs Lebroux, their elderly neighbour back in Secaucus. Secaucus itself. Scribbling on the concrete outside their little house with the chalks his mother had given him, falling in love with colour and marks and art for the very first time.

His mother.

His heart caved in on itself like it always did. The old familiar sting of grief, the pain of not seeing her, hearing her, feeling her touch, melded with the guilt of not achieving what she'd wanted for him, and the fear that she'd be so very disappointed in him now. He clenched his jaw, reflexively bracing against the direction of his thoughts that were one sure-fire way of getting his libido well and truly *doused*.

He looked back at Bella, peering at one of the seventeenth century's most impressive artists, getting as close as she possibly dared. Closer than she'd ever be able to in a gallery, that was for sure.

Was he surprised by her answer about her favourite painting? No, and *that* surprised him. It was a question that he never usually asked people. But with Bella he was just curious. Curious in a way that he knew was absolutely no good whatsoever.

She was sharp, in both intelligence and character. But he'd never seen her sharp with Maurice or Ali. Of the few connections he'd reached out to about her, she'd been described as invaluable, sweet, a problem solver and a fixer. 'The soother of ruffles,' one person had called her.

Except his, it seemed.

There was enough antagonism between them to light a city block. He was old enough to know what it was, and old enough to know better than to act on it. And having firmly told himself that, he turned back to watch Bella gazing at the Gentileschi, every thought and feeling showing across her face like words on a page.

Appreciation, wonder, sadness, regret, understanding.

What would she see in *his* work? And what would *he* see when she did?

There were one or two here, stored amongst the

greats and the not-so-greats. He classed himself with the latter, it went without saying. But he imagined the flush on her cheek, the brightness in her eye. The understanding. Without words, without explanation, just to be known, understood. To be enough.

Christ. Chase passed a hand over his face, hoping to wipe away his thoughts, and headed towards the part of the storage that was the reason he'd brought them both here.

Bella followed him as he found his way to the racks housing the section he was looking for.

Every gallery had one. He'd first discovered it as an intern at the Tate Modern in London and it had made him both sad and angry: the art that was 'shelved'. And ever since then, he'd made a point of visiting similar works whenever and wherever he could.

And he wanted Bella to see it too. Because he wanted her to understand what he wanted for Nayak. Because he was going to need her help to achieve it. But for that, he was going to have to trust her and just the thought of it made his gut clench.

She waited patiently behind him, unaware of his mental wrangling, as he pulled out a rack that looked just like any other rack in here.

He stood back, inviting Bella forward.

'What do you see?' he asked, feeling a little like a school teacher with his student, which just led his dirty, sex-starved mind down a path he had absolutely no intention of following.

'Expressionism, but early. On the cusp with Impressionism. I don't... I don't recognise the artist,' she said, sounding defeated, as if she'd failed a test, rather than passing it.

'That's not surprising. While some of her work is kept here, none of it ever made it into a gallery.'

Bella frowned as if not quite liking what she heard.

'Not even here?' Bella asked.

Chase shook his head.

'That's a shame. It's good. Bold, powerful. Physical.' She smiled up at him, as if having forgotten herself for a moment. 'Not *relentlessly*, but still. I... like it,' she said as if making up her mind. 'Why is it here?'

'It's part of a collection on loan to the gallery, but as it failed to reach critical acclaim at the time, lack of interest led to lack of awareness and it's not considered part of the acceptable cannon of Expressionism.'

Bella frowned, little angry lines between her brows. 'She was a female artist at a time when there were enough powerful men shaping the tastes and appetites for others,' she said, coming to the explanation herself. 'Could Nayak loan it out?'

'This one, quite possibly. But all the rest? There isn't enough money or time in the world,' Chase said bitterly.

She looked up, querying what he meant by 'all the rest'.

'Look around you. Rack after rack after rack. Each containing any number of three to thirty paintings, depending on size. How many artists do you think have work here? And how many do you think get to be the chosen few to be seen? Of those paintings, which will make enough money for the gallery to justify wall space?' he asked, his voice heated enough to betray the passion he felt about this. About marketeers and money makers deciding what was art and what wasn't. What would sell tickets and what wouldn't. What would make patrons and board members big fat bonuses, and what would cast an artist into the invisible pages of history.

'Who are these people to control who gets to see these paintings? Why is it up to an art critic or a professor to decide what is art, what is beautiful? Why aren't these paintings as accessible to everyone, from a child to a grandparent? Why aren't these incredible pieces of work as accessible to a mechanic and a school teacher as they are to—'

He bit his teeth together but it was too late.

'Me and my family,' Bella finished, unable to hide the hurt in her gaze.

He turned away guiltily. He'd taken his frustration out on her and Bella deserved better than that.

'You want to show what other people don't,' she said, circling back to the conversation they'd had in his office, her voice soft from behind him. 'In Nayak, you want to show the kinds of art that other galleries won't.'

He nodded, once. Definitively.

'You want to give the artists who don't get wall space a chance.'

'Yes,' Chase confessed, pleased that she understood. 'Not solely. I know Nayak has to garner enough financial and professional attention to make it work as a business, I'm not a complete novice. But I want people to experience what you did when you first came in here. The feeling that you were seeing something that not everyone else gets to see.'

'Exclusivity,' she tried.

'No, not quite that,' he said, struggling to define what it was he wanted the gallery to be. 'Something *intimate*,' he tried. 'Something gratifying, something near sexual, something individual,' he said, trying to put into words what he'd seen across her face as she'd delved deeper into the warehouse.

He looked to her to see if she understood what he was getting at. There she was, staring up at him with those big grey eyes, a tendril of hair having escaped somewhere along the way, her eyes flicking back and forth between his. He wondered if she knew they did that, eyes moving back and forth as if wanting to capture everything all at once.

His phone beeped, breaking the moment.

While he checked the message from Maurice, he saw her check her watch.

'Well, I have a better understanding of what you want for Nayak now, so thank you for that,' she said with a brightness that seemed more determined than real. 'I should probably get home.'

Chase winced and rubbed the corner of his eyebrow with his thumb.

'About that,' he said, somewhat regretfully because he actually *did* want her to go home in that moment.

7

Pretend to be weak, that he may grow arrogant.

— *THE ART OF WAR*, SUN TZU

'I don't see why you couldn't have just told me,' Bella groused, trying to keep up with the furious pace Chase had set.

'I thought you might try and back out of it,' Chase replied, his gaze on the street ahead of him as, once again, the pedestrians parted for him as if he were Moses.

'I wouldn't dream of such a thing. Team bonding is an integral part of best working practices,' Bella said hotly, even though she really *did* want to back out of it.

Chase pulled to a sudden and rather dramatic stop, flustering the flow of pedestrians around him, while she yanked herself back to stop herself from ploughing into him.

'It was Ali's turn to pick the location,' he said with a sigh.

'Why? Where is it?'

Chase pulled a pained face, making her laugh. Not because Chase was in actual pain, but he *was* clearly uncomfortable and that *was* amusing to her.

He looked boyish and rueful.

And then she stopped laughing.

'No, seriously. Where is it?'

* * *

Oh. My. God.

'Told you,' Chase whispered into her ear as he swept past her, taking off his coat and sliding into the booth ahead of her.

'This place is...' She trailed off, moving in a daze to the booth where the team sat under bright red and neon pink signage that took her right back to Just Desserts. But if Just Desserts had been her heaven, what was this? It was like Chinese New Year had thrown up in an American-style diner and no one had bothered to clean it up.

Ali leaned forward, sheer delight in her eyes. 'There's karaoke upstairs.'

Bella's mouth dropped open and nothing came out.

She was in shock, she decided, glaring up at the biggest Lucky Cat she'd ever seen. Gold against the lipstick-red painted wall, its paw waving up and down.

'I thought that was Japanese,' she said to herself.

'It is. But I don't think the designers of this place particularly minded that much,' Chase replied, surprising her that he'd heard.

'Because they're American.'

'Because they're American,' Chase replied, nodding.

Giant beautifully decorated fans were pinned to the walls while paper Chinese dragons hung from the ceiling. Somewhere a slot machines bounced and pinged, and servers yelled, everything working so hard that Bella felt her brain short-circuit as she gazed in half fear and half irrational excitement, curious as to what she'd find next.

'Oh,' Chase said in surprise, calling her gaze back

to him, only to find him looking right at her. 'You like it,' he accused. 'You *actually* like it,' he said on a laugh.

Bella glared a warning at him and he did that damned smirk again that pulled on something in her chest. Something she didn't want to think about because... of Astrid, because Bella couldn't, because he was absolutely everything she hated about men. Lying, cheating, charming snakes.

'Full of surprises,' Chase said to himself, turning to the menu in his hands.

Bella did the same, having to look again at the menu, half of which was all American diner food, and the other half a list of Chinese takeouts' greatest hits.

This was pure guilty pleasure.

And yes, Chase was right. She actually *did* kind of love it.

Immediately she thought of the girls and she wanted them here so much her heart thudded. She wanted to take pictures, but Good Bella would never be so crass.

But... she wasn't Good Bella any more, was she? She was someone who had got a job with the sole purpose of taking down her lying, cheating boss. That was most definitely not Good Bella behaviour.

So maybe she could take pictures because she was Bad Bella now?

I've been such a bad...

Bella cleared her throat, the line from Delia's book dragged from the recesses of her mind without warning.

'You okay? You look a little... flushed,' Chase asked.

'Do you need some water?' Ali said beside her, pouring her water anyway.

Bella nodded and gratefully took the glass, downing half the contents.

Where had she put that book?

A waitress came by to take their drinks order.

'Margaritas,' Ali cried.

'Frozen,' added Maurice.

Chase nodded his head in agreement and Bella thought, *Why not?*

Before long, four frozen margaritas were raised in a toast.

'Your official welcome to Nayak New York,' Chase declared.

Cheers turned into appreciative moans as everyone took a sip of exceedingly excellent margaritas.

'One week down and how do you feel? Ready to run for the hills yet?' Maurice asked.

'Not at all. I'm just getting started,' she said with a confidence she finally felt.

'So where did you to get to this afternoon?' he asked, his gaze curious.

'Market research,' Chase replied without taking his eyes off the menu.

Bella bit her lip as she felt Maurice's gaze on her.

'*More* market research,' she clarified, having already told Maurice about the galleries she'd visited yesterday.

Chase's eyebrow crinkled, but she doubted anyone noticed.

It then took nearly twenty minutes to wrangle everyone's food order and what ended up coming to the table was a mishmash of fried fabulousness, the likes of which Bella would never normally let herself anywhere near, let alone eat.

Bella asked Maurice about growing up in Martinique and what had brought him to New York.

'A man, darling. Isn't it always a man?' he replied with a knowing smile.

'And what happened to *the man*?' Bella asked.

'Lord only knows. That was nearly twenty years ago now.'

Ali started to tell Maurice a funny story about Ye-Joon, Bella smiling at the obviousness of her crush and more than a little envious of how uninhibited Ali was. She was free in just about every way, her expressions wild and wonderful, her enthusiasm seemingly endless. What would it be like to live like that? she wondered.

Ali tried to steal an onion ring from Maurice's plate, but he playfully slapped her hand away, causing her to scream. Bella flinched, but laughed along with the team, surprised when Chase donated his last ring to Ali.

Chase eyed her spring roll.

'No way,' Bella replied passively, causing Chase to narrow his eyes.

'I'd trade you.'

'Nope,' she said, shaking her head and biting into the delicious layers of flaky pastry, visibly relishing the garlicky pork and ginger-coated vegetables inside.

'Cruel woman,' Chase complained as the plates were taken away.

Dessert menus were placed on the table and Bella stared longingly at the red velvet cake. There was no way she should be even considering it, but...

'Tempted?' Chase asked, his gaze on her finger tapping beside the cake's description.

She'd be running off this dinner for at least a week as it was. 'I'm good, thank you,' she said, sitting back in the red vinyl seat full, reasonably happy, and very tired.

'And now for the best bit!' exclaimed Ali, jumping up and down and making the vinyl squeak. 'Kara—'

'Nope,' Chase said. 'I'm out.'

'Me too,' Bella said with a smile at the look of miserable disappointment on Ali's face. She turned to Maurice, her gaze pleading for him to say yes.

'Please, Maurice, *please.*'

Maurice peered down at her, eyebrow raised and Bella was fully prepared for him to flat out refuse when he instead said, 'Only if you agree to let me do at least one Madonna, one Kylie and one Celine.'

'Of course,' Ali replied with such seriousness that it was clear they had done this before.

And just like that, Bella and Chase were being rushed out of the booths with, 'Have a good night,' being yelled at them as Maurice and Ali disappeared upstairs to where the karaoke rooms were.

'Well, that was abrupt,' Bella observed as she picked up her coat. 'You don't seem surprised.'

'We've been here before. And I had to learn the hard way. You got off easy,' he accused, turning to pick up the end of her coat sleeve so that she could slip her arm into it more easily. Caught a little off guard, she shrugged into the coat and for a second she thought he might try and settle it around her shoulders, but he stepped back.

It was that precise moment that Bella realised she and Chase lived opposite each other and that they would basically be going home together.

No. Not home!

Just back. To the complex.

She swallowed, wondering if he was thinking the same thing or whether he'd realised just a little sooner than she had.

'Do you want to share a cab?' he asked, hesitating.

Did she want to be in an enclosed space with him, in the dark, late at night?

'I'd like to walk some of that meal off, but if you—'

'No, a walk would be good,' he said, nodding, not meeting her eye. 'Unless you had somewhere else you needed to be?'

'Yes, that's me. The secret party girl of Upstate New York,' she said wryly.

'I reckon the papers would have done an exposé on that already, had that been the case.'

Bella smiled, bitterness pulling at her lips.

'They've managed to do so much with what they've already had.'

Given what he'd read when he was looking her up online, Chase knew what she meant. He pushed open the door to the restaurant and waited for her to pass him before following her out into the cold.

'Though it's not a bad image,' he admitted as they came onto a quiet sidewalk, now that most people were already where they wanted to be.

'What?' Bella asked, the word a puff of white in the darkness of the evening.

'You as a secret party girl,' he said, smiling at what he saw in his mind's eye. 'I bet you wait until everyone's in bed, pull on a load of black clothing, some Doc Martens and go raving.'

Bella let out a laugh that half sounded as if it were against her will, and he was slightly delighted. He plunged his hands into the pockets of his long wool coat and tried to ignore the way that warmth began to spread from somewhere that had been cold for a very long time.

'Raving?'

'Yeah, you know. Sweaty club, angry music, full rage against the machine,' he growled out into the night.

She laughed again and she really had to stop doing that because...

'Dye my hair black? Never.' She shuddered as if the thought were more appalling than the current frigid temperature of a New York winter's night.

'I don't know. I can see it,' he said, tilting his head to find the angle to make it work. And he could. Startlingly pale skin, raven's-wing black hair and eyes like silver moons.

She looked at him as if trying to see what he saw. Trying to see that image of herself in his eyes and he knew he should shut it down.

They turned their backs on Harlem and Fifth Avenue, hugging the side of Central Park, and a comfortable silence settled between them.

'So, you don't have any messy stories about getting into trouble as a kid after raiding your parents' alcohol cupboard?' he asked, hoping that the tease in his tone softened the jibe.

A shadow passed across her gaze before disappearing.

'Ahh, no. No, that wasn't really... That wasn't what my childhood was like.'

'So what was it like?'

'When I was nine, my sister was diagnosed with Non-Hodgkins.'

His stride faltered for a second, his heart suspended in that moment for her, for all that could mean.

'Cancer?' he asked carefully.

Bella nodded, her gaze on the sidewalk, maintaining her pace.

'Things were tough for her and my parents, so it was easier for me to go and stay with my grandma in Massachusetts until she got better.'

Chase frowned. She'd been sent away? Like she had been last year following her wedding, he realised. An inconvenience to be removed.

'It's okay,' she said with a smile. 'They needed to focus on her, and Grandma could focus on me. She used to take me to galleries.'

'Hence the love of art.'

'Hence the love of art,' she confirmed. 'And of course, there were afternoon teas.'

'Of course,' Chase duly repeated. 'How long was your sister in hospital?' he asked, instead of, *How long were you sent away for?*

'A year and a half. And Bea got better, and I went home,' Bella concluded with a dazzling smile.

A smile Chase was seriously beginning to dislike. It was as if she used it as a distraction. But he saw the hurt beneath the glitter in her eye. He knew that hurt.

'My mother got ill when I was sixteen,' he confessed, wanting her to know she wasn't alone, wanting her to know that he understood. 'I don't know what it would have been like if I'd been younger.'

It had been hard enough then. Who was he kidding? It still was now. Every time he thought of his mother, he was hit with the kind of blinding pain that took his breath away. As if half of it was just shock that he could feel so much of it.

Grey eyes pulled at him like a thread and read him like a book.

'I'm so sorry.'

He wanted to tell her more. Tell her about what his mother had been like. About how his mother could recite passages of Shakespeare at the drop of a hat as if she were on the stage, and whisper poems by Edward Lear in his ear when he was upset or angry. He wanted to share with Bella the warmth and beauty that had defined his mother. But that wasn't 'the Miller way'. Miller men didn't air their laundry in public or speak their feelings even in private.

So all he did was nod, unsure what to do with her sympathy, other than let it wash over him.

He looked up to find the doorman from their apartment complex holding the door open for them, and they both muttered their subdued thanks. In silence they waited for the elevator without a word as they each tried to muscle through their own thoughts.

It arrived at their floor and he followed her down the corridor with a creeping sense of dissatisfaction without completely understanding the reason why he felt that way.

She pulled up opposite his door.

'Well, thank you for the warehouse,' she said, '*and for dinner.*'

'It's not as if I gave you much choice over either,' he admitted, his hand rubbing the back of his neck ruefully.

'Perhaps not, but thank you anyway. I feel I can get a proper start on reworking the overall comms strategy tomorrow.'

Her smile didn't reach her eyes as she nodded and said goodnight, and he decided that he didn't much like that look on her either.

He watched the door close behind her and let himself into his apartment. He pulled the scarf from his neck and shrugged out of his coat, tossing it over the back of the sofa as he walked to his view of Central Park. He wondered if Bella's view was the same. He imagined her apartment to be a mirror reflection of his own. No doubt neat as a pin, and as ruthlessly organised as she was in her job.

He walked towards the book shelf where he kept the bottle of scotch and his whisky glass and poured himself a drink. He sipped at the peaty alcohol, relishing the burn of it against the back of his throat, trying not to wonder about Bella. About the line of tension that seemed to permanently hold her so upright and upstanding. What lay beneath the false smile that distracted and dazzled people who couldn't or wouldn't see beyond it? What would smooth the furrowed line that appeared between her brows when she frowned?

It wouldn't be him, Chase answered himself grimly, that was for sure.

The thought that she'd ever find someone like him, paint-stained, and paint blocked, and not remotely suitable. No. Her fiancé might have walked out on her, but that didn't mean her tastes would change from the practically perfect son-in-law that could fit into an annual calendar of social events that a presidential candidate would be jealous of.

Despite the way she'd seemed to enjoy this evening's meal, Bella Carmichael had expensive tastes and no matter what Chase did, he was still the son of a mechanic and a school teacher from

Secaucus, no way near good enough for the likes
of her.

*   *   *

He was no good.

No good at all, Bella mused as she paced back and
forth in front of the floor-to-ceiling windows that, in
the apartment's dim lighting, only reflected her, su-
perimposed on a New York nightscape.

She didn't want to have walks home in the dark
with him. She didn't want to see what he wanted for
Nayak, didn't want to understand why he wanted that.
She didn't want to know about his mother, nor did
she want to feel some kinship with him, some hope
that she could be understood by him.

She shook her head.

She absolutely could not. COULD. NOT. Fall for
his charms.

She was here to do one thing and one thing only.
Get revenge. For Astrid. Who so desperately deserved
it.

And besides, if she didn't, then what would that
mean? For the girls? For Astrid who was winding
Aiden Carter up like a toy. And Paige, who was at this
very minute driving Bella's coward of an ex-fiancé out

of his damn mind. And Sienna, who was going to nail Paige's truly despicable piece of... *you know what*, in a way that he would never get over.

No. Bella would do what she needed to do: destroy Chase Miller professionally *without* falling under his spell.

Her phone vibrated from where it was nestled in her coat pocket. She must not have taken her phone off silent from this afternoon. Crossing the living room, she retrieved her phone and, seeing the most recent message from Sienna, Bella scanned back up to the top of the chain to the first unread message.

JUST DESSERTS WHATSAPP GROUP. 08.33 EST.

SIENNA

What's next in Operation Heartbreak?

ASTRID

I've been invited into the lion's den... Aiden's cooking dinner!

PAIGE

🙂

SIENNA

Be careful, Aiden can be pretty charming when he wants to be.

ASTRID

Well, technically he's cooking for Blake and me, but it beats a meet up at the rink.

PAIGE

Blake is going to be there?!

ASTRID

I'm sure there will be opportunities to get up close and personal with the right twin.

PAIGE

So long as you remember which one that is!

ASTRID

😏 Have you been speaking to Bella?

PAIGE

She may have mentioned you have something of a bad boy addiction…

ASTRID

I have it all under control 🐱

SIENNA

And I repeat, be careful!!

And finally, she began typing.

BELLA

Guess who has Chase Miller's computer password...

SIENNA

Ohhh, what are you going to do with it?

BELLA

I'm going to look for the magic bullet.

PAIGE

Wait, is that like a vibrator?

ASTRID

Chase has a vibrator?

SIENNA

REALLY??

BELLA

No!

It's the thing I'm going to use to bring him down.

SIENNA

Oh.

ASTRID

Shame, that would have been interesting.

BELLA

Don't need to know. We don't need to know!

PAIGE

I kind of want to know though...

8

It is a matter of life and death, a road to either safety or to ruin.

— *THE ART OF WAR*, SUN TZU

Chase sat at his desk, rolling his chair forwards and backwards. Something was off, but he couldn't quite put his finger on it. And it wasn't helping his mood at all.

Ever since yesterday when somehow instead of sugar, there had been salt in his coffee, actually *in* the sugar wrapper, which could only have been a mix up at the factory, he'd started dabbing his finger into the

white substance, and it made Chase feel like an
addict.

He checked his watch. He'd scheduled a team
meeting for 10 a.m., hoping that everyone would have
suitably recovered from the night before. Chase
barely recognised himself. Twelve months ago he
would never have imagined that he'd not only be arranging team meetings, but doing so, cruelly, the
morning after a night out. But Bella had been right.
He needed to let the team know about Zadzisai. It
wasn't fair to keep them in the dark.

Chase rolled back in his chair, still feeling like
something was off as Bella knocked on his door
looking alarmingly fresh at the head of the rest of the
team.

He gestured for them to come in. Ali entered
clutching her tablet, a notepad and the biggest can of
energy drink he'd ever seen. Maurice looked as if he
should have been wearing sunglasses.

'Morning boss,' Ye-Joon said brightly, bringing up
the rear.

The kid was a fucking ray of sunshine and as
much as Chase wanted to hate that, he really didn't.

'Ye-Joon. You've met our new comms director?'

'Yeah, just now. She's cool,' he said, bobbing his
head on his lanky frame.

Bella smiled at the compliment as if it really meant something to her and he felt a thump in his chest.

Ali could barely take her eyes off Ye-Joon and wasn't being subtle about it either. Bella's gaze tracked back and forth between the two. Ali might as well have had hearts in her eyes for how obvious it was. And Ye-Joon might as well have been hit over the head with a hammer for how oblivious he was.

As people got settled, he watched Bella retrieve something from her bag and pass it to Maurice beneath the line of the table. He mouthed, 'Thank you,' back before reaching for his water and swallowing what was presumably painkillers.

They were little things. Small gestures between them, but he couldn't shake the feeling that they'd become a little unit. A little unit that he was about to put under a huge amount of pressure.

He took a breath.

'Oh!' Ali exclaimed, reaching into her bag, and pulling out a cardboard box with pastries.

'Thank you, Jesus,' Maurice whispered, not so much under his breath as on it as he reached for the nearest and quickest way of loading his body full of sugar, fats and just a little salt.

Salt.

He grimaced and eyed the coffee station on the side table with suspicion.

He looked back to find Bella's eyes on him before she looked back down to her coffee.

'Bella?' Ali offered.

'No, thank you.'

No. Chase didn't think that a good girl like Bella would consume more than half her daily calories before 10.30 in the morning and as if in challenge, he purposefully leaned forward and picked out the one doughnut covered in the most sugar and took a huge bite, and he felt her gaze on him the entire time. She bit her lip and he nearly choked, and that was enough to remind him where they were and what he thought he was playing at.

He'd like to blame the hangover, but he didn't have one. He took a mouthful of coffee to wash down the sugar and cleared his throat.

'Okay. So, now that I have you all here, I've got some news.'

'You're leaving?' Ali accused.

'You're closing the gallery for the day and we can all go home?' Ye-Joon offered.

'Bella's pregnant?' Maurice said, causing Ali to squeal, Chase to laugh and Bella to gasp in horror.

'None of those things.' Chase was quick to recover

in time to see Bella looking at him in accusation as if what Maurice had said was *his* fault. 'At least—'

'No. Not pregnant,' Bella replied firmly. 'And I swear that if one, *one*, newspaper headline remotely even suggests—'

A chorus of 'no's filled the room without Bella having to finish the threat.

'Okay,' Chase said, calling attention back to him. 'I'm afraid we've lost Zadzisai,' he said, ripping the Band-Aid off in one fell swoop.

Maurice looked appalled, Ali bemused as if she knew she should be shocked but didn't quite get why, and Ye-Joon put his head in his hands. Ye-Joon had *really* been looking forward to working with Zadzisai's paintings.

'I'm sorry,' he said, genuinely, feeling responsible, because as gallery director, he really was. 'But I'm already looking, and I will find someone to replace Zadzisai as our featured artist.'

'Everything has to change,' Maurice said. 'The website, the promotional plans, almost the entire first magazine—'

'Neither the main pages of the website or the magazine have gone live yet, so we have time to change the copy there,' Bella said soothingly. 'We're still compiling mailing lists so no actual specifics have gone out to clients. We're actually in a really good place for this to have happened. It would be different if the information had been released...'

She trailed off a little towards the end of the sentence as if suddenly getting distracted, but despite that, Bella's words had the desired effect, soothing the ruffled concerns of his team.

'Absolutely. It's better that we know now so that we can make the changes we need.'

'But all the other artists were chosen because of how their pieces worked with Zadzisai's,' Ye-Joon said, worried. 'Does that mean we're changing everything?'

'I'm not changing a single thing until we have a new featured artist in place,' Chase said firmly.

'And... do you have an idea as to who that might be?' Bella asked hesitantly.

I'm working on it, wouldn't cut it.

'Not yet,' he admitted.

How can we help if you won't let us?

Just like then, Bella held his gaze now and he shoved the deep discomfort at putting his trust, his faith in other people aside and said, 'But I'm open to ideas.'

Maurice raised an eyebrow – though whether that meant he was impressed or derisive, Chase couldn't tell. Ali tapped her fluffy-tipped pencil against her sparkly notepad, eyes to the ceiling as if this was the pose of 'deep in thought' she had perfected from teen movies.

Ye-Joon frowned.

'Ye-Joon?'

He squinted. 'There is this girl – *woman*,' he hastily corrected under Bella's watchful eye, 'at college. She's... something else, man, like seriously. What she can do with a brush. It kinda reminds me of you, you know.'

Chase tensed against the emotional gut punch.

'BA? MA?' he asked.

'MA. Sascha Levy. Fine Art. There's something there, that's all I can say. You'd have to go see for yourself,' he said with a shrug.

Chase made a note, before saying, 'Look, I know that this feels like it stops us in our tracks but it doesn't. I'll be focusing on this, but I still want to see the mock-ups and copy for the remaining artists, as well as the marketing schedule for the lead in to the pre-opening by the end of the week.'

The team nodded and he got up as they began to file out, Bella hanging behind. Just as he'd expected.

'You want to go from Zadzisai, to an art student?'

Bella asked sceptically, thankfully having waited until it was just the two of them.

'I haven't even seen the work yet.'

'But you're considering it?' she prodded.

'Yes. I am.'

'Did you consider approaching another established artist? Someone that would at least have enough recognition to draw the kind of attention needed?'

'Did I think about it? Yes,' Chase said, returning to his seat behind the desk, because the hint of her perfume as she'd stood close to him had surprised him. He'd expected floral and sweet, but that was *not* what Bella was wearing. 'Of course I did,' he said, regaining his chain of thought. 'And did I think that any other established artist that would attract the kind of attention you're hoping for would run for the hills like Zadzisai? Absolutely.'

The conversation was beginning to grate and he needed her out of his office. The V of the silk shirt was tantalizingly close to revealing.

Pervert.

Bite me, he threw back at his inner voice.

'Look,' he ground out from between his teeth, 'let's go check out Levy and see what we think after that,' he said, trying to close down the conversation.

She pulled up, the shirt settling less indecently across her chest and he let out an internal sigh of relief.

'You want me to come with you?' she asked.

Pervert.

Chase cleared his throat. 'Yes. I would like you to come with me,' he said impatiently.

'Why?'

'Because you're going to need to see what I do, if we're going to sell this to the others.'

She gave him that glazed stare again and finally nodded her agreement.

'I'll let you know when we're good to go,' he said, pulling himself back into the desk on the chair that didn't quite feel like his chair.

'Okay,' she said, nodding, and walked smoothly out of his office, leaving a trace of that scent that he couldn't quite put his finger on.

* * *

It would be different if the information had been released.

Bella nibbled the middle of her top lip as she waited for the kettle to boil.

That was a very different kind of sabotage to putting salt in his coffee or destabilising his office chair. Both of which she'd done again that morning, slowly increasing the number of salt packets, and the inch in height of the chair.

But if that information *had* been released and it *did* get out it could damage Chase's career irrevocably.

But *how* to do it? And *who* to do it to?

Maurice came to the kitchenette and leaned against the cabinet.

'What do you think?' he asked Bella who was so lost in her thoughts, she replied, 'I think I want to see every article that's mentioned Nayak New York.'

'What?'

Bella spun round to look at Maurice. 'I... ah, I think if we're going to get ahead of this, then I want to see every article that's mentioned Nayak New York.'

Because if anyone had that, the archivist would.

'Yes, boss,' Maurice said warmly and he left her to go do just that.

Yes, boss. She kind of liked that, she thought, a smile curving her mouth.

Someone out there must dislike Chase Miller as much as she and the girls – and presumably his ex-wife – did. All that autocratic, I know best, must have put *someone's* nose out of joint. And she knew exactly who she needed to speak to about it.

BELLA

Are you free this afternoon?

ASTRID

On a work day? BAD Bella.

Of course I am, love.

But bring your leggings.

BELLA

Leggings?

ASTRID

You'll see... 😟

Less than three hours later, Bella walked, some-what nervously, into *Namast-ay*. She hadn't missed the women walking out on her way in, covered in sweat, bright red faces, one stumbling against the building.

She'd told Maurice she'd be working 'off site' that afternoon, which wasn't technically untrue. She was definitely working. Just against Chase rather than for him.

She searched the women dressed in workout gear, looking for a familiar face when—

'Carmichael! Get your cute tush over here right

now,' Astrid yelled across the serene, ylang-ylang scented foyer.

Old Bella would have been horrified. The coarseness, the brazenness. But new Bella, *her* right now, saw her friend and loved every minute of it. Bella hurried over to where Astrid was standing and they embraced like they hadn't just seen each other for brunch a few days ago. Bella felt herself well up a little at the rush of affection she felt.

'You okay?' Astrid asked without letting go.

'Yes. You?' Bella replied, also not letting go.

'Just about.'

And then they laughed and untangled themselves and sat.

'What is this place?' Bella asked, half on a laugh.

'This is the most extreme hot yoga in the whole of New York. It's legendary.'

Bella looked about her, even more worried than she had been.

'And this is where you bring me so we can talk about, our *you know whos*?' she whispered.

Astrid smiled at her. 'It's good to multi-task. Which is kind of how I feel taking on the Titan twins. Do you know what it's like facing that level of testosterone, not to mention all-round freaking hotness on an almost daily basis?' she said. 'I need to drain myself nearly of the will to live just to get my nipples to stand down, so distract me. What do you need?'

* * *

Bella and Astrid queued up in front of the studio with about another fifteen women, all wearing expressions that covered grim determination to fear, with just a few serenities to make it not clear that she should leave before the class even started.

'What do you know about Chester C. Carlton?' Bella whispered into Astrid's ear.

Once Bella had seen Chester's article on Chase from nearly four years ago now, she knew he was perfect. The piece was bitter, asinine and amusing rather than accurate. It had been in a culture section blog for an international newspaper so hadn't really caused any damage or impact.

But Chester C. Carlton was now working as an arts editor for a popularist lifestyle magazine having made a name for himself with bombastic, scathing write-ups of art and culture. He wrote like a food critic who hated food.

Astrid squinted in disgust. 'The man's a literary assassin. He's been called a "wit", but he's not funny in the slightest. He's just mean. Why do you ask?'

And then realisation hit.

'Oh! I like where you're going with this... But,' she said, looking off into the distance again. 'Your PR company won't go near him.'

Bella nodded, Astrid having confirmed all her suspicions. 'But I take it Carlton is the kind of man that would think I'm a stupid, spoiled socialite?'

'Absolutely. He'd think you're a stuck-up rich princess,' Astrid said in agreement. 'Wait!' she half yelled. 'You know you're *not* that, right?'

Astrid's concern made Bella laugh.

'Yes. I do,' she assured her. 'But that doesn't mean I can't play up to it to get what I want.'

The door to the studio opened and they all began to file in.

'Which is why he won't think it's strange that you contact him directly, rather than through the PR firm,' Astrid laughed maniacally. 'I *love* how diabolical you are. Just think what you could do if you used your powers for good.'

Bella nibbled her top lip. That was the problem though, wasn't it? She *had* tried to use her powers for good. And where had that got her? Dumped at the aisle, with her life plan burned to ash and no one there to help her pick up the pieces.

Until the girls.

Until she'd decided to be *bad*.
Fuck me, Daddy.
She really needed to find that book.
And then she walked into a room hotter than hell.

* * *

Two hours later, Astrid and Bella cut a somewhat erratic path down the sidewalk.

'I'm so sorry,' Astrid said, the words panting out of her mouth.

'Why was it so long?' Bella asked, almost imploringly.

'I don't know.'

'And hot,' she said, her skin still pink, even in the cold winter.

'So hot,' Astrid managed to force out. 'It's Blake's fault,' she groused.

'Only Blake's? I thought you said it was the twins plural.'

Astrid waved a hand, eyes averted. 'Tom-ay-to, tom-ah-to.'

'I hate you a little bit right now,' Bella admitted.

'I hate myself a lot of bits right now,' Astrid replied.

'Oh God,' was all Bella could express.

'Chase,' Astrid whispered.

'Oh *God*,' Bella groaned.

'No, Chase,' Astrid hissed, spinning her around to see Chase coming towards them on the sidewalk.

With a squeak, Bella turned, and in a wholly uncharacteristic moment of pure blind panic she pushed Astrid into the hedgerow of someone's front garden.

'Bella!' Chase called out.

'Yes!' she half screamed, half squealed as she turned to face him.

Chase looked a little startled by her response. Bella was a little startled herself to be fair.

'Sorry, I was...' She stuttered over her words, her mind horrifyingly blank.

'Are you okay?' he asked.

'Mm hmm,' she replied, trying to see if Astrid was okay from where Bella had shoved her.

A single hand rose from the greenery with a thumb sticking up.

'Bella?'

'Yup,' she said, the world tipping a little as she turned back to face Chase.

'Are you drunk?' Chase asked, clearly concerned.

'No!' Bella cried out in denial.

He barked out a laugh and finally her brain began

to work. She needed to get him out of here immediately.

'You're a menace, Bella Carmichael,' he declared.

'No, I'm not,' she replied hotly.

'You should not be allowed out by yourself.
Walking around New York pissed as a fart.'

Don't make a scene, Bella.

*We can't take care of you both, sweetheart. It'll be
much easier this way.*

But I'll be good, Mummy. Really good. Please?

'I am not a menace and I wasn't making a scene,'
she cried, feeling her emotions spin out of control.
'And I am not drunk, I went to a yoga class.'

'Bella, it's okay. I was just joking,' Chase assured
her, something like concern flashing in his gaze.
'Come on,' he said, pulling her into his side. 'Let's get
you home. Sound like a plan?'

She turned back to look at where she'd pushed
Astrid into a hedge and saw nothing, so looked up at
Chase and nodded. Unsteady on legs more than a
little wobbly after New York's most evil hot yoga class,
and on emotions that suddenly swept her to very
dark places, Bella allowed Chase to guide her home.

She could feel the warmth of him pressed against
her side, and couldn't help but wonder what it would
be like to live life unafraid of being an imposition. A

problem. A burden. What would it be like to want to burden someone?

She looked up at Chase, and thought how much of a shame it was that he was such a horrible, lying, cheating scumbag. Because, really, she'd quite like to burden him a lot.

9

If your opponent is of choleric temper, seek to irritate him.

— *THE ART OF WAR*, SUN TZU

Chase checked his watch. He'd arranged to meet Bella here after securing a meeting with Sascha through her professor. But he was early which gave him too much time to think. He stared up at one of New York's most respectable art colleges with a mixture of resentment and curiosity.

He'd got a scholarship to the UK and had never looked back. His mom had always wanted him to travel. To study abroad. To live up to his potential.

And now, here he was looking for someone else's potential because he couldn't even look at a canvas let alone a paintbrush.

Get over it, dude.

Ever sympathetic, his inner voice.

I *am* over it. That's why I've got the job as a gallery director.

And you're fucking that up too.

Bella arrived just in time for his inner thoughts to have a WWE throwdown.

Four days ago he'd bumped into her on the way home. And thank God he had because he'd hate to think what would have happened if he hadn't.

They were met soon after by Sascha's professor who led them through halls towards studios that smelled of paint, damp, coffee and nicotine, because kids still thought they were invincible.

'We've had our eye on Sascha for a while. Her promise was evident from the very beginning.'

Chase tuned him out and instead cast glances at the studio space. What had once been white walls – and would be periodically painted over again – currently looked like rough drafts of Pollock paintings. There were a few students still here in the afternoon. The die-hards.

He remembered. He'd been one himself.

Paint beneath the nails, knuckles grazed from pulling canvas across frames they'd made themselves.

A sudden memory of him and Dave falling into hysterics, because Dave had cut one piece of wood too small and didn't have enough wood left to fix it, and had mulishly decided to keep it, resulting in some kind of deformed rhombus. Their art teacher hadn't seen the funny side of it.

But they had laughed until they'd cried, gone to the pub and laughed some more.

Sometimes Chase wondered if that was the deepest betrayal from his wife. That she'd taken his best friend with her. Ruined all his memories of them.

'She's been working through here for the last six months,' the professor said. 'I'll just make the introductions and then... maybe if you could pass by after, we could interest you in our donation programme—'

'No,' Chase replied, without sparing the man a glance as he entered Levy's studio space.

His eyes consumed the walls as, behind him he heard Bella apologising to the professor and lying about a meeting that they had after this. Irritation and resentment burned and, after the professor left, he turned to block her path.

'What was that?' he demanded.

'What was what?'

'What you said to the professor just then,' he demanded, holding onto his temper by a thread.

Instead of backing off as he'd expected, she leaned in and whispered harshly, 'I was apologising for you.'

'Why?'

'Because you were rude,' she declared. 'And because if we're going to make Nayak New York a success then you need to *stop* being *rude*,' she exclaimed hotly.

'Do you want to know how much of their "private donations" go to providing scholarships for financially disadvantaged students?' he asked, her eyes registering confusion at the sudden about-turn of their conversion. 'Twenty-three per cent. Do you want to know how much of their "private donations" go to BAME students? Sixteen per cent,' he said as Bella stepped back.

'If I am going to donate to anything, then you can be damn sure that I want *all* my money going to where it should go, instead of lining the pockets of board members.'

'I didn't know,' she said, her eyes huge and glistening.

'No, you didn't,' he said, 'because you just give the

money, and as long as you're told it's for a worthy cause, you don't really care.'

He was wrong. He knew that the moment he'd said it. The 'you' hadn't been *Bella* specifically, but people like her. But that still didn't change things.

'Don't ever apologise for me again,' he warned frostily.

He turned on his heel, pushing down his anger at the professor and the discomfort at arguing with Bella, and stalked towards the studio space where Sascha Levy was eyeing him coolly, clearly having heard his disagreement with Bella.

'You do your research,' Sascha observed.

'Always.'

'It's about time someone put him in his place,' Sascha said of the professor that had left.

'That wasn't putting him in his place, sadly. But as my comms director says, I've got a gallery to make a success of.'

'And you're looking for art at a New York college? You've got bigger problems than your personality.'

'I think Bella would disagree with that right now,' he said, his eyes on her artwork.

Sascha Levy was a tall, angular young woman who wouldn't grow into her hard lines. But she was striking and defiant and Chase liked that a lot. She was going to need some of that defiance if he had any hope of pulling off what he wanted to, now that he'd seen her artwork.

Potential, the professor had said. Patronising ass didn't even know what he had here. The man had probably locked himself away at this college for nearly thirty years, never challenging himself, or his creativity, as much as his students did.

Christ, he was furious. He knew it wasn't the professor. It was being here. The energy, the creativity, Sascha's work on the walls, and fucking hating that it wasn't his. That he wasn't the one with the paintbrush, that he wasn't the one pouring out his inner essence on the walls and not giving a shit who saw and thought what.

He hadn't felt that way for *years*.

She deserved more time. Time that she'd probably take for granted, just like he had, but she was also ready. To *work, t*o sell, to show, for her pieces to be seen.

Chase was aware of the weight of Bella's gaze, flicking between them and the walls.

'You need a lot of work,' he said truthfully, but he could see it: what she really could be.

'What did you use here?' he said, walking over to one canvas.

As Sascha walked him through her process, he took it all in.

Monochromatic slashes, with texture and tears and energy. Fury, anger, hunger.

Relentlessly physical.

Something deep within him recognised her talent and cried out in joy at seeing it.

'You have more?'

'Yes,' she replied.

'Is this your only studio space?' he asked.

'I have... a space,' she replied a little cryptically.

He'd let her have that. Because every artist needed safety. Somewhere they could be completely them without fear of judgement, observation. Somewhere to experiment, somewhere to... *fuck up.*

'Some of these are good starting points, but we'd need more.'

'We?'

'Nayak,' he said.

'Your new gallery,' she said as if it were a little pet project.

He smiled at her. 'You can get cocky, that's fine. We've all been there, we've all learned the hard way. You're good, but you need work and direction and you know it.'

Sascha ground her teeth together, but nodded.

'And you're not getting it here.' It was a statement, not a question, but he was glad that she recognised it too.

'No, sir.'

'Don't call me sir.'

'Gotcha.'

Chase hid a smile. 'I'm going to find you some space, we'll take a few days and see where we get to. And we'll take it from there. How does that sound?'

'Amazing,' Sascha replied, for once the guard dropping from her eyes, and the prospect of working with someone she admired practically shining from her skin.

Christ, he felt old.

Potential.

Yeah. So damn much, it hurt.

'Can you give your details to Bella?'

'Of course.'

Behind him they shared information while Chase looked over canvases that made him ache from the inside.

He knew a place where she could set up for a chunk of time. He'd work with her. It would mean that he'd be less hands-on at the gallery, but Bella would be able to pick up what he had to let go of in order to ensure that they had a featured artist for opening night. He was half convinced that she'd do a better job than he would anyway.

'She's good,' Bella said when they hit the sidewalk, falling into step with him. But he wanted, *needed* to be alone.

'She's fucking amazing, but don't tell her that.'

'Why not?'

'Because soon everyone will be telling her that and she'll stop bothering to try,' he said, knowing firsthand how it worked.

'Is that why you stopped painting?'

Her question caught him by surprise. Everyone else pussy-footed around him, ignoring the gaping black hole in his chest.

'No, Bella. That's not why I stopped painting.' He barely managed to force the words out through the fist gripping his throat tight. He needed to get out of here.

He scanned the road, stuck out his hand and hailed a cab.

'I've got somewhere to be. You can head back to the gallery, or home, whatever works for you. I'll see you tomorrow.'

He didn't, couldn't, spare her a glance as he got into the cab and told the driver to take him anywhere but here.

Coward, his inner voice accused.

Damn right.

* * *

Bella stood on the sidewalk, watching the taxi get lost in a sea of cars, buses, cabs and trucks. Raw. She felt raw from their confrontation.

Don't ever apologise for me again.

Even now, the cool winter's dusk settling over New York couldn't dim the fierceness of the blush of shame on her cheeks. She railed against the telling off, wanting to have been in the right. Usually always in the right. But she wasn't. She'd been so eager to smooth the tension with the professor that she'd assumed Chase's rudeness was wrong. But it hadn't been.

And now she felt uncomfortable. Like her skin was crawling and she wouldn't be able to settle until he told her it was okay. She hated it. The fear of having done something wrong. And the fact she was concerned about being good for Chase? That was really worrying too.

She headed back to the apartment, unable to expel the nervous energy that rippled around her, forcing a smile for Isiah, the doorman, and wondering where Chase had gone to as she rode the elevator up to their floor.

She'd just let herself into her apartment, slipping off her coat and dumping her bag on the back of the island countertop, when her phone pinged.

ASTRID

Please tell me you're close to bringing him down.

I need some good news today.

Frowning Bella typed back.

BELLA

Everything okay?

ASTRID

Not really. But it will be.

BELLA

Want to talk about it?

Bella waited, but no reply came.

She checked the group messages, but there was nothing new on there either. She thought of how much Astrid meant to her. How much they all meant to her. Astrid deserved her vengeance, just as much as Chase deserved his *just desserts*. So, Bella the good girl ignored the feeling in her gut that she was missing something, that she didn't have all the pieces, that Chase wasn't behaving like the callous, egotistical, autocratic, cheating scumbag that she'd envisioned him to be, and fired off a message to Astrid.

BELLA

Don't worry. I'm on it.

Bella retrieved her laptop from her bag and pulled up the user ID and password she'd found in the personnel files.

CMiller
V. E. R. M. E. E. R. 1675

Surely if he was logged on, she'd just get a user error or something? She should have tried this with her own account, she realised, her finger hovering over the enter key. But she had to act now. She knew it. Or she'd chicken out, Good Bella overriding her need to get Astrid the just desserts she so desperately deserved.

She prayed to whatever goddess was listening and hit enter.

And just like that she was in. She exhaled a sigh of relief and about three years of her life expectancy.

Putting the laptop to one side, she grabbed her phone and logged on to her work email account, giving the draft email she'd composed earlier that day one last read.

To: ChesterCCarlton@LivingCulture.com
From: BellaCarmichael@Nayak.com
CC: ChaseMiller@Nayak.com
Subject: Nayak Exclusive

Mr Chester,
    I hope this email finds you well. As we gear up to the opening for Nayak New York, I am writing to arrange an exclusive interview between *Living Culture* and Chase Miller, Nayak's Gallery Director.
    Your magazine is absolutely perfect for the audience we are aiming to reach and would relish the opportunity to explore an exclusive, behind the scenes, sneak peek ahead of the pre-opening.
    We are very much looking forward to hearing from you,
    Bella Carmichael

Comms Dir. Nayak New York

It was commsy enough to pass, a little loose enough to suggest that she was every bit as terrible as most people seemed to think she was. In short, it was calculated and completed to perfection. But what was most important wasn't actually the body of the email at all. It was the CC line.

She hit send and, turning back to her laptop where she was logged on as Chase, waited for her email to appear in Chase's inbox. Her foot tapped on the metal support of the bar stool, her pulse pounding in her throat. When the email appeared in his inbox, she deleted it. She flicked into his deleted items and deleted it from there too.

She then pulled up his contacts, settings, and added Chester C. Carlton to his blocked email addresses before coming back out of settings, closing down Outlook and logging off Chase's account.

And in less than two minutes, she'd planted the seeds of what would look like Chase's self-destruction. If Chester C. Carlton disliked Chase now, he was going to absolutely hate him when the man couldn't even be bothered to show up to the interview he'd begged for. Let alone when they sent the new incompetent comms director who may or may not happen to let slip that they lost their featured artist because no one wanted to work with them.

Could she pull this off?

For herself? No. But for Astrid? For the girls? Absolutely.

* * *

Chase squinted at the whisky on the bar. He checked his watch and groaned. It was nearly closing time and he'd been here since... since whenever the cab had dropped him off.

He was in some godawful trendy hipster place where apparently it was cool not to be able to see the person next to you. Christ, he missed English pubs. The closest thing they ever came to a cocktail was a vodka and orange. And if you wanted a straw? You'd be laughed out of the pub. Hell, you were lucky if you got ice.

He hadn't done this for ages. Got trashed in a bar. Not since after Astrid disappeared before he could explain himself. He'd thought about reaching out to her, but what could he have said that would make it okay? That would make *any* of it okay. So instead, he'd spent nearly two days drinking himself into a stupor.

'Well, at least I didn't have to fly to France this time,' Tej said, taking a seat beside him.

Oh, thank God.

'Was that drunken growl supposed to be, *Thank you, Tej. I really appreciate it*?'

Chase nodded his head and then stopped when the room began to spin.

'I think I've drunk more than I thought.'

'That's a lot of thinking, my man,' Tej said, slapping him on the back and raising a couple of fingers to the barman.

'Is she good?' Tej asked of Sascha, taking a seat beside him.

He'd told Tej about her because he needed Tej to be okay with the risk Chase was planning to take. It was Tej's gallery, Tej's money, and Chase wasn't a complete asshole and had absolutely no plans to take such a risk without his permission.

'Yeah. Better than I was at her age,' he admitted.

'Better than you now?' Tej asked, like a punch to the gut.

'I'm nothing now,' Chase said, the humour burning away in the air like ethanol.

'Dude, it's not been that long.'

'Yeah, *dude*, it has,' Chase bit back, taking another mouthful of the whisky.

And even just talking about it, the cold sweat began to scratch its way onto his neck in painful pin pricks, his heart pounding in his chest as if he were facing down a wolf, rather than the inevitability of life without painting. Failure and fear, familiar, but still as poisonous and painful coursing through his veins.

'Okay,' Tej said, slapping him on the shoulder, as if he knew he needed to be punched out of his internal thoughts and back to the present. 'So what? You're going to avoid this kid?'

'I'm going to help her put together a collection that will launch her.'

'That wise?'

'It'll be good for Nayak. Come out of the gate swinging with the unexpected. Show that it's not like other galleries. Bella will be able to work up some excellent copy about how, in a world of the stayed and familiar, Nayak is breaking barriers and turning the art world on its head.'

Tej barked out a laugh. 'I think I got you two in the wrong jobs. You should switch.'

'I don't have the patience for what she does. But I will need her to step up if we're going to get Levy ready.'

Tej took a mouthful of his drink. 'I'll keep an eye

on her if you like. I'm sure she can handle it though.
She's handled you. That's enough to take down lesser
men.'

She's handled you.

I wish she would.

Chase bracketed his mouth with his hands, ex-
haling his thoughts into his palms. This was good. A
bit of distance between them was good. He'd be out
of the office much more and she'd be too busy to look
his way.

'A bad friend would let you get away with
avoiding my question. I'm not a bad friend, Chase. Is
it wise for you to help Levy, when just one meeting
with her results in this?' Tej asked, waving a hand between their glasses.

Chase swallowed. 'You are a good friend. Which is
why you're going to sit here and watch me get blind
drunk, get me home safely and pour me into bed and
never speak of it again. Just tonight,' Chase said,
shaking his head. 'I just need to get it out of my system,' he said, like a promise he hoped to keep true.

Chase held his breath while Tej considered his
request and then nodded once.

Chase signalled for another drink.

Is that why you stopped painting?

No, Bella. That's not why I stopped painting.

10

If fighting is sure to result in victory, then you must fight.

— *THE ART OF WAR*, SUN TZU

Bella hit the sidewalk at a jog, her breath fogging the morning air, ear buds Bluetoothed to her phone and playing a song that she hadn't heard since her teens. She thought of the girls' WhatsApp messages. Astrid seemed happy enough with the progress she was making with Aiden, Sienna was being extra careful with Harvey. He was such a slippery one that she needed to be. Because really, of all of them, Harvey was the one that absolutely everyone wanted taken down. Bella had already messaged Sienna offering any kind of help she needed. Because somewhere along the line, she'd actually discovered that she was quite good at this.

It hadn't taken Carlton long to take the bait. And when his email arrived, it had been full of false obsequiousness, in what Bella presumed was an attempt to lull them into a false sense of security about what she was 99 per cent sure would be a hit piece on Chase.

At least, it would be if she had anything to do with it.

And she did.

So, it would.

But reading through the WhatsApp messages again earlier that morning, she'd realised what was niggling at her. Paige had been unusually quiet and Bella couldn't help but wonder if something was wrong. It wasn't the first time that Bella found herself thinking of Paige and not Olly, or the revenge. And it was happening more and more.

Bella checked the time. It would be early morning in the UK and Paige should be up. She pulled her phone from the case on her arm as she did calf stretches just inside the entrance to Central Park. But every time she went to type something out, it sounded either too formal or too familiar.

Hi Paige. How are—

Delete.

Paige, how are things going—

Delete. Delete.

Hey hun—

Delete, delete, delete!

Hun?? She'd never said 'hun' in her life. Finally, Bella told herself off for being stupid and creating tension where there wasn't any.

BELLA

Just wanted to check in and see how you're doing. Hope everything's okay.

She put her phone back into the case on her arm and set out along the full loop that would give her at least six miles if she did it only once. She'd seen

Chase the day after the meeting with Sascha, looking and sounding like a bear with a sore head.

She'd also seen him roll back and forward on the chair that she'd doctored again since he'd last sat in it. But her greatest delight had been watching him hover over the coffee station in his office, eyeing the sugar packets suspiciously, tearing off the top of one and gently tasting the contents and promptly hurling it into the bin, accompanied by a wholly unnecessary amount of cursing for a place of business, in Bella's considered opinion. The cherry on top was the rather concerned glances Maurice sent his way, before masking his features in a 'business as usual' visage when he caught her looking at him.

But since then, she'd kept missing him. He'd sent emails and updates, and had assured her that if she needed anything he'd be available. Meanwhile, Ali had been in a state of perpetual bliss as Ye-Joon made use of his office space to work on the written part of his BA while also arranging the early deliveries of some of the other artists' work that would be showing their work for the opening.

And as much as she hated to admit it, she could see how Chase's vision was beginning to develop. And it was exciting. Her mind was waking up with the challenge work presented her with, under the creativity of it. But no matter how good it made her feel, she had to remember that once she was done with Chase, she was done with the gallery.

She ducked under a particularly low hanging tree branch, making way for a group of elderly ladies putting Bella's pace to shame, and upped her speed.

She'd been at Nayak almost a month now and while it still felt almost scarily new, she also couldn't shake the feeling that time was running out. She *had* to take Chase down before the gallery opening. She just had to.

Because a part of her was beginning to worry that she shouldn't be doing it. She'd seen him with other people, she'd seen him with Sascha, and while he was still autocratic and difficult, she wasn't sure that she was seeing the cruel, womanising, cheating bastard that she'd thought he was at the beginning of her time here. It was all going the wrong way. Familiarity was supposed to bread contempt. But what she was feeling wasn't...

Her phone beeped and she checked her smart watch. Seeing who it was, she pulled off to the side and took a beat on the bench, retrieving her phone to read the message.

PAIGE

Sorry I've been a bit quiet.

BELLA

Is Olly being awful?

She doubted it even as she typed it. Olly just wasn't horrible, even if he *had* left her at the altar.

PAIGE

No, no. Really… it's fine.

BELLA

I can call if you want?

There was a pause.

PAIGE

Would love that BUT Oliver's started yelling about Pavarotti escaping again and threatening to take him to the pound and Bunky will never forgive me. I should go help.

Bella didn't think that there was a pound for hamsters, but she got the idea.

BELLA

If you're sure you're okay?

PAIGE

Absolutely!

Are you okay though?

Was she? Yes, she was okay. But things with Chase were getting complicated and she wasn't sure what to do about it. She just... didn't want to tell that to Paige who had literally flown to another country and moved into the house of a man she was getting revenge against *for Bella*. Paige who had moved a menagerie of animals into Olly's pristine Cornish show home, one of which was a hamster of extreme girth and the other was a chaotic stray dog called Casper whose favourite thing in the whole world was a soggy tennis ball. She had done *so* much and Bella felt bad. And not the good kind of bad. She felt as if she wasn't quite meeting the standards she needed to. As if she wasn't playing her part.

BELLA

I'm good. I've finally set up that interview for the day after tomorrow.

And that will be the beginning of Chase's downfall.

PAIGE

Go Bella!! Astrid will be THRILLED.

Oh God, sorry, gotta run. Oliver is threatening to make

Pavarotti sleep in the garage. Talk soon xxx

Putting it in writing made it real. Telling Paige about the interview was making a commitment. One that, of course, Bella would follow through with. But it was different to sabotaging Chase's coffee and his chair. It was different to hacking his work account. This was properly, purposefully, ruining someone's career. Or at least, giving Chester C. Carlton the means to do so.

Astrid will be thrilled.

And what about her? Bella hadn't even asked about Olly. Was *she* thrilled that he was getting terrorised by a chaotic and utterly loveable redhead, a sugar-addicted hamster in need of a diet, and a dog that needed daily walks? What possible revenge would satisfy her?

The question pulled her up short, unknowingly

forcing another runner to side-step her at the last minute.

Bella just wanted him to *know*. To know how much that had hurt. To know what it was like to have the future they'd discussed taken away from her. To have the floor beneath her shake and crack.

But did she regret it? That he'd walked away from her?

She frowned and pressed on with her run at a distracted pace. Because surely marrying someone who didn't love her would have hurt more in the long run.

In the last few weeks, she'd been thinking of him less and less. But she wasn't sure whether that was because she was focused on her plan to bring Chase down or whether it just didn't hurt so much any more.

She thought about the life she'd wanted. The house, the children, the picket fence, and the charity galas, seeing it for the first time through a bit of a haze.

She'd *loved* Olly. She *had*. They'd been together for two years before the wedding. They'd had a friendship that had *deepened* their love. And yes, much of it had been spent apart, the long-distance relationship necessary because of her charity work in

Upstate New York, and Olly's socialising in California.

But as Bella slowly looped round to the starting point of her run, she realised just how much of their relationship had been about what happened *after* they were married. What life would be like *after*. What she would get *after*. And for the first time since the wedding had been cancelled, she wondered whether Olly might have perhaps been right to call it off.

* * *

Chase was a glutton for punishment. That was the only possible reason he was here, Chase thought as he got off the train at Secaucus. Immediately he felt as if he'd stepped into an Escher painting, as if the past and the present were colliding staircases of confusion.

Half of his brain still felt stuck in Sascha's studio. And he had to think of it like that, because every time he looked up to see someone else's art on the walls he felt like he'd been tasered. Full body electric shock and not for therapeutic, or sexual reasons.

He followed commuters off the platform, down the stairs and out onto the main drag and decided to walk. It wasn't that far. Forty-five minutes? He could do with stretching his legs.

Coward.

In absolutely no fucking rush whatsoever he started the walk back towards the house he'd grown up in.

When Chase had first made it big, he'd tried to give his dad some money, but it hadn't gone down well. His father was a proud, hard-working, blue-collar mechanic who looked after his home, his business and himself. The most Chase had been able to do was pay off his mother's medical bills and the mortgage on a house he knew his father would never leave.

Too many memories here, son.

The cold winter's breeze took bites from the tops of his ears and he hunched into his coat. He passed by places he remembered as a child. His mother on nearly every corner, collecting him from school, shopping at the grocery store, meeting up with a friend and making small talk while he played in the park.

Urban, but still local, his mother would say with pride. An English teacher at the local high school, he should have dreaded going to school, but secretly he'd loved it. Loved knowing that his mom was in the same building. Loved the fact that she was most kids' favourite teacher. Enough so that he wasn't actually given any grief over it either.

He passed a couple walking their dog and looked across the street to where a woman struggled to put a toddler into his car seat.

Get married soon and give me grandbabies, his mother had demanded. He'd been fourteen.

His father had nearly sworn the house down. *No fucking kids! Not until you're at least thirty.*

She'd slapped her husband with a dishcloth and his father had swept her up into his arms and covered her in a thousand kisses. His stoic, monosyllabic dad had done that. Because Daisy Miller could make even the hardest hard melt.

Christ, he'd wanted a marriage like that.

His mother had been beautiful. Thick dark, *Snow-White* hair, pale skin, and so damn kind it would break your heart. She'd filled the small square patch of grass at the back with as many plants as she could, hanging bird seed in the winter and any number of different kinds of food for whatever other wildlife could be found nearby. Half of the time, she was feeding the neighbourhood cats, but no one had the heart to stop her.

She'd loved hard, Chase thought, amazed by it, unable to imagine what it would take for him to love like that and that openly after the betrayal he'd experienced. No wonder his dad had all but disappeared in the wake of her loss.

Chase swallowed as his memories of the area turned into the ones of her last few months.

The weight loss, the nose bleeds. It had taken a while for her to be taken seriously by the doctor, in part because they didn't have a huge amount of money for healthcare but also because she didn't want to make a fuss, or cause a scene.

He'd never forget her apologising to a busy attending physician at the hospital, as if her fucking death was an inconvenience she needed to excuse. Wet heat pressed against the back of his eyes and his heart thumped painfully. Snatches of memories assaulting him from all sides now.

He never should have come back.

You're going to go to art college. You're going to travel the world. You're going to show them all. You're going to be famous. You're going to be an international success.

She'd said it with a wave of her hand, like a gameshow psychic, a jazzy husk to her tone, as if she were dropping prophecies upon him. Even now he could still feel the wires that connected her to the machines pressed between them as he tried to get closer and closer to her, even though she was getting further and further away. His father, poised on the threshold of the door to her room, desperate to give him some time with his mother but physically unable to leave the woman who had his heart for even a second.

When the university offer came through from the UK with a full scholarship, he'd thought it had been a sign from her. And everything he'd done since that day had been to make his mother's words true. He'd worked harder, been more focused, more determined than anyone in his year. He'd hurled his grief at canvases and slashed his fears into colour, grazing his pain into texture and...

And now that he couldn't, it was like it was all coming back to him.

He looked up to find himself outside his father's garage on Main Street.

'Been staring up at this place for a while, son.'

His father stood in the shadows, wiping one of his tools in a rag. It was the first he'd seen of him in about, *fuck*. Seven years? His father hated to travel and had never visited him in the UK. And he'd been so damn busy. He'd come here, years ago, with Annalise, and the thought just curdled his stomach.

'Yeah,' he replied to his dad. It was pretty much all

he was capable of saying. Seeing him again, it was both terrible and fucking wonderful. Terrible because of all the things Chase couldn't say. All the ways in which he'd lost a hold of his home, his wife, his art... And amazing because no matter what, his dad would always be his dad. In Chase's mind he experienced a thousand memories of running up to him and being swept up in his arms and in that moment he'd have sold his soul to do just that. To run so hard, and so fast, knowing – *knowing* – that no matter what, there were two arms that would take him up and make everything better.

'It's been a while,' Chase said instead, hoping a wry smile would make it easier. It didn't.

His father just nodded. 'I'm closing up. Are you staying for dinner?'

No, how are you? What are you doing here? How's life been treating you?

Where's your wife?

'Was thinking about it,' Chase hedged.

His father nodded again. 'There's enough for two.'

His mother had had all the words. She'd made everything pretty with them. She'd made his father smile and love and she'd made Chase see the world with a beauty he'd been chasing ever since she'd died. That was why he hated coming back to visit his dad. Because he remembered too much, hurt too much, felt too much.

'I brought something for you,' Chase said, pulling the bottle of scotch from the deep pocket of his wool jacket.

'Don't want none of that pish now. It'd better be the good stuff.'

'For you? Always,' Chase said, a genuine smile this time at his dad's gruffness.

His father scanned the label, a final nod deciding the evening. That was as much appreciation as Chase would get for a bottle that cost nearly three hundred dollars, but he'd take it. Because sometimes you didn't need all the words.

As his father pulled down the shutter and locked up, he said, without looking at Chase, 'Thanks for coming, son.'

Chase nodded, just like his father.

It was his mother's birthday. He couldn't have not.

11

The opportunity of defeating the enemy is provided by the enemy himself.

— *THE ART OF WAR*, SUN TZU

The five steps to running a con:

1. Look the part.
2. Give them the upper hand.
3. Give them something they want.
4. Get what you want.
5. GTFO.

JUST DESSERTS WHATSAPP
GROUP. 23.40 EST.

BELLA

See, I've done my research.

SIENNA

Where did you get that?

BELLA

Psychology USA

ASTRID

Hahahahaha.

BELLA

No, seriously. It was in their November issue.

ASTRID

You're still scary.

Bella had stayed up all night running through her plan. Whatever Chester C. Carlton wrote, it needed *not* to come back on her. Otherwise, it would look like *her* mistake and Chase would wiggle out of it. So, the article needed to very specifically be about him and not about a failed interview that *she* had set up. In fact, he needed to not mention her at all.

In all of Chester's hit pieces the main running

theme was that his negative expectations were always met; he wanted to like something but he suspected it was going to be awful... and it was. It was his brand. And here was the perfect opportunity. He suspected she was nothing but a nepo-hire socialite with two degrees bought by daddy and nothing between her ears but Prada and Versace.

So that was what he was going to get.

She'd video called Astrid the day before, wanting her input on what Bella had planned to wear. Thankfully Astrid had forgiven her for what was now being referred to as 'the hedge incident'.

She'd decided to go for monochrome. She needed to look like *more* of herself, not a caricature, so more jewellery than she would wear, more labels than she would like, more make-up and higher heels.

'Oh my God, it's perfect,' Astrid had screamed. 'I don't quite know how you've done it. I mean you look like you, but you look like... super annoying. Like the kind of person who would eat three quarters of a plate of food and send it back to the chef.'

'I would never.'

'I know you wouldn't, babe, but you look like you would, and it's perfect.'

The chat had descended into laughter at that

point and they spent another forty minutes on the phone just catching up, despite how tired Bella was leading a double life. Because seeing how much Astrid needed this had pushed Bella's conscience deep down to a place where it couldn't disrupt their plans.

She shook off that thought and stopped outside QT, the trendy bar she'd arranged for the 'interview'. Paige had called in a favour from a friend so that the venue was *not* under the impression that it would be actually used for an interview in case they got stroppy because it didn't end up being featured in the magazine. And it was absolutely perfect. Just the right side of chic to not be too trendy. Near enough the gallery to make it absolutely unconscionable that Chase couldn't make it, far enough away not to raise any suspicion from Nayak staff.

Bella braced herself. She could do this. She would do this. And then the dominos would soon topple on Chase Miller's career.

She pushed open the glass door by the fake elk horn handle that was, in Bella's opinion, a little macabre, but would probably appeal to Chester C. Carlton's style of literary assassination. At 11.30 a.m. the bar was eerily empty until a tall attractive blond with hair cut close to their head greeted her with a smile.

'Are you Bella?' they asked.

'Campbel?'

'Yes, that's me. Paige told me all about you.' The mischief twinkling in Campbel's eyes told Bella that they would be an accomplice to her mission.

'And me, you. This place is fantastic. I'm just sorry you can't get any free promo from it.'

Campbel waved her off. 'No worries. We do alright.'

Bella took in the décor. They must do more than alright. It was beautiful and she already wanted to come back here. With the girls. Maybe to celebrate once they'd all achieved their vengeance. *After* they'd been to Ali's restaurant and filled up on delicious fried things.

'I've got you set up back here.'

Bella followed Campbel past the bar and towards more standard seating tables, which, as she told Campbel, were perfect.

'Okay,' Bella announced. 'So, I'll head out, and if you could call me when he gets here. I'll probably wait at least ten minutes before "rushing in", with all the apologies.'

'Yup. Can do. Anything else?'

'Yes. Could you perhaps fill this with *cold* coffee?' Bella asked, producing a take-out cup. 'And, I'm sorry in advance for the mess. I'll clean it up, I promise.'

'Mess?'

* * *

Nearly fifteen minutes after Chester C. Carlton had arrived at QT, Bella rushed in, bag in the crook of her arm, several pieces of folded paper, phone and keys gripped in one hand, take-out coffee cup in the other, a single, elegant, wisp of hair out of place, and a blush on her cheeks not from rushing here as Chester would think, but from standing out in the damn cold for so long.

Chester C. Carlton had had the gall to be late.

But that only helped her cause.

Step 1. *Look the part.* Rushed, harried and utterly out of her depth was just what she wanted, because no one loves the fall of a socialite more than a journalist.

'Oh Mr Carlton, I am so sorry I'm late. There was a problem with the... no, you don't need to know all that, it's just... anyway. Mr Carlton,' she said again, as if trying to gather herself, 'it is so lovely to meet you. Thank you for taking the time to meet with... us.'

She bit her lip and not-so-secretly checked her watch, scattering papers all over the floor.

'Oh,' she said, letting out a squeaking noise that she'd never once made before in her life. It seemed to prompt Chester to action though as he helped to gather up the discarded papers. One of which was a printout email about Zadzisai, which she snatched back a little too quickly for Chester to get a good look at, but enough to make him curious.

'I'm sorry,' she said *again*. 'It's just that this is the first time I've set up a *real* interview with such a famous journalist and I'm a little nervous.' Her tone of voice was practically the definition of obsequious.

Chester C. Carlton grinned with delight, though whether it was the compliment or Bella's utter ineptitude, she couldn't tell.

'That's okay, sweetheart. You're doing great,' he said patronisingly.

Step 2. *Give them the upper hand*. Making Chester think that he could run this interview lowered his defences and made him overconfident, so when he gestured to the table, Bella knew he'd taken both the lead and the bait.

'Chase appears to be running a little late I gather.'

'Chase? Well,' she winced, a little. 'Mr Carlton—'

'Please, call me Chester,' he said, laying a hand on her forearm.

She smiled, hiding her grimace. This was what she wanted. 'Chester,' she echoed for him. 'I think... when it comes to artistic types, they are often so pre-occupied with their creative endeavours that other things... don't seem to mean as much.'

'Things like punctuality,' Chester said, smiling like the Cheshire Cat. 'I mean, I have met him before so...' he dangled.

'So you know,' she half cried in mock relief. 'You *know* how difficult he is,' Bella said, stretching the truth. 'And how... critical he can be.' Which was almost an outright lie.

'Oh absolutely. Superior and dismissive,' Chester added with a smile.

Well, kind of... but not really, she mused, replying, 'Yes,' instead. 'I am very sorry he's running so late though, so if you'll let me, I'll just see where he is.'

'Absolutely,' Chester replied.

Bella got up from the table and walked a little away. Enough to make it possible for Chester to try and peek at the paperwork she'd purposely left on the table.

She pressed a button on her phone that brought up the world clock.

'Yes, Chase? I know, I'm sorry,' she said, stuttering into her phone as if she were intimidated by him. 'But we have the... no, I understand but... yes. With Mr Carlton. No, I think he'd wanted to speak to you specifically. Oh... okay... well... No, yes, obviously I... Mm hmm.'

She flicked a glance back to Chester who was eating all this up. And now for the pièce de résistance, she cradled the phone in the crook of her neck, tore a strip off the paper sachet of ground pepper she'd found just for this occasion and sniffed the smallest pinch of it.

'Oh,' she exclaimed, accidentally out loud as the pepper reached the delicate lining of her nose. This wasn't supposed to hurt according to the internet. '*Oh*,' she said again before clamping her mouth shut. But finally, as predicted, though with a lot more inconvenience than imagined, Bella's eyes began to well with tears.

Bella caught Campbel's shocked gaze, and the last thing Bella saw before turning back to the table was an impressed thumbs up.

Chester's rather smug look turned to one of alarm when he caught sight of Bella.

'Oh lord, what happened?' he asked, standing up to usher her into the seat opposite him.

'He's... ehm, he's...' Bella didn't even have to fake it, she was practically choking on the pepper, tears streaming down her face – it was all becoming a little too much. A glass of water appeared at her hand alongside tissues from Campbel who seemed under the impression that her performance was Oscar-worthy.

'Oh my God, is he dead?' gasped Chester C. with rather more glee than horror in his expression.

She shook her hand and her head, causing tears to run in different directions.

'Not coming... he's not coming,' she finally spluttered out.

'Oh,' Chester replied, sitting back into his chair and Bella couldn't work out whether he was disappointed that Chase was still alive or not.

'I'm just so embarrassed,' Bella confessed, half truthfully. 'Mortified, even.'

'There, there,' Chester replied, patting the back of her hand.

'I've gone to such lengths to try and get some positive PR after...' She trailed off, glancing at Chester awkwardly.

'Oh hun, we all know about Julia.'

'Yes! Yes, Julia. That's what I meant.'

Chester opened his mouth and then snapped it shut again, eyes appraising.

'And now you'll have to print an article that writes Chase as a no-show and it will all come back on me, because you *know* how he's able to slip around things like that. I should have known better, I should have *done* better,' she said, leaning heavily into the *mea culpa*.

'Oh, no, I wouldn't do that,' he offered, not quite sincerely enough for her to be sure yet. She just needed to give him something bigger to write about.

'And you've been so kind,' she said, leaning across the table and intentionally knocking over the take-away coffee cup so that coffee spilled across all her paperwork.

She gasped in shock and, hand over mouth, as if it were all too much, she ran towards the ladies' around the corner, stopping where she could just make out the table reflected in the mirror behind the bar.

Chester looked after her and then back down and... picked up the bait, exactly as planned. Step 3 was an internal email she'd mocked up about Zadzisai pulling out of the running as featured artist. It would be enough for Chester to speak to the people he needed to and put a story together about Chase's incompetence. Bella had purposefully left Levy out of it, absolutely refusing to draw the young student into this at all.

But she knew she had Chester when he whipped out his phone and snapped pictures of as many of the coffee-soaked documents as he could. She came back around the corner just as he was putting his phone away.

'I really am sorry,' she said, offering to pick up a dry-cleaning bill if it had caught any of his clothes.

He assured her it wasn't necessary, and (a very important Step 4 – getting what *she* wanted) promised not to breathe a word of the interview before he practically ran for the elk horn-handled door. She didn't even need Step 5 in the end.

'Paige said you'd be good, but I must say, I'm very impressed,' Campbel said, bringing cleaning products to the table. 'I don't suppose you fancy trying to break up my sister-in-law and her obnoxious husband?'

Bella smiled, but once again didn't quite feel as victorious as she thought she might have been feeling.

JUST DESSERTS WHATSAPP
GROUP. 11.58 EST.

ASTRID

How'd it go?

BELLA

Like magic.

SIENNA

whoop whoop.

But there was still nothing from Paige.

* * *

Chase was on his way back from the studio. He'd spent nearly the entire day with Sascha, working on the unifying idea for the show, whittling it down to something concise and the deepest, purest expression of thought. Now, it was down to Sascha. He'd pop in over the next few weeks, but they'd done much of the hard work, focusing her creativity, developing artistic expressions beyond the constraints of her degree training, pushing and stretching that creativity to where Chase was sure she could be.

It was just...

The paint. The artwork. The creativity.

It was tearing him apart not to be able to meet his own creative needs. Fuck. *This* was why he'd got a job as gallery director. Because he'd still be in the world, still be able to be near it, but not have to force himself to be around others in the process of creating their art in the way that he no longer could. But now? Now helping Sascha create, hone, and refine her art was the only way he could save the job he'd never wanted in his best friend's gallery.

And now it was the only way he could save the job he'd never wanted, in his best friend's gallery. So yeah, he'd do whatever it took to make it work.

Whatever it took.

He hopped out of the Uber, thanking the driver, carrying the package he'd picked up on the way. He didn't know what he'd been thinking. Clearly, he hadn't been.

But as he'd left the studio, he'd recognised the bakery from the branding on the pastry box Bella had brought to the gallery at the beginning of the week, and he'd stopped at the window.

She might try to deny it, but Bella Carmichael had the sweetest tooth he'd ever known. He remembered her thumb tapping longingly by the description of the red velvet cake at the restaurant they'd gone to. Denying herself.

He hated seeing that. As if she didn't think she

was allowed a treat, an indulgence. No, Bella probably thought it was *bad*.

And before he'd even known what he was doing, he'd stepped inside the bakery and bought one red velvet cupcake.

And here he was, riding the elevator up to their floor, with a small cardboard box, wondering if he'd lost his mind.

It was okay to buy a member of his staff a treat, wasn't it?

Not when your motivation is questionable.

Questionable? he argued with himself. *I'm doing something nice.*

Two words. Bella. Tempted.

Oh fuck off, he told himself.

Perhaps this wasn't such a good idea.

The doors of the elevator opened and he walked slowly down the corridor. He didn't have to give her the cake, he mused. He could just...

But his hand was already knocking on the door.

Bella opened the door and his first thought was something was wrong. Her face was pale and her eyes were dull. Subdued was the word he was looking for. And in an instant, it disappeared under that familiar smile he was beginning to dislike so damn much.

'Chase? Is everything okay?'

'Yes, I just...' He didn't really know what to say.

Bella looked at the box, a little spark flickering in those grey eyes and he nearly laughed.

'I got this for you. As a thank you,' he said, the words coming to mind. 'You've been picking up a lot of my slack while I've been working with Sascha and this is a little – and by no means the least – thank you, for all your hard work.'

Chase took a breath as he noticed the flush on her cheeks.

'If we do make it to the opening, it will be thanks to you,' he added, truthfully. 'We, *I*, couldn't be doing this without you.'

Bella swallowed and he wondered if she'd said something wrong. He'd have thought that she'd be grateful. Or at least even a little snarky, but the quietness was new on her.

'Thank you,' she said, taking the box from where he held it out to her.

She took a little peak under the lid.

'*Oh*. It's red velvet,' she said, surprised.

'I thought you'd like it,' he replied without thinking.

She looked up at him and he was blasted by an unreadable grey gaze.

'Thank you,' she whispered.

And again he was struck by the thought that something was wrong. That she needed comfort, or reassurance. He opened his mouth but she cut him off saying good night and closed the door, leaving him half relieved. Because he'd wanted something then. Something he had no business wanting.

Her.

12

In war, the victorious strategist only seeks battle after victory has been won.

— *THE ART OF WAR*, SUN TZU

OPERATION TROJAN HORSE

- Bask in the glow of success!

JUST DESSERTS WHATSAPP
GROUP. 09.45 EST.

SIENNA

Oh

My

GOD!!

ASTRID

It's AMAZING!

@Sienna did you read it? @Bella
are you awake yet? @Paige where
are you??

SIENNA

I think it's the most incredible thing
I've ever read.

ASTRID

Hahahahahahahahahaha it's
ingenious. Bella you're amazing.

BELLA!! WAKE UP!!

Bella's phone buzzed and buzzed. She'd thought for one rather alarming moment, coming round from dreams about red velvet cake and Chase that she would never admit to a living soul, that it was an earthquake.

But no. It was just the girls. Bella pushed up out of bed, glaring at Delia's book.

Bella's thoughts had been too scattered last night

from Chase's ill-timed present for her to be able to fall asleep. She'd tried to turn to Sun Tzu, but he just wasn't cutting it. So, she'd finally unearthed Delia's book and started reading. She had thrown the book across the room in frustration at some point around three in the morning. And then at 3.15 she'd retrieved it again.

Her phone buzzed again and she reached for it, fearing something awful had happened. A quick scan of the messages still incoming confirmed that it had. Chester C. Carlton's piece had finally landed. And it had landed hard.

Bella clicked through the links to find it and... wow. She scanned the piece, her eyes growing bigger and bigger as sentences jumped out at her, her mouth hanging open in shock.

Portrait of the Artist as an Arrogant Man
By Chester C. Carlton

Having lorded his way through the fine art scene, subjecting any and all to such sneering levels of disdain as to all but ruin one's faith in humanity, Miller – presumably from boredom rather than any genuine desire to bridge the gap between patron and client, and piece and artist, has taken it upon himself to become 'gallery director' at large of Tejvir Nayak's new offering, the eponymous Nayak New York. The well-known property developer, presumably strong-armed into a vanity project for his best friend, seems almost wilfully ignorant of his employee's behaviour and as such, is playing a very dangerous game with his own reputation.

When rumours of near indecent levels of inappropriate behaviour reached my ears—

What rumours? Bella asked herself, scanning the rest of the piece.

Miller's well documented temper could only have been a surprise to an employee who had failed to do their research. He has apparently been terrorising staff, with one all but disappearing without a trace only three months into their job.

And now it appears his ineptitude has cost him the support of another life-long friend and fellow artist Zadzisai. But what could have caused such a rift? Nothing short of the biblical kind of hubris Chase Miller has long since been known for, surely.

JUST DESSERTS WHATSAPP
GROUP. 09.58 EST.

SIENNA

Do you think Chase knows? Do you think he's read it?

ASTRID

Oh God I hope so. Seriously Bella, you're a freaking genius!

Bella looked across her apartment as if she could see through to Chase's. Biting her lip, she padded her way out of her bedroom and towards her front door, her ears pricked for signs of... well. Anything, really.

Why wasn't she feeling as gleeful as Sienna and Astrid? Why wasn't she feeling the thrill of victory she *should* be feeling?

Because he's none of the things Chester C. Carlton said he was.

But he was still a cheating, lying...

A thump and a crash barged their way into her thoughts, pulling her up short about a foot from her front door.

Another loud bang cut through the silence of the early Saturday morning. And then the shouting started, curses strong enough to turn the air blue.

BELLA

He knows.

* * *

Ever since Saturday morning, Chase had fielded emails and phone calls from journalists, friends, enemies, artists, buyers, all with varying degrees of self-interest and rabid curiosity, threatening either to pull their current involvement from the gallery, or future *possible* involvement if they didn't find out '*what Chester was talking about*'.

The problem was, Chase didn't fucking know what Chester C. Carlton had been talking about. He didn't even know why it had happened. Yes, they'd crossed paths several years back and, okay, Chase was willing to admit that to say that he'd been abrupt was putting it mildly. And no, Chase had never liked to 'play the game' when it came to interviews, critics and social media.

But this? This was a wholly unprovoked attack

against him personally. It was a hit piece. Chester was refusing to take his calls, the magazine was refusing to take Tej's and the publisher was saying 'speak to our lawyers'.

Jesus, the whole thing was a mess. And that it had been released on a Saturday just made the whole thing that much harder. The online edition had hit just hours before it reached the news stand, and while for most it wouldn't have made front-page news, in the art world it was *everything*.

He'd spent all of Sunday evening clearing his inbox after spending three hours with Sascha in the studio. And how it was that a twenty-three-year-old art student was the sanest person he'd spoken to in the last three days, he didn't know. But he was damn thankful.

'Hit piece?' she'd asked.

'Hit piece,' he'd confirmed.

And that was it. She didn't need to know anything else. And he'd blocked it from his mind for those blessed three hours.

But it was 6 a.m. on Monday morning, Chase was already in the office and once again his inbox was full.

He rolled towards the drawer side of the desk to get his planner out, but the wheels were off and he rolled too far, whacking his knee on the cabinet instead. He let out a shout of raw frustration. Gritting his teeth, he flung himself back away from the desk, got up, glared at the chair because there was clearly something wrong with it even though he couldn't tell what, and rolled his shoulders.

Coffee. He just needed coffee.

He limped over to the coffee station and grabbed his coffee, sugar and realised that the water cooler was out. Huffing out a sigh, he went to the kitchen, filled a jug with water, came back, filled the coffee machine, waited for the light to turn orange, inserted the pod, nerves soothing as the scent of coffee filled the air from the pour. He tore the top strip off the sugar sachet, emptied the contents into the cup and took a calming breath before knocking back the scalding hot espresso and proceeding to spit the whole thing out back onto the floor of his office.

He had some weird out-of-body moment where he genuinely saw himself as a cartoon character with a huge red head and steam coming out of his ears. He wanted to rage, to break things, to *hurt* things. The abject horror of the last two days was finally getting to him and for a horrible moment he thought he might actually cry. Cry from rage. What the fuck was happening to him? Why was everything going so wrong?

Running a hand through his hair, he turned and found Maurice, Bella and Ali all standing staring at him in shock.

'Oh fuck off!' he shouted at the top of his lungs to no one in particular and they scattered like marbles.

* * *

Three hours later, Tej found him on the roof of the building, where he'd hidden from the rest of the staff since being caught throwing a tantrum like a little child.

'I always liked this view.'

'Tej, you like every view that isn't Mumbai.'

'That is also true.'

'How much shit did you get from your dad?' Chase asked, knowing that Tej would lie and say it was nothing. He hated that this was impacting Tej so badly.

'It was nothing.'

Chase huffed out a bitter laugh. He knew what he should do. He knew that quitting was probably the only way to make sure the gallery stood a chance at a half decent opening. But he'd quit so much. His art.

His marriage – not that that was entirely his fault. An-nalise had quit on him long before then. But he had quit London. He'd given up on so many things, in-cluding the dreams his mother had for him.

Christ. He had to stick at *something*. But not at the expense of his friend.

'Tej—'

'I don't accept,' Tej said with a shrug. Sometimes talking to Tej was like talking to someone with ex-actly the same brain. 'I don't want your resignation, Chase.'

'Tej, be serious. I'm going down and I'm taking this gallery with me.'

'The captain always goes down... actually, wait I'm *not* going down on you.'

'*I'm* the fucking captain,' Chase snapped back.

'No, *I'm* the captain, *you're* the gallery. And al-though I love you bro, I'm never going to go down on you.'

'It's *with*, not *on*, you muppet.'

'There's really no need to start name-calling.'

'Chester started it,' Chase announced, nearly at strop levels.

'It might have helped had you not called him an "insufferable egotist who wrote like he was being paid by the word and had debts to pay".'

'I said that?' Chase asked, half impressed with himself.

'Apparently so.'

'When?'

'Couple of years back.'

'Huh.'

'Seems fair, after reading that article.'

They both broke into smiles and standing side by side, looked down below at the sidewalk where people hurried back and forth. While that New York hum – absolutely unlike anything else in the world – played in the background. A mixture of building work, conversations, the roar of the subway, and something that could only be the beating heart beneath it all.

'Was it a hit piece? Yeah. Has it damaged Nayak New York?' Tej shrugged. 'Remains to be seen.'

Chase barked out a laugh. 'You know the PR firm is thinking about cancelling the contract.'

'Then they're not the right PR firm for us. Look,' Tej said, turning to Chase, finally with the seriousness Chase felt the situation warranted. 'If you want to leave, I get it. No harm, no foul. I wouldn't want you to stay somewhere that was unhealthy for you.'

Tej's pause wasn't for dramatic effect. That was the thing that meant the most to Chase. If he said it, he meant it. It was that simple. So, Chase knew that Tej wasn't trying to reverse psychology him. But he *was* giving Chase the opportunity to really think about it.

'But if you're only leaving because of some misguided sense of obligation, then fuck that.'

Chase could walk away now. Leave the gallery, leave Sascha, he knew that Tej and the team would honour their agreement with her, so that wouldn't be a problem.

Was this what he'd always wanted to do with his life? Absolutely not. Did that mean he shouldn't be doing it? As an artist, he'd got the chance to do something that so few people had. He'd got the chance to paint, to explore his creativity, to show his pieces in galleries and was lucky enough that a few very wealthy people had thought it worth the obscene amounts of money that they'd paid for it.

But he hadn't been able to pick up a paintbrush for over a year now. Even now, the thought of it all brought him out in a cold sweat. The gut-churning, nauseating, near paralysing *fear* of it all. That was *unhealthy* for him. But this? Whatever Chester C. Carlton wanted to write about, he *could* do this. He could be a gallery director for Nayak New York. And he would make it work.

Chase nodded. 'We go down with the ship.'

'We go down with the ship,' Tej echoed. 'Are you sure it's not *on*?'

'Yes.'

* * *

Bella followed Maurice, Ali and Ye-Joon into Chase's office, which usually felt spacious, but not today with Tej and the proverbial elephant in the room. She was confident that Chase would be announcing that he was stepping back from the gallery director position and that Tej would – in all likelihood – step into the breach until they found a suitable replacement. She'd drafted a comms piece stating as much after getting off the video call with the girls on Sunday.

As the first real piece of revenge against their exes it had been cause for celebration, which was why they'd all made the effort to video call. Astrid and Sienna had been drinking champagne, while a slightly subdued Paige had opted for a gin and tonic, having developed a taste for it after being in the UK for nearly two months now.

And all the while Bella smiled and took the credit for giving Chase his *just desserts*, she told herself that perhaps she'd feel something *more* when Olly got his.

'What did he say?'

'What did he *look* like? Oh God, tell me he looked terrible. The man is far too good looking for his own good.'

Bella had bitten her lip, not wanting to think about how Chase looked. Especially not the last time she'd seen him at her door with a red velvet cupcake. But since hearing the crashes and bangs from his apartment, she'd not seen or heard anything from him until she'd arrived at work that morning. At least now she'd be able to tell them. Now she'd be able to tell them how defeated he looked when he quit.

Only... Chase didn't look defeated. He looked mulish. And mulish wasn't part of the plan.

'There's no point beating around the bush. You'll all have seen or heard about Chester C. Carlton's article,' Chase began.

Everyone in the room nodded, Bella hoping that she didn't blush. She was, she was beginning to realise, very bad at *being* bad.

'As a result, we'll probably be fielding a lot of queries in the next few days. Bella, can you put something together that either sidesteps the query, or addresses it in a way that shows we're not taking it seriously?'

'Absolutely, I... ehm, what?' she asked, looking up at them. 'We're not taking it seriously?' she repeated.

'No.'

Bella's mind went completely blank. This had never happened before. She made plans. Executed them. And they went as predicted. Always. This... Chase *staying*... wasn't part of the plan.

'Why?'

Chase blinked.

Oh crap.

'No, sorry. I don't mean why are you staying, obviously, that would be...' She laughed, hoping no one heard how fake and awkward she sounded right now. She waved a hand. Maurice side-eyed her, Ali laughed with Bella, and Ye-Joon pumped his fist in the air, presumably in support of Chase.

Bella swallowed. 'I'll have something drawn up by lunchtime.'

'Excellent. And I'm going to need you this afternoon to sit down with me, Tej and Magenta,' he said, flicking the screen of his iPad.

'Sure, of course,' Bella said.

'How do you want to handle comms until then?' he asked, finally looking back up at her.

She blinked, hastily regrouping her scattered brain cells.

'If we get calls from journalists, it's no comment, for clients, Carlton is a disgruntled journalist with an axe to grind, and for artists there's no such thing as bad publicity,' she snapped out.

Chase looked to Tej leaning against the back wall, his arms crossed over his chest, who nodded, before turning back to the team. 'That works. Let's do it.'

Bella swallowed again and followed the team filing out of Chase's office back to theirs.

'I wonder what Chase did to that guy? The piece was terrible,' Ali whispered to Ye-Joon.

'These journos, man. They're all up in your business but if you piss 'em off, that's it. You're as good as done.'

'Bella,' Tej called. 'Can I buy you a coffee?' he asked with a laugh, pointing to the kitchen.

'Of course,' Bella offered with a smile. She turned to follow him and then her thoughts hit her, near stopping her in her tracks.

Oh God.

What if he knows?

What if someone had spoken to Chester? What if he'd told them about her involvement in the interview?

Ohmygod, ohmygod, ohmygod.

'Actually, can I...' she asked trying to excuse herself.

'This won't take long,' Tej assured her.

Ohmygodohmygodohmygod.

As she nibbled the centre of her lip, her heart went into overdrive and her cheeks burned.

'You okay?' he peered at her curiously.

No, sir. I am not *okay.*

I am about to sweat through my shirt, because I am FREAKING OUT.

'Of course. I just need some water,' she said, pushing a glass under the tap.

Get. It. Together.

She downed half a glass of water, took a breath and turned. She would face this, whatever it was, head on. She hadn't done anything wrong. Not really. And if she *had* been caught, then she'd simply 'silly socialite' her way out of it, like she had with Chester.

'Listen, I'm a little worried about Chase and I was hoping that you'd be able to keep an eye on him,' Tej said, with a rueful smile. 'It's not been easy for him to move from artist to gallery director and now this.'

'Oh, of course, that's no problem at all,' she said, offering her most compassionate smile.

Not been found out. Okay. We're back on track. It's all okay.

'It's just that I haven't really seen him like this since his wife cheated on him,' Tej shrugged.

'You mean, he cheated on her,' she corrected.

'No,' Tej said, with a frown and a shake of his head.

'Mmm,' was all Bella was capable of saying as her stomach dropped to the floor and her entire body was filled with dread.

'No, Annalise was sleeping with Chase's best friend. Poor bastard walked in on them just over a year ago.'

A ringing started in Bella's ears. Sadly, not enough to block out Tej's words.

'And as if that wasn't enough, Annalise tracked him down to where he was staying with this chick he really liked, and then told her that Chase was still married. All because Chase re-fused to agree to let her have the house that *he'd* bought in London. I'm telling you. *Nothing* could convince me to get married. *Nothing*,' he said, shaking his head, while Bella stared at him with bug eyes.

After about a minute, Tej collected himself. 'So will you?'

'I will?' Bella all but squeaked.

'Keep an eye on him.'

'Yes! Yes, I'll... I'll do that,' she said, staring at a blank space for nearly ten minutes after Tej left. Then

she rushed out of the office, without her coat or bag,
ignoring Maurice and Ali.

JUST DESSERTS WHATSAPP
GROUP. 10.39 EST.

BELLA

Code red.

Code RED.

HELP! NOW!

13

If you know neither the enemy nor yourself, you will succumb in every battle.

— *THE ART OF WAR*, SUN TZU

Bella rushed out into the frigid winter's morning, blindly hitting the call button on the Just Desserts WhatsApp group icon, hoping that at least one person picked up.

Oh God, she hoped it was Astrid. She *really* needed to speak to Astrid.

Astrid picked up.

And Bella burst into tears.

'Oh my God, love, what's wrong?' Astrid's voice floated to her from the screen that Bella couldn't see from the tears flooding her eyes.

'I've messed up. I've really messed up. *We've* really messed up.'

'What's going on?' Sienna asked as she clicked onto the call.

'Shit, Bella are you okay?' Paige's voice demanded.

'No, it's all wrong. It's all so, so, so wrong,' Bella said, near hysterical. She really wasn't good at being bad at all.

'Bella Carmichael, you stop crying this minute,' Sienna snipped through the phone, which had the desired effect. Bella sucked in a breath of air and swallowed the sob that had risen in her chest. 'Now find a bench, sit down and tell us what happened.'

'What is she doing in New York in the winter without a coat?' Paige hissed to Astrid, who simply shrugged, looking as confused as the others.

'He wasn't married,' she hiccupped. 'I mean, not really.'

'Who wasn't?' Sienna asked.

'Oh shit!' Paige exclaimed, realising who she was talking about.

'Yes, he was,' Astrid bit back. 'She told me. She had a ring and everything.'

Bella swallowed. 'She was after more money in the divorce. She'd cheated on him. With his best friend.'

And as she said each extra bit, she felt worse and worse and worse.

'Wait. What, Chase? Chase wasn't married? Oh *shit*,' Sienna said.

'No, he *was* married,' Astrid insisted. 'Because if he wasn't, then...'

'Then we just got revenge on a man who walked in on his wife shagging his best friend,' said Paige. '*Fuck*.'

'Can everyone *please* stop swearing?' Bella practically shouted down the phone.

All the girls stopped talking and looked at Bella, shocked by her or the situation, she didn't know. Bella wiped at her cheeks.

'I've got to get back to work,' she said, taking a deep breath of frigid wintry air.

'You're going back to work?'

'Fu— I mean, screw that—'

'That's still technically swearing—'

'You should get out of there. We'll make up some excuse for you. Just pack up and get out of there,' Sienna said.

Bella shook her head. 'I can't do that. I've literally destroyed this man's career. I can't leave it like that.'

Astrid bit her lip. 'You weren't to know.'

'I know but...' Bella took another deep breath, reason returning as she realised what she needed to do. 'I'm going to make this right.'

'How?' Paige asked.

'I don't know yet,' Bella admitted, her lip wobbling a little.

'I can be with you in minutes. Just say the word,' said Astrid. 'If you want me to go in there and explain the entire situation to him, I'll—'

'God no, I need to save his career while he still trusts me to do it. If he gets wind of this, there's no chance he'll let me anywhere near him or the gallery ever again.'

'Of course.'

'I just need time to think.'

'But if you need anything...'

Bella nodded.

'It's going to be okay,' Sienna assured Bella.

'It really is,' Paige echoed.

They just had to bring Chase's reputation back from the brink and assure that from the ashes of almost assured destruction, Nayak New York would rise like a phoenix.

She didn't have the faintest idea how, but if she could get him into this mess, then she would get him out of it.

She could do this. She had to.

* * *

Bella would never know how she got through the rest of the day at the office after Tej dropped the truth bomb on her. But she did know that she strong-armed the PR company back in line, barely letting Chase or Tej get a word in.

'What kind of PR firm can you call yourself if you fail to handle one single defamatory article for your client? *One.* Has anyone come out of the woodwork with anything other than rabid curiosity? No. Has Julia made any statements to any kind of misbehaviour on behalf of Nayak's Gallery Director? No. Have clients? No. Have fellow artists? No.

'And are you not currently representing one aspiring senator with several pending criminal charges and one banking CEO with five fraud charge? Yes.'

'They were just charges.'

'And this is *just an article*. Pull up your sleeves, and get to it.'

Despite taking a chunk out of Magenta for getting

cold feet, she and they *both* knew that ignoring the article would get them only so far. They'd brainstormed a few ideas throughout which Chase had rolled his eyes and groaned, stopping only when Bella had glared across the table at him. He was *still* frustrating her at every turn, even now that she was trying to save him rather than ruin him.

What they currently had planned for the promotion leading up to the opening would stay in place, but they needed something *more*.

When Bella had mooted the Harrison's annual charity gala at the end of the month, Magenta had scoffed, and Chase had growled. Tickets sold out usually on the day of release which was an entire eleven and a half months ahead of the infamous event that was the Met Gala of the charity calendar.

Cara from the PR firm had suggested that she call her father and the room had gone deathly quiet.

'I won't *have* to call my father if you do your job,' she'd said snappily and conversation had been quickly steered towards what Nayak could offer. It was at that point that Chase had reached his limit and she had closed down the meeting before it could get any worse.

As they'd left the office, she could have sworn Tej

you go girl'd her, under his breath. Chase had simply watched her, his gaze unfathomable.

Bella let out a half growl, half urgh, that sounded something like someone being murdered and stared at her computer screen two hours later. It was all very well and good to bring publicity to the gallery. But what they needed was something very specifically about *Chase*. They needed something redemptive. A Good News Story. Which of course he would hate. Which had her growling again.

'Go home, Bella,' Chase ordered as he stalked past the office that she was in alone.

'You're still here,' she yelled back.

'Go home. I need you back here bright, sparkly and slightly less murdery tomorrow,' he said, stalking back past the office on the way into his.

She glared at him, but he was right.

She needed to get out of here. She needed to get back to her apartment and she needed the girls.

* * *

'How's she doing?' Tej asked, passing Chase a beer and lifting the lid on the most delicious pizza any New Yorker had ever known.

Chase leaned back into the only seat in his office he could trust – because it wasn't on wheels and wasn't actively trying to kill him – and rubbed a palm over the stubble along his jaw. Shit, he'd forgotten to shave again.

'I'm a bit worried about her. She seems to be taking the article personally,' he admitted, looking to the top of the stairs he'd practically forced her down almost an hour ago now. 'It's a bit like she expects strangers to come up to me on the street and start throwing rotten vegetables at me.'

Tej huffed out a laugh around a mouth full of pepperoni, onions, cheese and olives. Now this he *had* missed while in the UK. Not Tej's verging-on-unholy topping combo, but the pie.

'There's still time,' Tej warned after swallowing.

Chase took a long pull on his beer, relishing the hoppy taste explosion on his tongue. It was better than the acrid bitter taste that he'd been left with following their meeting with Magenta. He'd promised Tej that he'd stay and fight this. But he was honest enough to admit that the PR firm's response had him a little more rattled than he'd been before.

Instead of the furore dying down, it was only seeming to increase, and just this little taste of it made him think about what Bella had experienced following the wedding that she'd had to cancel for her crappy, gutless fiancé.

She'd not had a PR firm, or a team of staff around her when the press had descended. Worse, she'd been sent away by her family because of the impact she was having on their charity work.

She'd borne rabid intrigue, spiteful gossip and running commentary bordering on slanderous with the grace and poise of a beauty queen. The last thing Chase had felt reading that one article was graceful or poised, and his respect for Bella and how she had dealt with things had skyrocketed.

He'd been worried that dealing with Chester's article was reminding her of all that. She'd seemed distracted, but determined in a way he'd not seen before. Obviously she was doing excellently in her role, and it wasn't just him thinking so either. Maurice had sent him an approving nod earlier, and Ali thought that the sun rose and set with Bella Carmichael. After her initial shock, she'd hit the ground running and handled the majority of the incoming queries herself which cannot have been easy.

But still...

'I'm surprised she hasn't tried to pull some kind of publicity stunt to try and redeem my reputation,' he thought out loud.

'Yeah, I can just see it now,' Tej said. 'Children?'

'Of course children,' Chase said, half laughing.

'It might not be so bad.' Tej shrugged.

'It'd be fucking terrible, Tej,' he replied without missing a beat.

Tej pulled a face. 'It happened on her watch. Maybe Bella feels responsible.'

Chase picked at the bottle's label. 'That how you see it?' he asked, keeping himself in check so as not to jump down his friend's throat in Bella's defence.

'Fuck no.'

'Good,' Chase replied, a little heat escaping into his tone.

The sudden strike of protectiveness unsettled him. Bella could certainly take care of herself. She'd proved that and then some. But...

I am not a menace and I wasn't making a scene.

He'd seen it. The vulnerability. The fear. He hated that for whatever reason, she'd not let herself be... loud. Be... relentlessly physical.

He coughed and spluttered as his beer went down the wrong way.

Tej ignored him as he died not so quietly, thumping his chest to try and ease the congestion.

'But think about it though,' Tej said, his eyes on him.

'What?'

'The children.'

Chase threw the label at him, which Tej expertly ducked, and reached for a slice of pizza.

* * *

'I vote we track down the ex-wife,' Astrid growled later that evening on the video call they'd all scrambled to get to.

All the girls replied with a strong and very definitive, 'No.'

Astrid looked awful. Bella knew that the guilt over her part in instigating his downfall was eating at her, but how could she try to assuage it when her own guilt was an iceberg-sized wedge pressing on her chest?

God, Bella was unspeakably thankful for them. The girls' support had been near constant since they'd discovered Chase's 'innocence'.

'I mean, I'm not sure he's entirely innocent, but certainly less so than we'd thought and planned for,' Sienna had conceded.

There was, the girls were beginning to discover, mitigating circumstances, degrees of guilt and therefore varying appropriateness of vengeance, all of which needed recalibration in Chase's case.

But they were all in firm agreement that he needed rescuing from their overly successful serving of *just desserts*, and that a serious act of redemption in the public's eye needed to happen sooner rather than later.

'It has to be natural. It has to come from him, otherwise he'll sulk and look even more like an ass,' Bella had told the girls, completely missing the way they smiled when she unconsciously cursed.

'What about money? Can't Tej throw some money at something?' Sienna suggested.

'I'm not sure that's going to help,' Paige pointed out.

'I mean, like, some good-will charity thing.'

Astrid scrunched her nose. 'But that's Tej, not Chase.'

'We're already on that. I have the PR team securing tickets to the Harrison's charity gala.'

Appropriate whistles, wows and awe were produced by the girls.

'It's a start, but it's not enough.'

'It needs to be about him.'

'But also not something he thinks is about him.'

He's less tetchy when he's doing things for other people.'

I want people to come in and have the same look on their faces as you did when you came in.

Chase, who was secretly working with Sascha. Mentoring.

'Everyone loves kids,' Bella said.

'Yes, well. Most people,' Astrid replied. 'You're not going to have him adopt a kid for sympathy?' she asked sceptically.

'What? No,' Bella replied, half outraged.

'Well, it's just that since, you know, you went all Jane Bond on us—'

'More like Bella*feld*,' Sienna interrupted with a laugh.

'Hey!'

'Sorry,' Sienna mumbled.

'We're just trying to pull you back from the dark side,' Astrid insisted.

'I wasn't that bad!' Bella cried out in defence.

'No, you weren't. You were that *good*,' Paige insisted unhelpfully. 'But you were talking about children.'

'Children. New Yorkers love nothing more than a gruff man that's good with kids.'

'Who doesn't?' asked Sienna like anyone who didn't would be utterly unreasonable.

'Yeah, but would Chase be any good with kids?' Astrid asked sceptically.

Bella thought back to the way he was with Sascha, and okay, she wasn't a kid, but Bella believed that he would be. She could see how much he would enjoy their unfiltered and uncensored creativity.

Chase disliked people for their duplicity. Something she was beginning to understand more and more, after Tej told her about his wife's betrayal. Children – young children – were much less likely to be duplicitous.

'But who in New York would let their children anywhere near Chase at the moment? He's toxic right now,' Paige pointed out.

Bella anxiously nibbled the edge of a nail bed that she promised to file down properly later.

'What if they think it won't get out?' Sienna suggested.

'What do you mean?' Bella asked.

'Like, what if you do an event that isn't an event, but then you're "found out"?'

'Ohh,' Astrid cooed, 'I get it. Like Chase is "caught" doing "good works".'

'Yes,' Sienna replied.

Finally catching on, Bella's mind moved at a million miles an hour. Words from all the research she'd done on Chase, sentences, opinions, the conversation at the gallery warehouse, the divide between who got to see art, to do art...

'What if we did something at the gallery with a local school?' she began. 'If we invited them to the gallery, got them to create some art and then while they're at lunch, we could hang their pieces on the walls and after lunch they can tour their work in our gallery?'

'Ohh, you could invite the parents too,' Astrid added.

'But how do you get that news out?'

'You don't have to,' Astrid said smugly. 'In fact, the harder you try to keep it a secret, the more likely the press will uncover it, especially if you do this soon.'

'But we can't guarantee that, can we?' Sienna asked.

'And I'm not actually sure I want to subject children to anything remotely press related...' Bella realised, backing away from the idea.

'No,' the girls all hastily agreed.

'But if we could make sure that it wasn't a press gang? If the news didn't get out until after the event, so the press would be nowhere near it. And of course, the "source" would want to protect the children and wouldn't name the school, but I'm sure some "photos" could leak.'

Bella could see it in her mind. Could see how much fun the kids would have. How good it would be and how well it fit with what Chase wanted for the gallery, for art, for a mechanic and a school teacher...

'Okay. What would that look like?' Bella asked and the girls got to planning.

14

In a position of this sort [...] it will be advisable not to stir forth, but rather to retreat.

— *THE ART OF WAR*, SUN TZU

OPERATION PHOENIX RISING

- Restore Chase's reputation.
- Make the gallery a roaring success.
- Stop crying when I see CM.
- Buy the next book in Delia's series.

'I cannot believe that you talked me into this,' he grumbled.

'Just shut up and smile,' Bella commanded.

Chase pressed his lips together. He didn't want Bella to see how much he enjoyed seeing her in boss mode. It was different to before. There was a determination to her that seemed to bypass her natural instinct to defer and pacify, which made Bella come to life in ways he'd just begun to imagine.

But that didn't make him any more comfortable or happy with Bella's idea to open the gallery to a local elementary school whose art funding had recently been cut. He'd stared at her, genuinely concerned how *on the money* both he and Tej had been with her plans to involve children in some kind of redemption scheme, but she had promised him that there would be no journalists and no press attention. This was just about imbedding the gallery into the local community in a way that aligned with his personal tenets.

He wasn't 100 per cent convinced and had begun to suspect that the perfectly poised Bella might be hiding a devious mind. Which was alarmingly appealing enough to distract him from his suspicions. Which was also why he now found himself staring at nearly thirty children aged four and five, all staring back.

At him.

And some of them weren't blinking.

The walls of the gallery were completely bare, Ye-Joon having worked hard over the last few days to take down and protect the artwork they'd put up while working on the layout of what would be the final placement for the pre-opening and opening.

Bella clapped her hands together, looking like a bright splash of colour in the sparse, white-walled setting of a weekday morning. She was wearing jeans, which surprised him. He hadn't seen her in a pair of jeans before. The rich burgundy silk shirt made her grey eyes glow, but he doubted it would last five minutes against a child with grubby hands and a paint-loaded brush. He was trying his hardest to keep his eyes off the way the denim hugged the curves of her backside, and felt the wide-eyed watchful gaze of a five-year-old catching him out.

But what caught his attention the most, was that her hair was down. It was the first time he'd seen it loose and there was so much more of it than he'd imagined. Rich, golden waves hit a few inches below her shoulders, not as long as the middle of her back, but not far off it either. But he couldn't quite understand why he was so taken by it, other than the fact that for the first time he thought he was seeing *her*. Not the socialite, not the perfect daughter or fiancée, not the comms director with something to prove. He saw *her*.

'So, who has been to a gallery before?' Bella asked brightly.

About half of the class put up their hands and Chase was slightly gutted by the sight. Every single one of them should have been to a gallery of some kind. But with the cost of entrance and travel to get there, with busy lives and cheap entertainment, it was harder and harder to get kids into spaces that were so heavily guarded against the noise that children would make, or the mess they could produce.

'And who knows what happens at a gallery?'

The children blinked back at her. Until they all started talking at once.

'Old people walk around a lot?'

'Kids get shouted at for making a noise?'

'People stare at pictures?'

'Children, remember to put your hands in the air if you want to answer or ask a question,' Mr Tawney chided, apparently remembering that he was there to supervise the children and not stare longingly in the direction Maurice had disappeared off to, having taken one look at a class of school children and run as far and as fast as he possibly could.

Chase coughed a laugh and caught Bella glaring at him.

'Galleries are places we go to see paintings and sculptures and other kinds of art,' Bella informed them with a smile, her voice pitched perfectly for the kids. She would have made a great teacher, he heard his mother say in his mind.

Chase swallowed.

'And what does *he* do?' a kid asked, pointing at Chase.

'*He's* my boss,' Bella replied.

'Why aren't *you* the boss?' the little girl asked, with a similar tone to that of a person asking to speak to the manager.

'Because she's a girl,' a boy replied with a snicker.

'Girls can be bosses too,' the future president replied, snippily, crossing her arms definitively over her chest in a 'because I said so' move that should have been enough to stop the conversation.

'But she's not a girl, she's a *lady*,' the boy pointed out.

Battle lines were being drawn, teachers were beginning to look to each other with concern as the situation threatened to escalate. The children moved subtly within the group on the verge of taking sides.

'Can ladies be bosses?' the girl asked, swinging

her attention back to Bella whose smile hadn't changed a bit, despite the way they'd dramatically veered off topic in barely three seconds.

'Ladies can be bosses. *Everyone* can be a boss if they want... they just have to work hard enough.' Which managed to successfully unite every single child in the room with a single disappointed groan as if they'd heard the sentiment many times before.

Teachers breathed a sigh of relief. A united front was better than fighting or out-right civil war. It took a little time to wrangle the kids into the seats at the tables they'd brought in for the visit, but eventually each child was settled down at the table they'd formed into a U shape and all that could be heard was the sound of pen on paper which was strangely soothing.

Bella knelt by a little boy, helping him choose some colours. Maurice passed through the gallery an unnecessary number of times to check on some spurious thing and tried not to fall over his own feet checking out Mr Tawney.

Chase could see that working, he thought with a smile.

He felt a tug at his pant leg and looked down to find a young boy staring up at him with large solemn eyes.

'Yes?' he said.

The kid tugged again.

Chase bent down and offered the kid his ear.

'I don't know what to draw,' the kid whispered, a confession that seemed pulled from Chase's own psyche.

He turned to look at the kid. 'You don't?'

The kid shook his head.

'What about an animal?'

The kid shook his head again.

'A flower?'

The kid scrunched his nose up and Chase hid his smile.

'A house?'

When he went preternaturally still, Chase clenched his jaw. Eventually the kid shook his head. He caught Mr Tawney's concern from the corner of his eye, but waved him off.

'What's your name?' Chase asked.

'Joseph,' the kid replied with a nod that shook almost his entire little body.

'Do you know what I liked to draw when I was a kid, Joseph?'

The kid looked at him as if trying to work out how Chase had once been a kid. Sometimes he wondered himself, but he pushed that thought aside and took the very small-sized child's seat at the table. Joseph laughed as Chase's knees rose above the table, but he came to stand next to him, until Chase kicked out the empty chair beside him for Joseph to sit on. Chase picked a piece of paper and his hand hovered for a second over a pen, before choosing one at random.

'Nothing,' Chase whispered to the kid as he started colouring in the page, finally answering the question he'd asked before. 'I didn't want to draw cats, or clouds, or airplanes,' he said, the pen moving the pen across the paper, while still looking at the little boy.

'What did you want to draw?' he asked.

'I,' he confided at a whisper, 'wanted to draw feelings.'

Joseph looked back at him. Wide, brown eyes full of wonder. 'Can you do that?'

Chase nodded. 'My mother said I could,' he confided. 'She said that I could draw anything I wanted to. Anything. And so can you. With this pen, nothing is right or wrong. And no one can take what you do with it from you,' he told Joseph, who ate up his words like they were the God's honest truth. And that, Chase realised, they were.

He looked down at the piece of paper beneath his pen and stared at the first piece of artwork he'd created since he'd caught Annalise and Darren in his bed.

'What do feelings look like?' the kid asked.

Chase pushed his piece of paper towards the kid. 'Mine look like that today.'

'Today?'

Chase nodded again as Joseph peered over at the colours, hovering over a forest green colour that merged into a deep grey, with slashes of red.

'Tomorrow they might look different.'

The kid nodded sagely as if he understood. For all Chase knew, he did. For all Chase knew, Joseph probably had it more together than *he* did.

They sat beside each other for the next half an hour, as Joseph filled pages with colour, getting more and more confident and happy as he did until Mr Tawney announced they were all going to the park for their packed lunches.

He caught the nod of thanks Mr Tawney threw his way for taking time with Joseph, but shrugged it off. As Bella and one of the teachers gathered up the pictures the children had drawn, he thumbed the edge of the page he'd filled with felt-tip pen scribbles, slid it from the table and slipped it into the bin before heading back up to the office. He felt Bella's eyes on him the whole way.

* * *

Bella, Maurice, Ali, Ye-Joon and one of the parent helpers spent the lunch time putting the drawings into frames and hanging them on the walls of the gallery, in between grabbing bites of sandwiches that she'd ordered in from a deli across the street.

Each child had at least one piece on the wall and once finished, they all stood back and oohed and aahhhed over the adorable pictures. But as Bella looked at the walls, there was something niggling at the back of her mind and she couldn't put her finger on it.

'What is it?' Maurice asked, noticing her distraction.

She wasn't sure. The walls were filled and the bright pops of felt-tip pen looked perfect against the stark white back drop. Innocence and an energy that pulsed from the room but...

She looked to where Chase stood watching her with a knowing smile.

'You know what's wrong with it,' she accused.

'There's nothing wrong with it.' Ali rushed to their defence, while the others looked around the gallery trying to see what she wasn't quite seeing yet.

He nodded, but didn't tell her.

'This has to be perfect,' Bella nearly whined, genuinely wanting the kids to like it, to *love* seeing their own work on the walls, completely forgetting that this had anything to do with his reputation or the article.

She'd seen how much effort the children had put into something so simple, just because they could. Because they'd been encouraged to play and be silly. Not to be means tested or assessed, but to put a little bit of themselves on a piece of paper and for it to go up on the... up on the...

'*Oh,*' she exclaimed, finally getting what was bothering her. 'We've done it all wrong. They all have to come off.'

Ali and Maurice went to stop her, but when she looked back to Chase, he smiled, more with his eyes than mouth, and gestured for her to do what he'd known was needed all along.

The others were confused until she took the nearest picture from off the hook she'd hung it on and lowered it by almost two feet. All of the pieces had been hung at adult eye level and would have left the kids peering up to see their work. It was something that had taken her a while to realise, but Chase had known nearly immediately, his awareness of *how* people accessed art so much stronger than others.

They all scrambled to rehang the pictures before

the kids got back from the park and their parents arrived. Maurice had procured some red velvet curtains that were absolutely perfect, and draped them across the small entrance to the gallery so that the class and their parents could gather for the 'grand unveiling' that Mr Tawney had advertised.

Bella welcomed them all back and Mr Tawney picked the girl who had decided that ladies could be bosses as well as girls, to cut the gold ribbon they'd tied across the velvet curtain and the children poured into the gallery with their parents.

And she had never seen anything more lovely. The look of delight across the children's faces as they saw their pictures hanging on the wall. Bella didn't know if they'd noticed the way that the pictures were hung at the perfect height for them, and then realised that was the point. They shouldn't *have* to notice.

Children held the hands of parents, of each other, of teachers, moving around the room in beautiful chaos, so unlike the way that adults moved progressively painting by painting around a quiet gallery.

Today, Nayak was full of gasps of delight and conversation that *wasn't* hushed, it was full of colour and brightness and noise and everything Bella wanted to see in a gallery again already.

She smiled as she looked around the room, until

she noticed the little boy that Chase had been working with earlier standing alone looking unsure. She was about to cross the room when the boy looked up, a look of happiness passing over his features and he ran smack-bang into Chase's legs.

'Look,' the boy said, his face angled up at Chase.

'I did,' Chase said, smiling, understanding the little boy immediately.

But the child still grabbed Chase's hand and drew him half way across the gallery, almost as if he were dragging a stuffed toy behind him. Bella watched half fascinated as the boy pointed at his drawing. Chase and the boy came to stand opposite the small frame that encased his drawing, both wearing almost identical expressions of seriousness on their faces as they 'looked'.

'If I had ovaries, I think they'd have just exploded,' Mr Tawney said, suddenly appearing at her side.

She let out a huff of surprised laughter, but knew exactly what he was talking about.

'I'm afraid that you might not be his type,' she offered regretfully.

'Oh, he's not mine either,' Mr Tawney confided, casting a longing glance over Bella's shoulder to where Maurice was studiously ignoring them. 'I was thinking for you.'

'Me?' Bella spluttered. 'Oh, no. No, no, no, no, no.' She dropped the denial about them like confetti.

'Mm hmm,' Mr Tawney replied wryly.

'No, seriously,' Bella replied, half panicked.

'Me thinks she protesteth too much,' he stated with a wicked grin and left her standing in the middle of the gallery reeling at what he'd just said.

15

There are roads which must not be followed.

— *THE ART OF WAR*, SUN TZU

They were still finding coloured felt-tipped pens in corners and beneath chairs long after the last child, parent or teacher had left. Chase told Ye-Joon to wait until later in the week to start putting the pieces back up on the walls in preparation for the opening. They were still working from photos of Sascha's paintings to perfect the layout, but he wasn't worried.

But with the children's drawings all taken down, he was once again surrounded by stark white walls, staring at him like a blank canvas.

His heart rate picked up, just like it had earlier even with just a coloured pen.

What did you want to draw?

I wanted to draw feelings.

He released the breath he'd been holding, trying to rid himself of the discomfort the memories brought.

'Night!' Maurice called, an excited smile lighting his features as if they all didn't know he was going out for dinner with Mr Tawney.

'Good luck!' Chase called out behind him as Maurice waved him off with a hand.

Ye-Joon was next, Ali skipping after him, peppering him with questions and looks of adoration that the poor kid didn't know what to do with.

That left Bella.

Bella who'd looked almost relaxed today. Bella in *jeans*. He smiled. Until he didn't. Because those jeans had looked good. Really damn good.

'You were good with the kids today.'

Her words came from behind him. Sneaking up on him just like she had.

'So were you,' he said truthfully, turning to find her standing beneath a spotlight, looking up at him with those grey eyes of hers.

'It's part of the job description,' she said ruefully.

Chase frowned. 'As comms director?'

'Pampered socialite,' she clarified.

'You're not that,' he dismissed with a shake of his head. 'I'm sorry I ever said it.'

She scrunched her nose and a shrugged delicately. 'I'm a little bit of that,' she admitted kindly.

'You've been working very hard. Do you miss it?'

'What, you actually believe that pampered socialites do nothing all day?'

'Tell me,' he asked, just to hear her speak a little more. Just to draw out any kind of conversation with a woman that was fascinating him far too much for his own good.

'Oh, you know. We sit around all day drinking tea, eating cupcakes, planning good works in the community...' she said loftily.

'PTA?'

'Oh absolutely. And making sure that our children are at after-school activities and our husbands are...'

Bella trailed off, filling the gallery with a heavy silence.

'Playing golf,' he offered to fill the space. He hadn't meant to touch on her past but in some ways, they'd been skirting around it all for a while now.

'Golf in the Hamptons,' she added, picking up the

threads of the story they were weaving for her fictional life of privilege, before he could apologise. But as the details rose in his mind, they all felt strangely wrong for the Bella standing before him.

'And what about you?' she asked and he smiled. A hand at the back of his neck.

'Me? The classic, tortured artist,' he said with a little bitterness that surprised him. 'I pour everything I have into my art, while raging against the system,' he said, blurring the line between fiction and fact. 'So much so,' he said, swallowing, 'that my wife becomes resentful and cheats on me with my best friend.'

Bella stared at him with those glowing grey eyes.

He didn't know if she already knew, and right now he couldn't tell from that unfathomable stormy gaze. But whatever was or was not happening between them, he'd wanted her, needed her, to know that about him.

'It's such a fucking cliché,' he admitted. He'd hoped for humorous, but instead it had sounded helpless. He clamped his teeth together to stop any more words from escaping. It went against a lifetime of habit, of *the Miller way*, but something about Bella made him want to break the mould his father had given him. He braced himself for her sympathy. But she just waited. As if knowing that now the dam was breached, it would all come pouring out with only her to stem the flood.

'She was an artist too. A ceramicist. A good one,' he acknowledged, 'but not a *great* one,' he replied truthfully. 'And ceramics are harder than painting already so...' He shrugged. 'We should never have got married,' he admitted now to himself and to Bella. 'I was...'

Get married soon and give me grandbabies.

Another way he'd failed his mother's dreams for him.

'Rushing headlong into things I shouldn't have,' he said, picking up the threads of the conversation he'd started. 'And after the success of that first show, things just snowballed for me. I loved it. Pouring everything I had into my pieces, not realising just how much Annalise hated it. Resented it.

'She had this image in her head of us, struggling together. Of being passionate artists, living off our creativity and whatever crazy indulgence we could find,' he said, finally looking back and seeing how difficult it must have been for her. That he hadn't been what she'd thought she was getting. And with each success he'd had, she had drifted further and further away. And he hadn't noticed. He hadn't noticed how much that had hurt her. And he should have. Dan had.

Chase swallowed.

'I'm sorry that she couldn't be happy for you and what you'd achieved,' Bella said and deep down something caved in on itself, her words soothing a hurt he'd not allowed himself to acknowledge, let alone speak of.

'Do you miss her?' Bella asked.

'No,' Chase replied truthfully. 'I should. But I don't. I feel... relieved.' The word emerged on a heavy sigh, guilt and hurt and loss and... relief, all knocking him for six. Yes, they had betrayed his trust, and trust was still something that he found difficult to contemplate. But he wasn't blind to the way his own actions had helped form the problems in their relationship.

It takes two people to ruin a marriage.

That was what Annalise had said to him the day she'd found him in the hotel room with Astrid and she wasn't talking about her and Dan. She'd meant that Chase had ruined things for *her*. That he'd ruined her plans, her life, her future, the things *she'd* wanted. And that was what she'd wanted to do to him. With Dan, with Astrid.

And Chase would never put himself back in that kind of situation again.

'Relieved and thankful. Marriage is not for me. Not again,' he said firmly.

He knew what prompted him to say that.

He knew he wanted Bella to know that.

Bella was the kind of woman that still wanted marriage, children, the Hamptons.

He wanted her to think, to know, that he wasn't what she needed. Wasn't what she wanted when she looked at him with those unreadable eyes of hers.

She opened her mouth to speak, but then the sound of her phone ringing from her bag stopped her.

With an apologetic smile, she checked the screen and frowned.

'I'm sorry, I have to—'

'Of course...'

And just like that she was gone.

* * *

'Hey Paige,' Bella said as she exited the gallery, her mind still half on the conversation with Chase. With what he'd shared and what she'd felt, but the fact that Paige was calling was unusual enough to make her concerned.

'Hey,' Paige said brightly. 'How'd it go today? Did it work?'

'Oh, it was *amazing*,' she replied, pulling her scarf around her neck with one hand and closing her coat with the other, heading back to the apartment without giving a single thought to the pedestrians stepping out of her way. It had been *so* much more successful than even she'd dared hope for.

'That's... awesome,' Paige replied. 'You must be... thrilled.'

Bella frowned, the unusually stilted response catching her attention.

'Paige, what's wrong?' Bella asked.

'I don't... I can't... Oh Bella...'

'Paige, it's okay,' Bella rushed to reassure her. 'Whatever it is, it's okay,' she insisted.

A near sob came down the phone, pulling Bella up short. 'Are you hurt? Did Olly hurt you?' she demanded with alarm creeping into her heart. She didn't think for a second that Olly was capable of such a thing, but that didn't mean that something hadn't happened.

'No, no. He didn't. He's... he could never.'

'Is *he* hurt? Did something go wrong with the payback plan?' she demanded.

'No,' Paige replied, and Bella breathed a sigh of relief. 'He's fine.'

Whatever had happened could be fixed. Once Bella knew what was *actually* wrong, she was absolutely sure that they would be able to make it fine.

'It is about Olly though,' Paige said, stuttering her way through the words. 'I've, we've... I...'

Something turned in Bella's chest, a knowing, without knowing. A strange kind of hurting that was for something that was about to happen, rather than from something that had already happened.

'About two weeks ago... God, I don't know how to say this...'

'How to say what?' Bella asked, as her stomach twisted.

'Something happened. Between us. We kissed.'

Paige's words were drowned out by a high-pitched ringing in her ears. As if Bella was reeling from a physical blow.

'And I'm so, so, sorry. The last thing I would ever want to do is hurt you. Oh *fuck*, I'm a terrible person and a shitty friend.'

'No,' Bella said. 'No, you're not,' she said automatically, her lips strangely numb.

'I *am*, and you were going to marry him and he jilted you via text on your wedding day and—'

'It's okay,' Bella replied robotically. 'Are you...' She cleared her throat. 'Do you have feelings for him?' Bella forced herself to ask, collapsing onto a bench on the sidewalk.

It shouldn't matter, but it did. If it had been for nothing, if it had just been a fling...

'Yes. No. I don't know. I'm so confused.' Paige sounded miserable and she didn't want that, but...

'If he feels the same way, then I'm happy for you both,' Bella said, remembering the messages of congratulations she'd received from friends and family on her engagement to Olly.

She blinked, hoping to clear them from her mind and a tear escaped, to roll down her cheek.

We're so happy for you.

Thrilled for you and the future you'll have together.

Congratulations Mr & Mrs Prendergast.

Her breath shuddered in her lungs.

'Bella—'

'I have to go, but I'll talk to you soon, okay?' she said and hung up before Paige could reply.

She stared at nothing as the cars passed, their lights glowing in the early dark of a winter's night, unhearing of the noises of the people that stalked up and down the sidewalk around her.

I'm happy for you both.

Are you? Really? she asked herself.

She wanted to be. She wanted to be the bigger person, to rise above her own feelings and wish them well. But she couldn't. Because she was... *angry*. Her whole being vibrated with emotions that she didn't know what to do with.

It wasn't because Olly had moved on, because Bella had always known he would one day. But it was Paige. It was *Paige* that she felt she'd lost. Not Olly.

Somewhere over the course of the last weeks and months, she'd stopped thinking about Olly so much. She'd stopped thinking about what she'd lost when he'd walked away from her.

But this... this was different.

This hurt in a new way.

Because it felt a little as if Paige had chosen Olly over her. Because it felt a little as if it didn't *matter* how good she was, or how hard she worked to make everything fine, to achieve her goals, to fix everything. To make sure that she didn't disturb what other people got to have. And if that didn't matter... then what was she doing, *all the time*, being so damn *good*?

Her phone buzzed in her pocket, but she ignored it. It would be the girls, they'd be worried about her.

The last thing they need is to worry about you.

She didn't want them to be worried.

But a small, mean, part of her *did*. Just for once, she wanted to be the one that people cared about. Just for once she wanted not to have to make herself invisible in order for them to feel better.

Her eyes hurt and she blinked, the cold feeling from the back of her eyelids making her aware that she was cold. Really cold. She got up, stiffly, not bothering to check her watch to see how long she'd been sitting there.

She didn't even think as she walked into the liquor store and grabbed the nearest bottle of wine. She paid for it without noticing the curious glance she got from the guy behind the counter. As she passed Isiah she barely waved hello, not noticing the frown of concern he gave her as he watched her walk to the elevator.

She walked blindly down the corridor and let herself into her apartment.

I'm so sorry.

Me too, Bella thought, wondering why the sting of hurt seemed so much worse than when she'd realised Olly had left her at the wedding.

She would never begrudge Paige her happiness. She damn well deserved it. And Bella meant that, truly and completely. But that didn't mean that she didn't hurt and wonder when it was that *she* would get to be happy.

She grabbed a glass from the cupboard, not even caring that it was a tumbler and filled it near full with wine.

Stop it right now. No more tears. You don't get to feel sorry for yourself when your sister is in a hospital bed and your parents are worried out of their minds.

She swallowed down half the glass and ignored the way that it hit her empty stomach and sloshed. She shrugged off her coat, only just realising that she still had it on, and let it fall to the floor. She stood in the kitchen and downed the rest of the glass of wine.

For just one night she didn't want to be Good Bella.

She kicked off her shoes as she refilled her glass and walked to the window, looking out into the night to see if she could see the hospital where her sister had been treated. It was on the other side of the park, and too far up, but if she squinted, really hard, she could imagine that she could see the lights.

When she went back to refill her glass, she realised that her phone was buzzing again and, ignoring the screen, she put it on silent. She tipped the bottle to the glass but nothing came out. She shook it, but only a drop clung to the mouth of the bottle.

It wasn't enough. She wasn't nearly drunk enough.

She spun on her heel and left her apartment, crossed the hallway and knocked.

She knocked and kept knocking.

'Hold on,' she heard from the other side of the door. 'Christ, hold on!' the angry shout came again, making Bella realise that she hadn't actually stopped knocking.

She frowned at her knuckles. They hurt a little.

Chase yanked open the door with one hand, the other clutching the edge of a towel hung low around his waist.

She blinked at him, seeing him, not really seeing him, but knowing that she *should* be seeing him because in her mind she flashed to a scene from Delia's book where the heroine walked in on the hero in the shower.

'I don't need that right now,' she said to herself more than him, and pushed past him into where she knew the main area would be.

'Bella? Are you okay?' he asked, not yet closing the door, as if he hoped to get rid of her as soon as possible.

'Yup, I just need...' she said, peering around the

room and locating the wet bar she knew he'd have well stocked, 'this.'

She searched the bottles: vodka, gin, Jack Daniels, and... scotch. She wouldn't be able to stomach the taste of gin, JD was too sweet and vodka, tasteless. She wanted to feel this as she drank it.

Relentlessly physical.

She snapped her mouth shut and grabbed the bottle and turned to leave, pulling up short just before she crashed into Chase's very wet, very naked chest.

He eyed the bottle in her hand and the look on her face and shut the door behind him to stop her from leaving. He scanned her from head to toe, quickly and efficiently as if he were checking for injuries.

'Are you drunk?' he demanded.

'Why do you keep asking me that?'

'You didn't answer the question. Are you drunk?'

'No,' she replied. Not enough, anyway.

He stared at her in that way of his. As if he wanted to see more, when most people were only happy with what she showed them. And while she longed for that, needed it in a way she could barely put into words, she didn't want that now. Not tonight.

'I'm not quite sure what's going on, but if you're planning to drink that? You're not leaving,' he informed her.

'I'm not a child, Chase. You can't keep me here,' she said in a tone that even to her own ears sounded frankly childish.

'It's my alcohol, Bella. If you want to go and buy your own, by all means,' he offered.

His sudden attachment to a bottle of scotch was strange but now that it was so late she wouldn't be able to buy any. If she wanted alcohol, this was the only way.

She glared up at him, trying not to look at the way his body looked in just a towel, his hair still wet from the shower he'd been taking, swept back and sleek against his head. The hair dusting his chest, dark swirls across his pecs and down the centre of his torso, sweeping around toned muscles. Lean. He was lean rather than muscular, but she couldn't help herself from following the trail of hair to the edge of the towel around his hips and—

'Bella.'

'Yes?' she said, finally drawing her attention back to his face.

He frowned at her as if he was worried. Then narrowed his eyes.

'If you leave, I'm coming after you,' he warned as he finally moved away from the door. 'Stay there,' he commanded.

16

Sun Tzu doesn't know what he's talking about.

— BELLA, DRUNK.

He shouldn't have let her in the damn door, he thought as he hastily pulled on a pair of jeans and a tee. Though, to be fair, once he had even the slightest inkling of her determination to get blind drunk, there was no way he'd been remotely willing to let her loose without a chaperone either. So, that was where he found himself: hurrying to play chaperone to a wannabe wayward socialite.

Not that she was a socialite in the way he'd once meant. Their conversation from the gallery came back to him. He frowned. What on earth had happened between then and now, that she turned up like this on his doorstep? And thank God it had been his doorstep, he thought with relief.

Until he returned to the living room to find Bella pacing in front of the window. The restless energy was new on her. It drew her body in different lines and colours. Chase passed a hand over his mouth, watching her as she walked back and forth unseeing of the view beyond the window, the sight of which made him clench his other fist.

It was getting harder and harder to deny his attraction to her, but that didn't mean a thing right now. Because the woman who hated being out of control was currently doing her very best to get completely shitfaced.

'Bella, do you want to tell me what's going on?' he asked, with a sigh.

She bit the inside of her cheek, considering his question. Eventually she shook her head, her hair swinging across her face as she spun elegantly back to the view.

He opened his mouth to argue, but stopped when she spun back to him, only slightly off balance.

'I'm a good person,' she said, as if he'd accused her of not being one.

'I know.'

'I *am* good,' she stressed. 'I'm a good daughter, a good friend, a good colleague. Mostly.'

He wasn't sure about the mostly, but he was fairly confident about the rest. And couldn't even remotely imagine her being a bad daughter.

'I'm good even when I'm being bad,' she announced.

Chase didn't mean to intentionally scoff out loud, but when he looked up at her staring mutinously at him, he realised she'd heard.

'I've been bad,' she said, swinging her glass towards him, rather recklessly as far as the carpet was concerned, and he couldn't help but laugh.

'I've been bad!' she insisted over his chuckle. 'I've done things,' she said, and he supposed it was supposed to sound ominous, but it just made him laugh harder.

'Bella, your definition of bad is not making the bed in the morning,' he stated, leaning back on the sofa and enjoying the flush of indignation rising on her cheeks.

She opened her mouth to speak but couldn't seem to find the words.

'That's okay, Bella,' he said. 'It's okay if that's who you are.'

'But it's not okay. Because... because...'

He watched her grapple for an answer and slowly the humour of the moment twisted and changed. Because she was reaching for something he could damn near see written on the air between them, but that she couldn't quite bring herself to say.

'Because it doesn't get you what you want,' he read in her gaze.

Grey eyes glittered like snowflakes in the setting sun. The idea that Bella's wants had been discarded... not with her asshat ex who had left her alone to confront a mess of his making. The way she was, the person she was... he could see it. Could see why she moved through the world trying not to make ripples. Christ, given what happened when she was younger, her sister's illness, he could see how wanting anything for herself would have been hard.

And suddenly he wanted to see what Bella was like when she made ripples. When she *tried* to. Now, that would be something.

'So, what is it that you want?' he couldn't stop himself from asking.

She looked at him, confusion in her eyes, morphing to sadness.

The only people who didn't know the answer to that question either never allowed themselves to stop and ask, or had never expected their wants to be met. And with a sucker punch, Chase realised that Bella was the latter.

'I want my friend to be happy.'

He wasn't sure who this friend was, but Bella was missing the point. 'What do *you* want? For yourself.'

She held his gaze until she couldn't. Her head dropping and with those little shakes as she stared at the carpet, she replied, 'I don't know.'

The silence that hung between them wasn't uncomfortable. But he also wasn't sure that he believed her. She might have thrown a wall between herself and her wants but until she was ready to admit that they were there, that they were valid and that it was fine to have wants and to go for them, she would only be living a half-life.

And as someone who had reached for his wants, had them in his grasp and lost them, he truly knew what that half-life was like to live. And it was no life at all.

'I...'

Say it, he dared her mentally. Tell me what it is you want.

'I want to get really, *really* drunk,' she announced before necking the rest of her scotch.

And he smiled, even if he was partially disappointed that she hadn't been able to say what it was that she wanted, because he was also partially relieved. There was enough beginning to build between them. Honesty might be the thing that tipped them over the edge and he wasn't sure that either of them needed that right now.

* * *

Bella was going to die. She hadn't even opened her eyes yet. Surely no one could survive this much physical pain and nausea. Every single time she inhaled she thought she might actually pass out.

She reached up to press a hand to her forehead. It felt feverish and she groaned again.

'Here. Drink and swallow.'

She tensed and inhaled a gasp of shock.

Who? What? Wait...

Chase?

The sound of a glass being placed onto the bedside table made her flinch and she scrunched her closed eyes even more shut. Where was she? And, more importantly, why was Chase there?

'Ahh. Memory blank? Well, you did have a fair amount to drink last night.'

Scotch. That was why her tongue felt like a carpet. Urgh.

Scotch. Paige. Olly... *Chase.*

She whimpered.

'Drink the water, take the pills and get in the shower,' Chase ordered before leaving her alone.

She remembered going to his door. Remembered the towel around his waist, the scotch. His sofa.

Her heart lurched. Why was she in a bed? Whose bed was she in? Oh God, was she even wearing clothes? She lifted the covers, glaring down at bare legs and arms. She was wearing her underwear and a vest, but still... how had she?

No. Nononononononononono.

She shoved a hand over her own mouth to stop the sound from coming out.

What had she done?

Her breaths came shallow and quick. Which only made the nausea worse. There was a genuine possibility that she might actually be sick. She looked around the room, recognising her things, so at least she was in her own apartment. But if he'd brought her home, why was he still here?

'Stop overthinking, Bella, and get in the damn shower,' Chase called through from the other room.

She whimpered again and gingerly made her way to the bathroom.

Oh God, oh God, oh God.

Bella spent the two minutes she allowed herself in the shower to try to figure out a way of getting rid of him. But when she emerged, nearly five minutes later, washed, dried, moisturised – which didn't help nearly as much as she'd hoped – she still hadn't thought of a way to get rid of him.

She needed to think. She needed space. She needed not to think of him standing there in a towel and nothing else.

She dressed quickly and went looking for him in the other room, trying not to squeal in horror when she saw him on the sofa reading Delia's book.

'Oh Jesus Christ,' she said, before she could stop herself.

Chase's eyes snapped to hers and he laughed. 'Bella! Language.'

'Get out,' she snapped while holding onto her head to make sure that it didn't fall off.

'What kind of person would I be, if left you alone with what I'm fairly confident is one hell of a hangover?'

'I'm fine,' she insisted, hoping that she wasn't about to throw up.

He cocked his head to one side and she scrunched her eyes shut again, hating the way that made her feel almost sea sick.

'Could you... not,' she said, gesturing to him with her hand – the other one was still holding onto her head.

'Fat, sugar, carbs and fresh air,' he declared.

Bile rose in the back of her throat. 'I don't think I can,' she admitted, the hand holding her head moving to her stomach.

''Tis the only way, I'm afraid.'

She whimpered again.

'Don't worry, I've got you,' he promised, holding her coat out for her to put her arms into.

It was probably easier just to do what he said, rather than to try and think for herself, so she decided to go with it.

'Out of curiosity,' he asked as he ushered her down the hallway, 'what's the last thing you remember?'

She felt the blood drain from her face. 'Why?'

'No reason,' he replied, rather too innocently for her liking.

'I remember you putting ice in my whisky glass,' she offered.

What do you want? For yourself?

Her head throbbed, trying to remember what had happened after, and the blank space made her back away from the elevator.

'Actually, I think I should just stay—'

He turned her back to face the elevator and pushed her forwards as the doors opened.

'You need food. I'm 90 per cent sure that the contents of your stomach are currently wine and scotch, and that the last thing you ate was half a ham sandwich from yesterday's lunch.'

'I hate you a little bit right now.'

'I can live with that,' he said smugly as he pressed the button for the lobby.

* * *

By the time Chase led her from the freezing cold into the warmth of the diner, Bella had decided that she'd happily murder him. They'd barely said a word on the fifteen-minute walk. Partly because she was still trying not to throw up, even if she did have to admit that the sharp slap of near freezing cold air was actually helping.

'Chocolate milkshake, cheeseburger with fries, and onion rings, twice,' he told the waitress who came to take their order.

'Twice?' Bella hissed as the waitress turned away with a knowing smile. 'Twice?' she repeated again when Chase chose to ignore her.

'Yeah, you need it. Boss's orders.'

Oh God.

Was it normal to feel so... turned on in the middle of a hangover? Like the worst ever hangover? Was a horny hangover even a thing? Not that he was turning her on. Not really. It was just the book. She couldn't be attracted to a lying cheating...

Only he wasn't. He hadn't lied. He hadn't cheated. Not really.

Oh God, it was such a mess. She gave in and leaned her forehead on the table.

'So, this is what's going to happen,' Chase said. 'We're going to eat this incredibly delicious food, as slow as you like, but you're going to eat it. And then you're going to look at the messages that have been blowing up your phone since last night. Then you're going to walk back to the apartment—'

'Cab,' she interrupted.

'*Walk,*' he stressed. 'And then you're going to curl up on the sofa and finish the book you screamed at me for reading.'

Oh.

My.

God.

'Just kill me,' she begged. 'Get it over with and kill me,' she groaned, her forehead still attached to the table.

The sound of his laughter rolled over her in warm waves and she didn't hate it. Not really. It felt kind of nice to joke with someone.

'It's not bad actually,' he offered. 'I especially liked the bit when she put one knee the table and said, "Daddy, can you—"'

'Chase,' she exclaimed, cutting him off as the server placed plates loaded with food on the table.

'Oh, you got that far already?' he asked with a knowing grin, popping a fry into his mouth.

Bella grabbed her milkshake hoping to cool herself down – not from the memory of that particular scene in the book (which she had read, by the way, *twice*) but from the thought of *Chase* reading that scene.

She whimpered again, but stopped the moment that she saw Chase tense. She swallowed a mouthful of thick, sweet milkshake as if she could ignore the moment as easily.

'So, your friends are worried about you. Should I be?' he asked, after clearing his throat.

Bella took a shuddering breath. 'No. It's fine. I'm fine.'

'You know how some people have a swear jar?' Chase asked, drawing her gaze back to him with the about-turn in the conversation.

She nodded.

'I want to have a *Bella's fine* jar. Five dollars for every time you say you're fine.' She rolled her eyes at him, but he held her gaze. 'Was it one of them that did the bad thing? Is that why they're worried about you?'

Bella nodded again.

'Does it still hurt? The bad thing?' he asked.

Bella considered his question. Because from the moment Paige had told her she'd been upset with the wrong thing. Or at least, probably not what everyone expected her to be upset by. It wasn't Olly.

Because she'd begun to suspect that Olly might have been right to leave. They should never have got as far as a church aisle, let alone a marriage. He'd been grieving and she'd wanted someone to love her. That wasn't a foundation for a future.

'Not in the way that it should,' Bella admitted.

He raised an eyebrow and nodded as if impressed.

She opened her mouth to explain and he held a

hand up. 'It's okay. I don't need to know. I just wanted to make sure you were okay.'

She bit her lip. 'I'm okay,' she told him, and she realised that he trusted her to tell him the truth. And that, surprisingly, it *was* the truth.

He nodded again. 'Okay. Now, tell me. What's your favourite scene in the book so far?'

And she choked on a laugh while swallowing her milkshake.

* * *

Chase watched Bella head back towards the apartment, looking much better than she had first, last night, and then again, this morning. The breath shuddered in his lungs and he clenched his jaw. What kind of woman has a racy romance on the same table as Sun Tzu? He'd seen about seven different sides of her in the last twenty-four hours and none of them had done anything to make her less appealing to him.

Which was a problem.

A problem that wasn't because he hadn't had sex since he'd been with Astrid nearly six months before. He was a man, not a monster and was perfectly capable of going for stretches of time without someone to scratch an itch. The problem was that Bella wouldn't be an itch. She'd be an addiction.

On the surface she was composed, graceful and sophisticated, but Chase was beginning to suspect that in reality she was none of those things. They were learned behaviours, things she'd done either to protect herself or someone else. *Behind* that... beneath those layers was the Bella he wanted to know.

Beneath those layers, Chase was almost 100 per cent sure that she'd be pure liquid gold pouring through his fingers and coating his soul until he couldn't escape. And Christ, he didn't think he was ready for that. He didn't think he'd ever be ready for that.

* * *

UNREAD MESSAGES

ASTRID

Bella if you don't let us know that you're okay RIGHT NOW I am going to call the police.

Bella, seriously. I'm getting a little worried. We just want to know that you're okay.

SIENNA

Honey, are you okay? Paige feels awful. I know that you probably don't need to hear that right now, but she does.

PAIGE

Bella, I just… I don't know what to say other than how sorry I am. Your friendship means so much to me. I hate that I've jeopardised that.

Bella stared at her phone. She had twelve missed calls. Five from Astrid, three from Paige and Sienna, and one from Olly. She fired off a message to Astrid and Sienna letting them know she was okay. They would get in touch with Paige to say that they'd heard from her, she was sure. But before she spoke to Paige she needed to make this call.

The phone rang and her pulse raced. She didn't know why she was nervous. They'd messaged a few – painfully civil – times, but this was different.

'Hi.' Olly's voice, warm and soft, and sorry, poured down the phone. It was so familiar Bella ached.

'Hi,' she replied, her voice breaking on the word.

'God, B, I'm so sorry.'

Wetness pressed against the back of her eyes, but

the tears weren't sad, they were a kind of release that she hadn't known she'd needed.

She'd *needed* to hear that. Needed it in a way that she hadn't known.

'I know,' said, tucking her chin into the scarf warding off the wintery bite of the cool air in Central Park.

'She didn't... we didn't...' Olly trailed off, unable to finish his sentence.

'I know it wasn't intentional. I do. And... it's okay.'

A puff of air punched into the static of the phone's ear piece.

'Bella—'

'No. Really,' Bella said, feeling the truth of it. 'It *is* okay. I... can actually see how you two work. *So* much better than we ever did,' she continued, nodding to herself as she made her way back to the apartment.

'It's okay to yell and scream, B. I can take it. I deserve it twice over. You don't have to be so damn *fine* all the time.'

'Yes, I'm beginning to understand that,' Bella said with a small sad laugh. 'Do you love her, Olly?' she asked.

'I'm not sure,' he hedged. 'It's... complicated.'

'Yeah,' she agreed. 'In more ways than you know,'

she said, thinking of how Olly might feel if – *when* – he discovered the truth of how they all met.

'What?' he asked.

'It doesn't matter. What matters,' she pressed on, 'is this. You can't hurt her, Olly. She's been through it. Really through it, you know.'

'I know. She told me about the revenge porn.'

'She did?' Bella asked, unable to hide her surprise.

'Yes.'

'Oh. Well... that's good then. So you get it,' Bella said, her tone morphing to serious in line with her feelings. 'You understand why you need to figure out how you feel. You understand why you need to get sure. Because you can't play with her, Olly. If you do, if you hurt her, I will track you down and do things you couldn't even imagine,' she warned, absolutely no humour in her voice at all. 'Paige deserves the world and if you don't give it to her, I will make sure that you regret it.'

Olly swallowed down the phone and rushed to reassure her that he wouldn't hurt her, that he would give her the world, and that when they next met in person, Bella would know how sorry he was that it hadn't worked between them, but not sorry that it had brought him to Paige.

'Okay,' Bella replied, finally feeling the first thread of peace she'd felt in the last eighteen hours. 'Now, can I speak to Paige?'

'Sure. Hang on a second.'

Down the line she heard muffled sounds as she impatiently waited to hear her friend's voice pour down the line.

'Bella? Are you okay?' Her friend's voice poured down the line.

'Yes, Paige. I am. Really,' Bella promised, feeling relief and knowing that she actually meant it.

17

Anger may in time change to gladness; vexation may be succeeded by content.

— *THE ART OF WAR*, SUN TZU

Bella had changed. Before, if Bella argued with him or wanted to contradict him, there was a certain reticence about her. As if she were holding back.

Well. She sure as shit wasn't holding back now.

'This is unacceptable,' he said, trying to keep his anger at bay.

'You are wrong,' she stated defiantly, grey eyes flashing glitter. Again.

'I'm your boss,' he reminded her for what felt like the hundredth time.

'That doesn't mean you're not wrong, Chase,' she all but growled. *Growled*! At him!

'The kids don't like it when Mummy and Daddy fight,' Maurice sing-songed as he passed on the way to the kitchenette where Ali and Ye-Joon were looking on in concern.

Chase bit back a sigh. 'We should take this to my office.'

'Why?' Bella demanded. 'You think they can't see us in there?'

'When did you get so mouthy?' he demanded.

'When you stopped caring about the reputation of yourself and this gallery,' she whisper-hissed back.

'What?' he demanded, fully outraged now. 'I care!' he yelled, leaning into the argument now. 'But what I *don't* care for, is using children to try and redeem it.'

'The children are safe, the school is anonymous, and the picture is so far away that you can't identify anyone other than you,' Bella mutinously yelled back.

'I had no warning, Bella. None. I woke up this morning to this.'

He slapped the newspaper down on the counter-top, the article face-up and centred around a photograph of the little boy holding his hand and staring at his picture, framed and up on the wall.

Bella shrugged and gave him a look that basically wondered what the hell his problem was.

'It's a balanced article on the importance of local galleries working with local, underfunded and over-stretched schools, to help breach the barriers to art.'

'But you didn't *tell* me about it,' he growled, unable to confess why the fact that he'd been kept in the dark about it felt like a betrayal.

'Because you wouldn't have agreed to it,' she pointed out.

'Precisely.'

'And you would have been wrong.'

His hands flew to his temples.

Give me strength.

'I'm mad at you for doing this,' he said, stating the obvious.

'For doing my job?' she threw back at him. 'Because that's what this is, Chase. My job. Our job, in fact. To make sure that this gallery opens with the greatest success for Tej and for the artists that we show here. And part of *that*,' she stressed, entirely for his benefit, he was sure, 'is making sure that *your* reputation is damn near squeaky-clean.'

He clenched his jaw, his teeth aching under the pressure. 'Fine.'

'Fine,' she shot back.

'But no more PR stunts.'

Bella narrowed her eyes and he wanted to throttle her.

'What is it this time?' he demanded, anchoring his hands on his hips so that he didn't accidentally actually do just that.

She inhaled and held her breath.

And the longer she held it, the more he worried.

'We're attending the Harrison's gala at the Pulham Hotel, this coming weekend.'

'No, *we're* not,' he said, cutting a hand through the air, not even having to think about it for a second. 'You can go without me.'

'No, I can't. Magenta came through and got us *two* tickets. So, we're going.'

'We are absolutely fucking *not*, Bella.'

'You don't need to swear.'

'You did,' he pointed out.

'I did not,' she denied hotly.

'Yes, you did,' he needled.

'When?' she demanded, outraged and he didn't know what was funnier. Her outrage that she'd cursed and wasn't aware of it, or the twists and turns in this conversation.

'"Damn near squeaky-clean",' he quoted for her.

She thinned her lips and, clearly, chose to ignore him. 'Tej has already paid for them,' she said instead.

Chase's head snapped up. 'What?' he asked, not because he hadn't heard, but because he needed to clarify it before he got on the phone and tore his friend a new one. Because Tej knew how much he hated even the idea of a gala, let alone going to one.

'Because he knows that these are the things that you have to do as a gallery director, Chase.'

Your role. Your responsibility. Things you need to do.

She was backing him into a corner and he didn't like it one bit.

'I was nice to you,' he pointed out, reminding her of the weekend.

'I know. And whether you believe me or not, this is me being nice to you,' she said, more gently this time.

'Christ, I'd hate to see you when you're being mean.'

Something flashed past her eyes, but was gone before he could really register it, because he suddenly realised what he *was* registering. Rich grey eyes, staring up at him, the smooth creamy skin, glowing with just a touch of a flush, and her lips slightly parted as if in expectation or want.

He turned on his heel and left before he did something stupid, like try to kiss her.

* * *

Bella's heart was thundering in her chest as she watched him leave the kitchenette. She'd expected an argument, had been ready for it. She'd prepared all her responses to every conceivable objection he might have... she just hadn't been ready for *her*. For how *she'd* feel when she went head to head with him and it had been...

Exhilarating.

Exhilarating and fascinating, because she usually got things done by smoothing waters, making it easier for everyone, slowly moving the pieces on a chess board so that it happened organically. Doing it this way – confronting Chase – was like smashing up against a wall and seeing who would cave first. And it had been him!

He had done what she'd wanted him to do, not by being quiet, but by being determined and loud and unapologetic and... *demanding*. And it was so intoxicating that she felt light-headed.

ASTRID

How did it go?

BELLA

I did it! He agreed!

ASTRID

Whoop whoop! I had absolutely no doubt whatsoever.

Does he know about the prize?

BELLA

...not yet.

ASTRID

Ah, he'll be fine.

BELLA

He'll have to be.

ASTRID

Yeah he will! You go girl! ☺

But he's okay? I feel pretty bad about the whole vengeance thing.

BELLA

Me too. But yeah, he seems okay?

How are things going with Aiden?

ASTRID

Oh, you know. He's being his usual charming self.

BELLA

And Blake?

Bella knew that things had got tense with Aiden's brother Blake who, according to Astrid, was the complete opposite to Aiden but just as much of a pain.

ASTRID

Turns out Blake is a pussycat

Bella frowned. *Really?*

BELLA

You mean to say you've tamed the lion?

ASTRID

Something like that 😉

Bella laughed, slipping her phone back into her pocket and picking up her coffee as Maurice came into the kitchen.

'Ali's got the mock-up of the layout for the Nayak's first brochure. I thought you'd like to see it.'

'Absolutely,' she said, smiling as they returned to the office. Now that the plans to help boost both Chase and the gallery's reputations were underway, Bella was knee-deep in finalising content for email bursts, newsletters, and what would be the website's live content, once it transitioned from the 'coming soon' phase, which would happen the following week. Once that was done, she could shift her focus towards active comms in order to create a decent client list and a broader audience.

Which needed her attention because as much as Chase wanted to stick his head in the sand about the damage the article had done, the newsletter numbers had dropped considerably and website hits were almost exclusively driven by people being nosey following the article.

Which was why the Harrison's charity gala was so important – and why she was so thankful for Magenta for coming through for them. They were raising money for families living in poverty in New York and even if Chase grumbled and moaned, he couldn't argue with that.

Tej had thought it was a great idea when she'd spoken to him to sound him out about it and the cost – and of course, permission to use the gallery for the prize. Bella bit her lip, still uncomfortable about es-

sentially going behind Chase's back in order to or-
ganise it. But she knew he'd try and shut her idea
down. And he couldn't. Not if they were going to
make the opening a success.

'You need to pace yourself,' Maurice said, later
that day. 'We have time,' he insisted.

And Maurice was right. She had loaded up her
work plate and was approaching it like an all-you-
can-eat buffet with a time limit. But she couldn't help
it. She needed to. Because when she wasn't working...

Chase was standing in front of her in a towel and
nothing else.

Or popping a fry into his mouth with that wicked
look in his eye.

Or running his fingers through his hair.

Or scowling.

She really liked it when he scowled.

What was *wrong* with her?

She fanned the flush rising on her cheeks and
tried to ignore the look of curiosity that Maurice was
casting her from the side.

Eight months ago she'd been about to marry Olly,
with nothing more than a future of children and a
white picket fence on her mind. Now, her ex-fiancé
was getting together with her new best friend and she
was lusting after the ex-lover of her *other* best friend.

A man who very much didn't want a white picket fence and children. A man who was the complete opposite of her and everything she wanted.

She groaned out loud, rubbing her eyes with the heels of her hand, and a cup of camomile tea appeared by her side.

'You should go home, Bella.'

She jumped at the sound of Chase's voice, and he stopped back with his arms raised as if to say, I mean you no harm.

She looked up to find that the rest of the office was dark, and her team had gone home.

She put a hand to her chest to try and sooth the sudden shock to her heart, belatedly laughing and saying, 'You startled me.'

'Clearly,' Chase said, a smile pulling at the corner of his mouth, before his gaze stilled. 'Am I such a terrible boss that you have to work so late?'

'Awful. Horrible. Evil boss,' she said, trying to hide her smile as she closed down her computer reluctantly.

* * *

Chase had purposefully put a wide birth between him and Bella Carmichael. No more drinking buddies, no more disagreements at the office. He was on his best behaviour. And if she noticed a difference in their interaction then she had chosen not to say anything.

He was blaming the book. He should never have picked it up.

But when he'd seen it lying open on the side table, he'd been curious.

Fuck me, Daddy. Please? I've been such a bad *girl.*

He shivered. He actually fucking shivered. Less at the thought of the character and more from the thought of Bella reading it. Bella *enjoying* it.

Every time he looked at her his pulse dropped a beat and his chest caved. And it was no good. Nothing was helping. Not even distance, because every time he went home he knew she was on the other side of the corridor.

With that damn book!

The problem, he decided, was that he had too much time on his hands.

Sascha was well on her way to creating a strong enough body of work for the opening and he knew that any further input from him would be unnecessary.

He thought that Tej might have suspected something, from the way that he kept asking after Bella. It had taken on a slightly teasing tone in the last few calls and Chase didn't like it one bit.

Tej – of all people – knew why he needed to keep his distance. He was trying really damn hard to get his life back on track. He couldn't afford to mess it up by having any kind of relationship with someone he worked with.

But that didn't seem to mean a thing when every now and then he'd find himself tracking her progress between her desk and the kitchenette. Or when he found himself in their office, and he couldn't resist nudging her pen to an angle that was sure to frustrate her, and getting far too much enjoyment from the way she huffed and put it back.

Or the way he held his breath when she passed by him so that he didn't have to be assaulted by that mouth-watering scent that he still couldn't quite identify, and could never ask her about. Because that would make him look as unhinged as he was beginning to feel around her.

Christ, get a grip, he told himself as he checked his phone and re-read the message she'd sent him on his phone.

Room 365

They were supposed to head to the gala together, but Chase had been running late and Bella had decided to get ready in the room that came with the gala tickets, rather than trek halfway across New York to get to the hotel.

It made things different, to pick her up from the room. Made it feel like a *date*. And he didn't want it to feel like a date. Bella still hadn't told him what the gallery had offered as part of the blind auction, and he had a feeling that he wasn't going to like it. But as long as it didn't involve him, then really he didn't care. Because as much as he was ready to admit, Bella was doing good things for the gallery. Things that he should probably be doing, if he'd not been so distracted by his work with Sascha.

But now that Sascha was pretty much standing on her own two feet, he could return to his duties, and Bella could return to hers.

He checked himself in the mirror of the elevator that took him to the third floor of the spectacular Pulham Hotel, tugging at the suffocating black tie around his neck, feeling awkward and wanting the whole thing over as soon as humanly possible.

The elevator arrived and he scanned door numbers to find the suite Bella was in. What a monumental waste of money – to rent rooms as part of the dinner ticket. The majority of people attending had apartments in the city, and if not, certainly enough money to arrange to return to wherever they'd come from. And for the life of him, he couldn't understand why Bella had even wanted to use the room to get ready in. A dress. Some make-up. Surely it wasn't that hard?

He found the room and knocked, impatient and irritated already.

'Hold on!' Bella called through the door.

And he waited nearly thirty seconds before she opened the door saying, 'Sorry, I was doing my...'

Her words trailed off as she took him in from head to toe. And he honestly couldn't hold it against her because he was utterly speechless.

18

On hemmed-in ground, resort to stratagem. On desperate ground, fight.

— *THE ART OF WAR*, SUN TZU

Bella ran the mascara wand over her eyelashes in the hotel bathroom mirror, careful not to disturb her eye make-up. She must have got ready for nearly one hundred gala dinners before, but none of them had made her feel like *this*.

Butterflies swept in circles around her stomach, and little shivers danced across her skin, fluctuating her body temperature from high to low with every breath.

She blinked and a spattering of black freckles appeared across her eyelid.

Biting back a curse, she reached for the cotton bud she'd dipped into remover and went to work fixing her mistake. *This* was why she'd agreed to use the hotel room provided, because it had to be perfect. *She* had to be perfect. This was the way she would help redeem her mistaken revenge against Chase. It was imperative that by the end of the night, she had undone the damage to his – and the gallery's – reputation. And Bella clung to the lie she told herself: that she was nervous because of what was at stake and *not* because of Chase himself.

Bella's phone vibrated with a message from the girls and as she read the 'good luck' from Paige who had come back to the group messages after they'd spoken last week.

PAIGE

What are you wearing?

Bella had sent them a picture.

SIENNA

OHHHHHHH!

ASTRID

I want your stylist. I want the dress,
but I also want the name of your
stylist.

SIENNA

You're going to look amazing in
that.

PAIGE

Really amazing.

Just like a blonde Audrey Hepburn!

Bella laughed, swirling the beautiful black satin
skirts around her mid-calves and smoothing her
hands down the fitted bodice. She hadn't ever used a
stylist. She'd watched and learned from her mother
for what clothes to wear, how to wear them, what
event suited what style. She'd already checked, and
thankfully her parents weren't coming tonight. She
didn't think she could be the Bella she needed to be.
Not in front of them. Not when so much was on the
line.

Which was why she absolutely had to ignore this
silly... crush... that would make her heart lurch and
her stomach fizzy and her pulse jump and her skin
flush just at the sight of him. Because it didn't mat-

ter. Because he wasn't what she wanted. He couldn't be.

The man was moody, irascible, short-tempered, slightly arrogant and made her uncomfortable in ways no one else ever had. Surely that was a bad thing, right?

Marriage is not for me. Not again.

And it was all she'd ever wanted. Someone to love *her*. Someone to choose her.

A knock on the door crashed into her thoughts and startled her.

'Just a minute,' she called out, hoping to buy herself enough time to get her pulse back under control.

It's not forever. It's just for right now. And I want you. Right now.

The quote from Delia's book came back to haunt her just when she didn't need it to.

She shook off the thought. Her only goal tonight was to ensure Chase's reputation was redeemed. Everything else was just a distraction.

She pulled open the door. 'Sorry, I was just...'

Oh crap.

He looked incredible.

Chase filled the doorway, his six-foot height drawing her gaze upwards. His hair, thick, wavy, and carelessly tossed made him look debauched. Because even dressed in formal wear, a black, superfine wool of his jacket clinging to his body in a way that looked near indecent, it was the way his tie, not a bow tie like others would be wearing, but a classic tie that looked as if it had been yanked loose in frustration.

Sexy. It looked sexy. *He* looked sexy.

Every pulse point on her body began to throb at the same time sending hot and cold shivers that flashed over her body in waves becoming harder to ignore.

She avoided his gaze, because the heat in his eyes was burning her where she stood.

'May I?' she asked.

And although he didn't say yes, he didn't stop her when she closed the distance between them and reached for his tie. The scent of his aftershave, warm from his body, filled her and she bit her lip to try and stop herself from taking big gulps of it.

Taking the knot in her fingers, she freed the tails before looping them back into a perfect knot at the centre of his collar. She just managed to stop herself from smoothing her hands down his chest, but only by fisting her hands. She felt his gaze on her as if he'd known what she wanted, as if he could see it in the way her body tried to hide the tremor across her body with a roll of her shoulder.

She'd come back here at the end of the evening to retrieve her things, but for now she reached for her clutch.

'We should get going,' she said to the room. She still couldn't meet his gaze, half terrified of what he might see there. Terrified that he might act on what he saw there. But his lack of answer drew her back to him unwillingly.

Oh.

His gaze ate her up. Hunger and want barely restrained, marking his jaw with an angry tension that *delighted* her. *Enflamed* her. He made her want to fight. Bite, lick, touch, scream. All these things that good society girls just didn't do.

Relentlessly physical. That's what it meant.

Him.

Then he closed his eyes and when he opened them again, it was hidden. A small perfunctory smile graced his lips and he gestured for her to lead the way and she couldn't decide whether she'd imagined it or not.

* * *

The Pulham was almost entirely given over to the Harrison's gala. As one of *the* social events of the year, there were a lot of familiar faces to Bella. It was, in fact, the first time she'd attended something like this since the non-wedding, and she could see, if not imagine, all the whisperings and gossip that followed her and Chase as she led them through the reception towards where the auction items were being displayed.

'Is this okay for you?' Chase asked, low in her ear from behind.

No. I feel on display and as if my mask is cracked and everyone can see.

'Bella.' His hand on the crook of her arm stopped her.

She turned and smiled. 'It's fine,' she assured him.

'Five dollars.' His hand was out between them, demanding payment for the 'Bella Jar'.

She huffed out a low laugh. 'It's not ideal,' she admitted with a shrug of her shoulder. 'But...'

His gaze darkened. 'But we need it because of my reputation and the impact that's had on the gallery.'

'No, I didn't... I didn't mean it like that,' she said, genuinely. 'I was going to say, that they'll get over it. Someone will do something else and it will draw their attention, and this won't matter one bit. It's how it all works.'

'And you don't mind that it's like that?' he asked,

as they moved side by side towards the room where the items up for auction were on display.

Chase tried to ignore the way that being so close to her made him so... *aware.*

'It's the way it works. It isn't about whether I mind or not,' she said in a way that made Chase angry.

The way Bella simply accepted things infuriated him and confounded him at the same time. But what really bothered him was that it was his fault. They wouldn't have even needed to be here had he not, however many years ago, picked a fight with a journalist he knew was simply looking to make his name by being ruthlessly bombastic and careless of the careers he'd wrecked along the way.

That he'd brought her back here, to be the focus of gossip and whispers, made him distinctly uncomfortable.

'We should go,' he said, causing her to spin around to confront him.

'Absolutely *not*,' she hissed. 'We are here to do a job. This is part of that job. Nayak is contributing to the silent auction and has paid for the dinner. We will both represent the gallery perfectly, do you hear me?'

'Yes, ma'am.'

'Don't call me ma'am,' she whisper-hissed, but her eyes softened, making her look a little less 'murdery' than she had been before, so he followed her towards the room where the auction items were.

It almost looked like a mini gallery with items displayed on a plinth, or on the wall. Experiences had photographs and booklets, pieces of art were framed, there was jewellery, pieces of famous clothing, all donated by some of the wealthiest people in America, about to be bought by the wealthiest people in America, to raise money for the poorest.

Tej had given him strict orders to bid on as many things as possible and although Chase had money, serious and well-earned money from his art, the wealth here was inconceivable. Bella moved through the items as if she was supposed be here, but he felt that he still had paint and oil stuck beneath his fingernails.

Bella cast him a look from a few feet away where she was looking at one of the items.

'What's wrong?'

He tried to shake it off, because Bella was right; they were here to do a job, they were here to represent Nayak, to represent Tej. Chase could handle it. For tonight.

He scanned donations that must have cost an eye-watering amount, and he realised he didn't know what they'd put up for auction. He wandered towards

Bella who was looking at a Rodin, when it caught his eye. A projection on the large white wall, acting like a canvas, of the front of Nayak New York.

He watched as the fancy video walked the viewer through the gallery. Images of some of their artwork already secured for the opening was shown in glimpses. A voice-over invited the watcher to bid on 'An Evening at the Nayak', where the winner would get an evening that started with cocktails and an exclusive one-on-one tour of each piece in the gallery with each piece's artist, followed by a Michelin-star dinner, *in* the gallery, and a weekend stay at the penthouse of Nayak Apartments, New York and...

The buzzing in Chase's ears drowned out the rest. He was furious.

'What is this?'

Bella looked at him nervously. 'I know you're angry—'

'Angry?' he demanded, struggling to keep his voice down. 'I will not have my artists prostituting themselves in this way.'

Lightning flashed in Bella's gaze. '*Prostituting*?'

'They should not have to perform for these people,' he insisted. 'That is not their responsibility.'

Bella reared her head back as if he'd lashed out and shook her head. 'They wanted to do this. They were genuinely happy to help raise money,' she informed him. 'And while I understand where you're coming from, not everyone is as hostile towards people with money as you are.'

He clenched his teeth together. 'That's not what this is about.'

'Really? Then would you feel the same way if the person who won the bid was *not* rich? Would *that* be okay? For an artist to spend one-on-one time exploring the meaning behind their artwork?'

'I would absolutely be okay with that, because they don't get to have access to that any time they like, whereas these people click their fingers—'

'I will grant you that there are some people here like that, but not everyone. And your only criteria for disliking them is that they could afford to be here. Not because you know them, or are familiar with their work, or how hard they work to help others.'

He bit his tongue. She was right. But so was he. His gaze bore into hers. 'You didn't tell me about this because you knew I would be upset.'

'Yes,' Bella replied. 'But I also know that a one-to-one with someone rich enough to win this bid is life-changing not only for the charity, but also the artists in your gallery. Is it really so bad that we not only get to help families who desperately need it, but the artists too?' Bella asked. '*You* did it. You met someone who changed the journey of your art. Is it so bad that we give the artists in Nayak the same chance?'

He stared at her, not having seen it like that before, and his head swam. Was he holding the artists *back*? What kind of gallery director was he, if he let his own prejudices prevent them from moving beyond what he could help them achieve?

'Chase?' Bella asked, concern in her gaze.

'Fine,' he bit out, wanting a bit of space to think this over.

'Fine as in "Bella Jar" fine?' she asked, wincing hopefully.

It was damn near impossible to argue with her. Especially as it was so different to when he'd argued with Annalise. That was lava-hot rage and cryogenic levels of cold, furiously slammed doors and silent treatment on both sides. But Bella was like the tide, she might not keep her cool, but she explained herself, her thoughts. She used her words to open doors, and show him corners, there was heat and fire, yes, but it didn't burn everything down, it brought everything *in*. And they could agree to disagree which was why it *was* impossible. She drove him mad. In a way that made him want to consume her whole.

She waited. She stood there and waited until he

wrestled his feelings and thoughts back together. She gave him the time he needed to be able to answer coherently, where Annalise hadn't, because it always had to be her way, on her time scale, on her terms. Even the end of their marriage.

'As in, fine, I'm okay with the donation, if not entirely with how this came about,' he grudgingly admitted. There was understanding in her gaze and he almost wished there wasn't. Because it was that that would get them into trouble, he just knew it.

He watched her move around the space, making bids on auction items. He'd wanted to hold onto his anger. Needed to. Because without it, his desire for her began to spin out of control. And when their gaze met across the room, wide glistening grey eyes capturing his, he saw surprise, accusation, and something he shouldn't see.

Want.

* * *

No one would know, to look at Bella Carmichael, that inside she was trembling. Having placed bids on behalf of Nayak on items she didn't actually care about, she made her way towards the dinner knowing that he was following her.

Bella located their seats at the table, feeling Chase's gaze on her the whole time. She smiled and introduced herself and Chase to the other people on the table, one of whom – Amanda – she vaguely knew from the 'circuit' of gala dinners and foundations. She tried to focus through the painstaking small talk that seemed all the more derisible with Chase beside her.

To her surprise, Chase entertained the table with stories of various artists he'd known, or met, galleries he'd showed at and art scene insider gossip. He charmed the women at the table and involved the men. Amanda was practically drooling in her soup by the end of the first course and Bella was irritated beyond belief.

It was exactly what she'd wanted though. Chase, proving that he was nothing like the article. The redemption not only of the gallery's reputation, but his too.

So why was she practically flinching every time Amanda laughed at something Chase said?

ASTRID

How's it going?

BELLA

A little too well. I think Chase is
flirting with someone.

ASTRID

Is that a problem?

Yes. No. Bella bit back a groan.

BELLA

Of course not.

ASTRID

You sure?

BELLA

Yes. I am.

Three dots appeared. Stopped. Appeared again
and stopped again.

ASTRID

I just... thought that you might
have...

BELLA

What?

ASTRID

You know. Fallen for his charm.

Panic rose in her chest as she typed angrily onto her screen.

BELLA

What charm?

ASTRID

B, I know exactly the kind of charm
Chase has.

Bella hated the sudden twist of jealousy that thankfully flamed out as brightly as it had come into being.

ASTRID

And I also know the kind of woman
that would interest him.

Bella's heartbeat picked up. She didn't want to be having this conversation, certainly not at a dinner table with Chase sitting right next to her and practically frowning at her and her phone.

ASTRID

And I want you to know that it's
okay.

Because I know you'd feel bad and
I know you wouldn't do it if you
thought it was bad.

Because, B, you're a good girl –
one of the best I know – and it's
okay to be good. And it's okay to
be happy.

Oh shit. Bella felt tears press against the backs of
her eyes.

ASTRID

So if you find yourself wanting to
have something with Chase, then
know it's okay.

That's all. Love you. Xx

They'd not talked about it. Bella certainly hadn't
said anything to Astrid or anyone else about the feelings she was beginning to have for Chase. No. Not
feelings, because she knew that they weren't right for
each other, but she couldn't deny it any longer. She
wanted him. And Astrid had just taken away one of

the last barriers preventing her from doing anything about it. With trembling fingers, she tucked her phone back into her clutch, aware of Chase watching her with hooded eyes.

'Is everything okay?' Chase asked, his voice low for her ears only.

She nodded. Wiped the corner of her eye with the pad of her thumb, cleared her throat and nodded again.

Waiters appeared, clearing the dessert plates, and offered coffee and digestifs to those who wanted them, ahead of the silent auction announcements.

She tried to avoid looking at Chase, but as the lights went down in the room to spotlight the MC for the dinner, she couldn't help herself. Her gaze came back again and again to the profile she could just about make out as the spotlight swirled around the room to highlight each winning bidder.

She took in the line of his jaw, the slight angle of his nose, the furrow to his brow and the tension across his shoulder. She wanted to touch it, trace her finger along it. She wanted to know whether his skin was as warm as she imagined, as rough as she imagined. Whether he was as rough as she imagined.

The muscle at his jaw flexed.

'If you don't stop looking at me like that,' he whispered harshly, without looking her way, 'I'm going to have to do something about it.'

Air stuck in her lungs, her heart leaped in her chest, turning beneath the clear warning in his tone.

'What?' she stammered. 'What would you do?' she whispered back.

After an interminable minute, he turned his gaze on her and every single part of her body was engulfed in heat and flames that drenched her in desire from head to toe. She felt sick she wanted him so badly.

But no matter how much she tried, she couldn't drag her gaze away from him.

The muscle at his jaw flexed again and his gaze flickered between her mouth and her eyes.

He stood, pushing the chair back, the noise near shocking in the quiet of the room listening for the MC.

'Come with me,' he said, taking her by the hand, pulling her from the chair and near dragging her out of the room.

And this time Bella didn't care that they drew attention from the other guests. She didn't care that they had left the dinner before what was socially appropriate. She didn't care that people whispered or stared or looked after them as they left the room. All she cared about was whether finally she could rid herself of this thing, this living breathing thing in her chest that wanted him and only him.

19

If he is secure at all points, be prepared for him. If he is in superior strength, evade him.

— *THE ART OF WAR*, SUN TZU

Chase led Bella out into the foyer of the Pulham Hotel, his mind so full of her, he didn't even know where they were going. Her scent, her gaze, her breath, her hand in his and the feel of her skin.

Mindless. He was mindless with want.

He saw the elevators and remembered.

'Give me your purse,' he asked.

She handed it over to him without question. He

opened it and found the key and gave her back the purse, before leading her over to the elevators.

He held her hand in his, but couldn't look at her. Couldn't, because if he did, he wouldn't be able to stop himself from kissing her. From consuming her.

The doors opened and he gestured for her to get in. He turned to face the young couple who had come up behind them and glared at them until they walked to another lift and he didn't care. He pressed the button for the third floor and waited until the lift began to move before pressing the stop button.

The lights dimmed to emergency lighting and somewhere in the background was the faint sound of an alarm.

Finally he turned to her, pulling her towards him, taking her face in both hands, seeing the open desire staring back at him, and did what he'd been wanting to do pretty much since he'd first set eyes on her.

There was no gentle way into what was going on between them. It wasn't pretty kisses and gentle sups, this was everything, all at once and still it wasn't enough. They met, open-mouthed and desperate, her moans clashing with his groans, tongues, seeking, filling, wanting, fingers desperate for skin, slipping behind clothes and grasping at whatever they could find. He was going to burst out of his body. That was how she made him feel. But no matter what kind of madness this was, he forced himself back.

'Fuck,' he cursed, 'that was better than I'd ever imagined.'

He bit his lip, to stop himself from kissing her again, and tried not to feel a crowning glory at the way Bella looked. Ravished. Her lips puffed and pink, her glorious hair tangled from his hands, her breath coming in pants that matched his own – but it was her eyes. They *glowed* silver.

He held up the key between them. 'You can take this,' he said. 'You can take this, and go to the room, and I'll take the elevator back down to the foyer and we'll never have to speak of this again. Not if you don't want to,' he promised her. 'Or I can keep it. And we'll both go to the room. And you won't be going home until the morning.'

Bella's gaze flickered between him and the key he held up. He needed her to know that this was her choice. He needed her to make that choice. And whatever choice she made, he would honour it and accept it. But for the love of God, he hoped she chose him.

He watched the tension fill her. Saw it in the line

of her jaw and the stiffening of her shoulders. She closed the distance between them and her arm reached forward and he closed his eyes, regretful but understanding. Only for them to spring open when the lift jerked back into action. She'd released the stop button on the elevator and come to stand by his side.

Leaving him with the key.

He let out the breath he'd been holding and gripped the key so that Bella couldn't see the way his hands trembled. He was like an addict already, unable to control his body or his desire.

The elevator arrived at the floor and he followed her out, closely, as if just the heat from her body was enough to sustain him. She reached the door as he lost himself in the curve of her neck. She waited as he remembered himself and passed the key over the lock. Bella pushed open the door and crossed the threshold.

He held himself back by the doorframe, casting a quick glance at the spacious room that had a small living area over by the window on the opposite side of the room to the bed and the open-plan shower and en suite. Jesus, the things he wanted to do in that shower. With her.

He'd read too much of that damn book. It had made him debauched.

Bella reached the middle of the room and turned to face him and dropped a match to every single coherent thing in his mind, when she politely asked, 'Would you like to come in?'

More than fucking anything.

He nodded, slowly, surely, and came into the room, closing the door behind him without taking his eyes from her. Some of the hysteria had burned from the edge of his need, like alcohol fumes into the air, but in its place, mindlessness had become conviction.

He *needed* her.

He crossed the room, her hungry gaze on his every move, making him feel powerful, making him feel wanted, making him surer of this than he had been of anything else he'd ever done. He didn't stop to give her space, he got right in there, scooping her up into him, against him, needing to feel her around him.

He went to kiss her, and the leash of restraint yanked him back barely an inch from her lips.

'You deserve words and poetry,' he admitted, knowing he wouldn't be capable of pretty words right now.

'I don't want words and poetry,' she said, her

breath coming in short pants, her eyes alive with the same need he felt. 'I just want you.'

Christ, he was lost.

* * *

The words were barely out of her mouth, when Chase's lips found hers. She opened for him, wanton and wanting, delighting in the way his tongue filled her, sought her, found her. *That's* what it felt like. As if she'd been found, after wandering lost for years. Seen after being overlooked.

His hands were everywhere: lifting her up, holding her as she wrapped her legs around him, one fisted the skirts of her dress, the scrape of his knuckles against her thigh sending shivers across her body.

Bella pulled at him and pressed against him, against the hardness she felt at her core, the feeling releasing a moan she hadn't realised she was fighting. She'd *never* felt like this before, and she was half terrified that even skin to skin wouldn't be enough. What she wanted from him felt endless. Unstoppable, *insatiable*.

He could kiss her for an eternity and she'd never grow bored. Each second felt like a revelation, a new learning, a new feeling. His finger teased the hemline of her panties, and she ached for him. Her breasts strained against the neckline of her dress, and she cried out when he grabbed her ass. The only thing stopping her from begging for more, was his mouth on hers.

Chase was entirely different to anyone she'd been with before. He took, filled, consumed, but nothing that cost her. He made her feel powerful. He took only what she would give and she would give him everything if he asked. She knew it with the kind of startling clarity that stole her breath.

He pulled back, concern in his gaze as he asked her, 'What's wrong? Did I—'

Bella shook her head, unnerved by the fact he'd sensed the turn of her thoughts, and pulled him back into a kiss that made them both forget. She pulled at his shirt, tugging it loose with clumsy fingers and tried to free buttons, as Chase simply reached up and pulled the top of her dress down, exposing one breast. He wrenched his mouth from hers and pressed open-mouthed kisses to that breast, igniting a line of fire from there to her core, stealing her breath and making her wet. Her heart pounded and her skin felt electrified as she shifted in his hold.

When he stared moving, she thought he'd take

her to the bed, but instead, he stalked backwards to the large armless chair that faced the room. He sat down with her still wrapped around him.

'I want to see you like this,' he said, looking up at her.

Her hair fell like curtains about them and he reached up with one hand to fist it before his wicked tongue teased the nipple of her exposed breast. Unable to help herself she ground down against the hard length of him between her legs and moaned as he growled against her skin.

He drew the rest of her dress down and palmed one breast as he sucked on the other and she felt *ravished*. He feasted on her and she loved it. He was skating the edge of control, they both were, and instead of wanting to run it made her want to rush headlong into it for more.

She teased herself again and again against him. Chase's hands flew to her hips and he thrust beneath her, letting her know how affected he was, letting her know what was to come. Her pulse thundered in her ears and throbbed beneath her skin as she bowed her head to kiss him and groaned as he thrust against her.

His hands slipped beneath the skirts of her dress,

and clutched her ass and thighs, thumbs creeping towards the seam of her panties.

'Christ, Bella.'

His words fell against her lips, and she knew he'd discovered how wet she was for him.

Need hung in the thick air between them.

'We can still stop here, Bella. If you want,' he offered, his hands on her skin, burning brands she'd feel for days.

His eyes were deep dark bitter swirls shining near gold when he looked at her. Bella knew that this was crazy. For so many reasons, she could hardly count. They should absolutely be stopping here. They could still walk it back. But the way her heart ached at the thought of it...

Bella shook her head, her eyes on his, knowing that the seriousness she felt was etched across her features.

'I don't want to stop.'

'What do you want?' he asked.

Everything.

Whether she answered out loud, or whether he read it in her eyes, Chase wrapped an arm around her and met her in a kiss, chest to chest, core to core, tongue to tongue.

He yanked her thong, the thin silk snapping and

Bella cried out when his fingers slipped into her, teasing and touching and pressing. He drew her to her knees and told her to stay there, while he worked his trousers and briefs down and off his legs, bringing her back down while she tried to release the zip of her dress.

'Wait,' he commanded and her fingers stopped. 'I want to be the one to take it off you,' he confessed, his eyes on her body as if he were waiting for secrets to be revealed. Her hands dropped to her sides and she watched his careful study of her with fascination.

He released the zip and gathered the dress in his hands, lifting it over her head and casting it aside. He looked over her entire body, frantically almost. As if he were worried she'd disappear. But then she became distracted by his body, the dark swirls of hair across his chest she remembered from his apartment. His body, lean, strong, not bulky, with muscles from the gym, and doing things to her she'd never experienced before. Her skin felt too small, as if she'd jump right out of it if he touched her.

His lip quirked into a smirk and she looked up to find him staring back at her, his eyebrow raised. 'Like what you see?' he teased.

She nodded, biting her lip, and his eyes burned.

'You look truly debauched, Bella Carmichael. It

suits you,' he said, pulling her down to him and Bella felt as if he'd told her that she was the most beautiful woman in the world.

He reached for the wallet he'd put on the table by the lamp and retrieved a small foil packet and tore the corner with his teeth. She shifted back as he rolled the condom onto his length, her fingers itching to take him in her own hand. But when she looked back at Chase, the *intent* in his gaze burned not from frantic, drastic need but relentless want.

With one hand he lifted her gently onto her knees, positioning himself beneath her, his gaze never leaving hers. She felt watched, observed. Seen. His thumb circled her entrance, teasing her, leaving her wanting, until one finger, then two, thrust into her and she cried out. Her legs trembled as she held herself there, wanting to push down on his hand, pulse racing as he filled her with fingers that were just a taste of what was to come. It wasn't enough. She wanted more. She wanted it all. As if reading her body, he gripped his cock with the same hand he'd brought her to near orgasm with, and teased her entrance with the tip. Every pulse point in her body throbbed with anticipation.

Until finally, he allowed her to lower herself onto him slowly, in control of the way he stretched her muscles, sinking around him to take him in. *All* of him. Her head dropped to meet his, their foreheads pressed together in a shared pleasure that words couldn't capture, until finally she whispered, 'Fuck,' and she felt his smile against her lips.

'I love it when you talk dirty, Carmichael.'

She smiled as he pulled her down around his length even more and he groaned while she sank into the feeling of completeness. It was as if she'd found something in herself that she hadn't known she was missing and she never wanted to move ever again. Until Chase anchored her against him and rolled his hips.

* * *

Bella cried into his mouth and he'd never heard anything more incredible. It had been a while since he'd last slept with anyone, but he knew, instinctively and instantly that this was different. It was some al-chemical reaction bonding them together even if he was resistant to it.

Dragging his mouth from hers, he looked up, her hair having fallen around them, golden strands encasing them, his eyes fastened on her, unable to look away. His gaze devoured her, every nip she made on her lip, every moan that fell from her mouth, the way that her eyes closed as if trying to hide her pleasure from him, but was utterly unable to.

The way she felt around him, the way she felt above him, he worshipped her with his hands and mouth, the taste of her indelible on his tongue. Every nuance, every moment was different, a cacophony of moments of her that he wanted to capture on canvas, in paint, pen, pencil, charcoal, anything he could get his hands on.

And then he felt her begin to tighten around him and all coherent thought fled. They became pure sensation, as he lifted her ever so slightly, allowing him to thrust into her in chaotic pumps that took them close to the edge of something as inescapable and inevitable as it was incredible.

Her moans of pleasure filled his ears and his groans became growls as he pushed them both to the brink. Sweat-soaked skin slapped against sweat-soaked skin and when Bella thrust out her hand against the window behind them, holding herself in place above him just where she wanted him, just where he hit that spot, it shoved them into the path of an oncoming orgasm that crashed over them in a wave that washed *everything* away.

'That was...' she tried, her voice harsh from her cries. 'That was...' she tried and failed again.

'I don't know what that was,' he whispered, his own throat dry, 'but I want to do it again.' His heart turned when she laughed. He pulled back so that he could see her and kiss her and simply explore her. His cock pulsed from that simple contact and he knew they couldn't stay like that for much longer.

'I'm going to have to move you.'

Bella shook her head and he felt his own reluctance.

'I know, but I need to deal with the condom,' he said, pressing a kiss to her lips. He reached for the throw on the sofa and pulled it across her, before heading to the bathroom.

He disposed of the condom, washed his hands, and looked at himself in the mirror. What they'd shared... it wasn't just something that could be one night. He didn't know what it meant, but he knew it made him worried. Worried about her. Worried about what it meant for him. She wasn't someone he could see himself walking away from.

Bella knocked on the open door, something like nervousness in her gaze. And he understood it. Christ, he felt it himself. But instead of facing it, he leaned into the shower stall and turned on the hot spray of water, pulling her gently with him to stand beneath it.

As the water cascaded down over them, he took her mouth, the slick slide of their tongues merging with watery caresses. Christ. Already he was hard for her. Already the fire stoked by just one touch burned through the water. His lips hungrily consumed the skin on her neck as he pressed open-mouthed kisses to her collarbone and chest. His hands palmed her breasts and her cries urged him on.

What was this madness? he wondered, his entire body burning with need.

'Condom,' he said against her skin, groaning just from the thought of leaving her.

She stilled in his hands, frustration etched on her face.

His forehead dropped to hers. 'I only had one in my wallet,' he admitted.

'That's okay,' she said, smiling softly as if that was it. That was all he was after. He frowned, wondering at what the hell the guys she'd been with before now had been up to.

'That doesn't mean that I'm done with you,' he warned her, eagerness spreading through his body at the way her eyes lit up.

He kissed her with the fervour of a dying man,

before turning her in his arms and gently pressing her against the shower wall. She shivered as he pressed a kiss to her neck and trembled when he told her to hold on.

He dropped to his knees, and parted her legs, drawing her hips back towards him.

'Chase—' She shook.

'Don't worry. I've got you,' he promised her. 'Just trust me.'

And then he leaned forward and pressed open-mouthed kisses against her core. His fingers found her clit as she cried out, her body tense and near fraught with need.

She tasted incredible, but it was the way she shifted in his hands, as if unable to keep still, unable to bear her own pleasure. His tongue delved into her folds, teased her entrance as one hand palmed her ass cheek and the other teased her clit. Hot, wet and sweet, he'd never been so turned on in his life. He was at risk of coming just from the sound of her pleasure.

She pressed herself against him and he smiled, tonguing her thoroughly, spreading her just a little wider for him, until finally, spectacularly, she came undone on his tongue, her breath rhythmic sobs that he felt right down to his balls.

Tremors wracked her body as he took her into his arms and out of the shower. He dried her carefully, while the daze slowly receded from her gaze and led her back into the dimly lit room. He drew her beneath the covers, tucking her against his body, knowing that his own needs could wait. Would wait, until they knew exactly what was going on between them.

20

When envoys are sent with compliments in their mouths, it is a sign that the enemy wishes for a truce.

— *THE ART OF WAR*, SUN TZU

Bella opened her eyes to the sight of the empty bed beside her. Her heart jerked, the level of hurt near shocking, and warning enough. *He'd left?*

'You shouldn't think so hard so early in the morning.'

Chase's voice startled her, making her jump and then laugh, and she tried to hide her foolishness by squashing her face into the pillow.

He was still here.

She peeked out at him from the pillow to find him smiling at her. He was holding a cup of coffee and there was a room service tray in the corner of the room.

'You're a feeder,' she complained as her stomach rejoiced.

'We didn't get much at the dinner last—'

Bella's gasp of horror cut him off.

The dinner! Oh God, she'd completely forgotten!

They'd left early. The *whole* point of the event had been about redeeming Chase's reputation and ensuring the gallery was back on track and instead, they'd left before the end.

Her hand flew to her head, her thoughts so frantic they were giving her a temperature. It was another mess she was going to have fix. She needed to call the PR firm and—

'You're doing it again,' Chase chided. 'I told the Harrisons that it was a family emergency.'

'You can't do that,' Bella cried.

'Well, I *did*, so it's done,' he said with a shrug.

'You can't lie about things like that.' She wanted to throw the pillow at him where he stood looking far too good, the shirt from last night open mid-way down and half-tucked into the formal trousers.

So, it hadn't been an aberration. Just looking at him made her entire body hum, expectant shivers pushing at her skin and wanting more.

'It's fine. When I called them this morning, they said they'd raised a record amount of money and they were extremely thankful for the Nayak's donation – which we *will* talk about tomorrow,' he said, with a warning point of his finger. She bit her lip. 'But apparently it was an extremely popular donation,' he conceded.

They hadn't messed up, no one was upset, she didn't have to fix anything. In fact, Chase had handled it for her. He hadn't waited for her to fix it, or solve it; he'd done it himself. And God that made her feel...

Her phone buzzed somewhere in the room, but she ignored it. So did Chase.

It made her feel *things*.

'Last night,' she started, her throat rough from the pleasure he'd made her moan with. Just the thought made her skin flush. 'Last night you gave me a choice,' she tried again, forcing the words out.

His eyes, hot and heavy on hers, grew serious, and he nodded slowly.

'And' – she shrugged, not quite sure how to say it – 'if you want to just leave it here...' She trailed off.

She didn't know what to say, what the correct words were to ask whether this was a fling or something more. Good girls didn't have flings. But Bella wasn't a good girl any more.

When she looked up, Chase shook his head, slowly, something determined in his gaze.

She bit her lip, hoping to hold back the smile. 'You don't want to just leave it here?'

'Nope.'

She swallowed.

'You?' he asked, and she shook her head, quicker than he had. People had always wanted her poise and grace. Chase seemed determined to make her messy and chaotic.

'But,' she said, thinking about the next few weeks, 'I'd rather not tell the staff. At least, not until the gallery is open,' she said, cutting off her thoughts. Not wanting to think about what would happen after the gallery was opened.

'Agreed,' Chase said, finally releasing himself from where he stood, putting the coffee down on the table and stalking towards her with a wicked glint in his eye.

'Do you want to know what else I did this morning, while you were sleeping?' he asked, slowly unbuttoning his shirt.

She bit her lip and nodded her head.

'I bought some more condoms,' and she squealed as he came down on her and covered her with kisses that started out as teasing and silly, but quickly grew hot and needy and *perfect*.

* * *

ASTRID

I don't need to know the details, love, but I do need to know that you're okay. That's all. Promise. Xx

BELLA

I'm okay. Promise. Xx

The dinner had, despite her concerns, indeed been a success, Nayak New York getting good mentions in the press from the Harrisons and attendees of the dinner who had seen Chase and Bella.

Maurice was happy with the newfound confidence for the gallery and now that pieces were coming in thick and fast, Ye-Joon was spending more time here, making Ali happier too.

The website had gone live and the sign-up rate for the newsletter was higher than had been predicted, and the guest list for the pre-opening night was already nearly full, which would hopefully push some over into the actual opening, scheduled for two days after.

Tej had opened his little black book for Bella and she had rifled through it, making a careful selection of who she could invite. She'd thought about asking Astrid about Blake and Aiden, for a hot second. The 'Twin Tornados', America's ice-hockey giants, would attract an entirely new audience to the gallery. But then realised she couldn't. Because if Chase ever knew about her friendship with Astrid, or the revenge plan, he'd never forgive her. So for however long this thing ran between them, it had to be a secret.

And not just from Chase.

Although Astrid knew – or at least, suspected – Bella hadn't told the other girls yet and... and she was going to keep it that way too, she'd decided. Bad Bella ignored the unease Good Bella would have felt about it. Because being good had got her dumped and being bad apparently got her some incredibly good sex and Bad Bella was *not* complaining.

But deep down, she wrestled with it. She had come to terms with Paige and Olly because they had fallen in love with each other. But was it better or worse that she and Chase weren't in love? Because she couldn't be in love with Chase. And he certainly wasn't in love with her.

But the girls had been so worried about her when it had come to Olly and Paige, and now Bella had gone and done the same thing to Astrid. Only it *wasn't* the same thing... and then Bella was back in the same circle of thoughts as she had been over the last few days, which made her just want to bury her head in the sand.

And for the first time in her life, she did. She stopped returning calls, saying that she was just busy in the run up to pre-opening and opening. And she was. It wasn't a lie. But it wasn't the truth either. Because when she wasn't working...

Chase walked past the office and she couldn't help but track him with her eyes. He was dumping another coffee in the kitchen, because he was *still* finding salt sachets in his sugar and she hadn't swapped them out yet. She found herself smiling, until she felt Maurice's gaze on her. She cleared her throat and returned to the report she'd been working on.

* * *

Chase ended the call with Sascha, surprised as well as relieved that she'd been able to finish the collection so soon. He promised to visit the studio tomorrow, but the list of things he had to do before the pre-opening and opening were growing and he couldn't help but be frustrated by it. His hope to feel a sense of excitement or accomplishment as they neared the opening were beginning to fade. But Chase didn't exactly have another option at this point and besides, pushing ahead with the gallery still felt a million times better than just the thought of his own art again.

'It's okay to grieve it,' Tej had told him at the very beginning. But Chase had shoved those words away. Because if he grieved, it meant he'd lost it. And he refused to even consider that. If he didn't grieve, it wasn't gone. He could always go back to it. But the further and further he got from his last painting, the more fear, the more anxiety, the more pain built up to a point so overwhelming, he could hardly breathe.

It wasn't even about being a success. He'd set fire to all the money in his bank account if he could paint again. Hell, he'd go work in an office for the tax man, if it meant he could pick up a brush again.

He checked his watch. Just after five-thirty, and Bella wasn't at her desk. They'd all started working late in the run up to opening. There was a sense of urgency, not panicked or rushed, but focused and driven. It was good to see what they were all accomplishing together, but a part of him felt separate from it. As if they'd have been perfectly capable of doing it without him.

He gave one last glance at the email he'd received that afternoon from Zadzisai's agent who'd apparently had a change of heart and now wanted to headline the opening. He wasn't ready to sort through his feelings about it yet, so he locked his computer and got up, stretching his arms above his head, cricking his neck, and surreptitiously trying to see if Bella was still in the office.

Ever since the gala dinner, they'd hardly been able to keep their hands off each other. Surely he should have got used to her by now. Surely at least familiarity should have made him less... *hungry*.

Christ, just the thought of it had him achingly hard. He grimaced, adjusting his trousers and left his office. He wanted to check on the latest layout they'd been testing around the life-sized photographs they had of Sascha's work.

They'd been experimenting with a series of moveable walls that would create separate areas for different pieces. One was almost entirely enclosed where Chase was considering either the quadriptych from Lit Lake or the instillation from Itashi.

He found Bella in the far corner, her gaze flitting between one of the pieces from Lake and the enlarged photo of Sascha's piece pinned up against the wall next to it.

Her hair was down, partly because every time she tried to put it up, he'd find a way to pull it loose again when no one was watching. She was wearing those jeans again, the ones that hugged her ass and made him damn near feral, but the open-knit cardigan she wore looked soft and innocent in a way that made him want to peek beneath it.

He came to stand behind her, aware that the rest of the staff were still upstairs for now, if not for much longer. She behaved as if she hadn't noticed him, but peering over her shoulder where she had nestled her tablet to take notes from, he could see the way her skin pebbled. Goosebumps that trickled across his own arms.

Then he saw her notes.

'You want to move it?' he asked a little surprised.

She craned her neck to look back at him. 'I'm not sure. But there's something about it that's bothering me and I can't quite figure out what it is.'

He stared at the positioning of the pieces, trying

to see what she saw, but couldn't. He liked the pieces where they were.

She smiled, and rolled her eyes as if sensing that he was about to dig his heels in. 'Don't worry, I'm not going to argue about it. Not yet anyway,' she warned.

And he was pleased. Because he *liked* arguing with her. It was a mental exercise that pushed and pulled and when it spilled over into their bed, it usually became something glorious.

With one ear on the staff upstairs, he dropped his mouth to the crook of her neck, pressing kisses against the flesh exposed by the loose neck of her cardigan.

Bella gasped, and he felt it shoot through him.

'Chase.' His name on her lips was half warning, half plea and it was like a red flag to a bull. Unable to stop himself, he wrapped his hands around her, drawing her back against his chest, hands slipping beneath the knit and meeting smooth cool skin.

Nought to sixty, every time he got his hands on her. That's what it was like. The rush, that same heady feeling when he lost himself to a painting and looked back to see what he'd discovered. She was like that. A fresh painting, a surprise discovery, every single time.

She unfurled against his body, and he thrust one

hand between her legs, and the sound she made was near indecent. Christ, he could barely contain himself. It didn't seem to matter how much he got of her, he still wanted more.

He drew her backwards, slipping behind the screen wall set up in the corner of the gallery, turned her in his arms and claimed her mouth like a starving man. His tongue thrust boldly and she welcomed every bit of it, of *him*. Her fingers fisted his hair and he relished the difference between the near-glacial poise she maintained at work, and the incendiary wildness she met him with out of it.

He pulled down her cardigan and bra and took her breast into his mouth, knowing that he should stop, knowing that they could be caught any minute. She moaned and he quickly clamped a hand over her mouth, without stopping. He teased her nipple with his tongue and palmed her breast with his hand and she was like fire twisting in his hold. He felt her press against the hand that covered her mouth, but not trying to escape, and the tug of desire that passed through his body tightened his skin and heightened his senses.

'Is anyone here?' they both heard Maurice call out.

Chase's gaze flew to Bella's, her eyes wide with panic, her body trembling beneath his touch.

'They must have left,' Ali responded from the other side of the screen wall and a streak of wicked heat shot right through him.

Bella's breast still exposed, he blew across the skin, slick from his tongue. She shivered, her eyes fluttering, her body unfurling once again. Her eyes flared like sparklers, and she shook her head in warning, but it was too late. The idea had already taken hold and Chase was helpless to stop it. With one had still over her mouth, he used the other to flick the top button of her jeans and draw the zip down, his fingers slipping into her panties and into the cross-hatch of curls between her legs.

'Chase usually says goodbye,' Maurice said, confusion clear in his tone.

He circled her clit once, marvelling at how wet and ready she was. Bella pressed against his hand again, shifting as if unsure whether to pull away or to open for him, but he'd learned to read her body in the last few days, the flicker of her pulse, the near plea in her storm-grey eyes; she wanted this as much as he did.

He bent his head to her ear and whispered, 'Tell me to stop.'

'Maybe they had an off-site meeting,' Ali mused.

And after what felt like an eternity, she shook her head. She didn't want to him stop. *Thank God*. He thrust two fingers into her wet heat and she rolled her head back against the wall, whimpering against his hand, her nipple taut and pink, enough to tempt him to take it into his mouth. He crooked his fingers as he thumbed her clit and drew on her nipple and she nearly collapsed beneath him.

'That must be it,' Maurice said uncertainly. But their steps retreated, the lights flickered off before the door closed and the lock turned firmly.

The gallery was cast in shadows, lit vaguely by the lights out on the street, but the darkness hid them from the view of any passerby. Bella let out a shuddered breath that was half laugh, half relief and Chase smiled, before crooking his fingers and watching her entire body respond. She was so physical like this – so restrained during the day and he wondered what it had cost her to do that. To separate the two so powerful parts of her so distinctly.

'Condom,' she whispered to him and he laughed.

'You've got a one-track mind, Carmichael, and I like it,' he whispered back, reaching into his pocket.

Bella shimmied out of her jeans as Chase rolled the condom over his length. They came back together in a clash of tongues that teased and teeth that nipped and hands that grasped. He lifted her up and wrapped her legs around his waist as he pressed her carefully back against the wall. And when he positioned himself at her entrance, she rolled her hips and he buried himself deep. His curse melded with her moan and they ceased being separate. Together, they moved, the pleasure just as shocking, just as new as it had been that first time.

She rolled her hips and he flexed deep within her and when he ground into her, and reached that spot that no one had ever found, together they were thrust into a starburst so bright it blinded them both.

21

In battle, there are not more than two methods of attack; the direct and the indirect; yet these two in combination give rise to an endless series of manoeuvres.

— *THE ART OF WAR*, SUN TZU

Bella waited for the guilt to start. The shame at her wanton behaviour. But it didn't. And she was beginning to suspect that she wouldn't. At some point in the night, Chase had pulled her to his side, cradling her hand against his chest, and possessively claiming her thigh that was draped across his body.

She relished how much he wanted her, enjoyed how much she wanted *this*. And she marvelled at who she was with him, exploring wants and desires she'd never have before admitted. Or even behaving in ways she'd have never allowed herself to. Arguing with him, being loud, not just in bed, but in the office, on the street. She didn't care what people thought and...

Oh.

She didn't care what people thought.

'You're doing it again,' he groaned as his body began to move beneath hers, his hand sweeping up and down her thigh as if trying to soothe her.

'Doing what?'

'Thinking. Shhhh. You're too loud with it.'

She smiled into his side, and he groaned again and pulled her over him. He growled into her neck and bit her playfully and she giggled from it.

'No, you can't make me,' he said, shaking his head. 'I won't do it.'

'Won't do what?' she asked.

'No more sex!' he exclaimed, holding her to him with strong hands around her middle. 'I can't take it any more. All you want to do is fuck me senseless.' She squealed at his language and he laughed, but carried on. 'You only want me for my body. Admit it,' he said, digging dextrous fingers into her ticklish ribs.

'No!' Bella cried out.

'Admit it,' he demanded as he tickled her even more.

'Okay, yes I admit it,' she cried with laughter.

'Say it,' he demanded, pinning her with his gaze.

'I did.'

'No, say it,' he stressed.

And she pressed her lips together to stop herself, but he only tickled her more.

'Say it.'

'All I want to do is fuck you senseless,' she cried out, a flush across her cheeks and heart.

And he laughed, victorious. 'I love it when you talk dirty, Carmichael,' he said, taking her mouth with his before tossing her to the other side of the bed playfully.

He slapped her bare ass, hard, and told her to get up.

Shock, delight and the brief sting of pain short-circuited her brain and he, unknowingly, left her panting in surprise on the bed as he started the shower.

'Come on!' he called from the bathroom. 'We have places to be.'

* * *

'Places to be' turned out to be a six-mile Saturday-morning run, followed by breakfast back at the diner that he'd taken her to before. The waitress smiled, remembering them, and they had exactly the same order, even though Bella complained about the calories, but not hard enough to keep her from the chocolate milkshake, the burger, the fries or the onion rings.

That was followed by a trip to the Met and even though it should have seemed like a working holiday, they browsed exhibitions that spanned hundreds of years, art, architecture, installations, ceramics, and cultural exhibits, relishing the sense of hushed awe and appreciation. They avoided crowds who ignored the ban on photography and snapped pictures like strobe lighting. They smiled at pieces they liked, argued over pieces they didn't, and she enjoyed watching Chase take in art, but felt the distance between him and the work. As if he was taking a step back from it, from allowing himself to have it, or be near it.

'Are you in here?' she asked impulsively.

'I am standing here, so technically, yes.'

She slapped his arm. 'That's not what I meant, and you know it. Are you, your *paintings*, in here?'

He closed his mouth, trying to keep the smile – she could tell – but the light had gone from his eyes. He nodded.

'Can we go see it?' She didn't need his permission, but it felt like something she wanted.

He sighed, checking his watch and she already knew his answer.

'I was really hoping to get to the market before it closed,' he said, his disappointment feigned.

'Another time,' she said, and he said, 'Sure,' pulling her slowly back towards the exit.

As they pottered around the market, picking up bits and pieces for dinner that evening, Bella didn't forget the way he'd avoided her answer, the urge to fix the hurt, the need to make it better for him growing in her like a flower.

She wasn't blind to the way he had never talked about his art or his paintings, or how they didn't fill his apartment. It was as if he, rather than her, had only been there for three months. His apartment was impersonal and undecorated and somehow, for an artist, that struck Bella as so very wrong.

She was still thinking about it several hours later when she was finishing up the pasta sauce she was making for dinner while he poured himself a glass of wine.

'Would you like one?' he offered.

'Please,' she said, nudging an empty wine glass toward him. He filled it and passed it back, leaning against the countertop to watch her.

'What?' she asked.

'Bella Carmichael, domestic goddess. It suits you,' he observed, raising his glass to hers in a toast.

They'd spent the whole day together, laughing, teasing each other, arguing about paintings and carbonara versus spaghetti vongole; they'd talked about everything and anything that wasn't about work or the future.

The future she didn't want to imagine where he discovered that she was the one behind the article, that she was friends with his ex-lover. She knew what that future looked like in her worst nightmares. But Chase was running from something else, and she didn't know what, but she wanted to fix it, to help him.

'Chase—'

'Don't. Please don't,' he said, looking down at his glass.

She didn't try to pretend not to know what he was asking. And she felt mean, because she was going to push him, because she knew how important this was.

'Why aren't you painting?'

* * *

Chase clenched his teeth together. He'd known she wouldn't be able to let it go. She wasn't that kind of person. She liked to fix things and he liked to leave them the hell alone. It was the Miller way.

And he knew that he could push it off, her question. She'd let him if he really didn't want to talk about it. But for the first time, he realised that he *did*. It had been pressing against his mind, the back of his tongue, ever since he'd been helping Sascha find her way through to her collection, and even before that. Ever since Bella had stormed into his life and demanded more from him.

'It's block. Creative block,' he admitted. 'I haven't been able to pick up a paintbrush in over a year.'

He couldn't meet her gaze, so he locked his sight onto his hand, swirling the pale Citrine wine around the glass.

'I'm so sorry, Chase. That must be extremely painful.'

He shrugged as if it didn't matter. As if it didn't

feel like more than half of him, of who he was, had been AWOL for twelve months.

The silence between them wasn't awkward, but it wasn't peaceful either. Her presence was like a gentle press of a palm on his skin. Gentle, but insistent.

'It started after I found them in bed to—' He bit his lip, knowing what he'd been telling himself, what he'd told Tej, but unable to lie to Bella. She didn't deserve that from him. 'No. It started before that,' he admitted. He'd been blaming Dan and Annalise for far too much for far too long. 'It started about eighteen months ago. At first, I just tried to ignore it. Pretend it wasn't happening.' He rolled his shoulders, trying to shake off the guilty feeling in the pit of his stomach.

'I became pretty unbearable to be around when the painting started to fizzle out,' he admitted, hating the shame and the guilt and the memory of those months. The arguments with Annalise, the way he'd shrug things off with Dan. Because how could he tell his wife that he was worried about his painting when her career had disappeared at the expense of his? How could he tell his best friend that he was struggling when, as his agent, he was as much dependent on him for income as his wife? Christ, no wonder they'd sought solace in each other while he'd been behaving like an adult-sized child throwing a tantrum.

He nodded to himself. 'Completely unbearable. I was angry, I shouted, I kicked things. Trashed my studio,' he remembered with shame, rubbing his chin with the palm of his hand, hating how terrible just the memory of it made him feel.

'Then, when I found Dan and Annalise together... I was devastated. I literally had no clue it had been going on,' he admitted, shocked even now, still unable to quite believe it. 'Everything began to slip through my fingers. And for a while, I tried to pretend that it wasn't. I attended pre-existing exhibitions. I spent a few months travelling between them. I even met someone. She was pretty great, but even then I knew I wasn't ready or able to give her the more that I knew she was looking for. But I ignored that too,' he said, guilt and bitterness heavy on his tongue.

'And then, when Annalise managed to ruin that, I just... She hated me so much. For not being able to give her the life she'd wanted to have with me. And after she scared Astrid off, and after the divorce came through, it just became easier to blame *them* for my lack of painting. And really, it wasn't long before I nearly forgot that it had started before I'd found Dan and Annalise together. Because... because then it wouldn't be my fault,' he tried to explain.

'Your fault? The marriage?' Bella asked, turning off the stoves and coming round to where he'd backed himself up against the counter.

He shook his head. 'My fault that I didn't live up to what my mother wanted,' he admitted, clenching his jaw to hide the way his lips trembled, blinking back the wet heat that pressed against his eyes. The way that the sliver of pain near split his heart in two.

Bella's hands swept back the hair that had fallen across his eyes, to gently lift his gaze to hers. Eyes open, accepting, understanding. *Christ*, he didn't deserve her. There were plenty of things he did deserve, but not Bella Carmichael.

'I'm pretty sure that your mother would have just wanted you to be happy,' Bella said, looking sadly up at him.

'Yes.' He nodded. 'She would have wanted that. But she also wanted more for me.' In his mind's eye, he saw it, her hand marking an arc in the hospital room. *You're going to be famous.*

'I think that every parent wants the world for their child,' Bella offered. 'And I think your mother tried to plant for you the seeds for a future she would never see outside of her imagination. And I think that if she knew for even a second that would become a burden rather than a hopeful dream, she'd be devastated.'

He nodded, not trusting himself to speak. Because she was right. He'd been so focused on being the success his mother had always wanted him to be, that he hadn't really thought about just being happy, about what that even looked like to him.

Instead, his creative block had latched onto anything as an excuse to make the guilt and anger at not being able to paint so much worse. It was a kind of sadomasochistic self-flagellation, thoughts that came so thick and fast that they choked him, leaving him utterly overwhelmed and incapable of anything.

Bella's lips pressed against his, the heat of her body pushing away the darkness and the voices. A moment of calm in the chaos that he didn't deserve but clutched to like a lifeline.

'Thank you for sharing that with me,' she said against his lips and as if being given a green light to end the conversation, he turned from receiving to giving and before he knew it they were in bed and the dinner was left on the stove for the next two hours.

* * *

Bella teased the hem of her rollneck a little higher hoping that no one could see what was hidden beneath.

A love bite.

She had a love bite. At twenty-six.

She felt a knowing gaze on her, but it wasn't coming from Chase. She looked up to find Maurice staring at her. Perhaps she and Chase weren't being discreet enough. Maurice raised a wry eyebrow as if to say, 'You think?'

Ali entered Chase's office just ahead of the man who had given her more orgasms last night than she could count and Bella fought the blush on her cheeks hard. And failed.

'Are you okay? You're looking a little—'

Maurice cut Ali off before she could finish. 'It's a little warm in here.'

Ali looked between them and shrugged before dropping down next to Bella, who was absolutely re-fusing point-blank to make eye contact with Maurice who was now fully smirking.

Chase was the last to enter, muttering about never making coffee again, and Bella remembered that she *still* hadn't fixed the sugar sachets in his room. The problem was that she rarely had time here alone. She and Chase would leave together after the others had gone home, not because they waited for the opportunity, though there was maybe a little of that, but mainly because they'd been working so hard in the run-up to the pre-opening event, which reminded her.

'Maurice, Ali? Can I have the final list of your invitees for the pre-opening by the end of today?' she asked. 'And Maurice, if you could speak to Ye-Joon—'

'I'll do it!' Ali cried, bouncing on the sofa, with her hand practically in the air, delighted by any excuse to speak to the crush who now blushed every time she looked his way.

'Okay,' Bella replied with a laugh.

Chase sat down, eyeing his coffee warily, as if it may or may not commit grievous bodily harm at the first sip.

'Okay,' he said, finally dragging his eyes away from the coffee. 'I wanted to let you know about an email I received from Zadzisai a few days ago.'

Bella smoothed out her features before the frown she felt gathering could take place. Chase hadn't mentioned it, but it wasn't like he had to. It wasn't some secret he wasn't telling her. Not like the secret she was keeping from him about Astrid and the girls and why she'd first come here.

She bit back a mental curse. Having a good-girl conscience was a real pain sometimes.

Maurice nudged her with his knee and she refocused.

'It seems that they have changed their minds and would like to return as featured artist for the opening.'

A whoosh of air left Bella's mouth, not quite a gasp, not quite a sigh. Maurice did manage to frown and Ali looked a little confused.

'What about Sascha?' Ali asked. 'What about all the material that's ready to go out? And the website?'

'Can we peddle it back at this point?' Chase asked Bella.

Even while she reeled at the thought of dropping Sascha, Bella ran through the amount of work needed. 'Nothing has actually gone out to the mailing lists, the website is live, but hasn't reached phase two of the update in terms of specific artist details, beyond the current images. But...'

How? How could he consider doing that to Sascha?

'I'm not making any decisions right now,' Chase assured them, 'I just want to know if a) we can do it, b) whether we want to, and c) what would be the right thing for the gallery. So. Thoughts. Maurice, take it away.'

After a beat, Maurice leaned into it. 'Technically we can do it. Technically it would be the most sensible thing for the gallery – Zadzisai brings a lot of attention and kudos, not just with clients and guests, but other artists too. But do we want to?'

'No,' Bella said. She blinked when all eyes landed on her. 'I know that it would make the most sense, I know that...'

But it would sell out everything that Chase stood for. She didn't want to watch him turn into one of the corporate raiders that he had been so disdainful of, just because he'd been forced into it by that shitty article she'd practically written herself. She didn't want to sell out Sascha who had worked day and night, pushing herself, to get ready for the opening.

'I get that this could cost the gallery in the short term,' she pressed on. 'It doesn't make the most business sense, turning them down. We'd obviously do initially much better with Zadzisai. But I can't help but worry about what it would cost us in the long term.'

And why was she thinking of the long term? For this gallery? She had come here, hoping to ruin the life and reputation of a man she had thought a monster for making her friend suffer. And now? Now she was planning for after? With Chase? And the gallery?

'How long do I have, before I have to make a decision?' Chase asked as if considering both positions.

'Twenty-four hours,' Bella said decisively. 'Any longer and we risk losing the momentum needed to capitalise on either Zadzisai or get enough info out on Sascha. But I don't like it,' she said, finally.

'Noted,' Chase said, making marks on his tablet and moving onto the next topic while avoiding her gaze.

22

O divine art of subtlety and secrecy! Through you [...] we can hold the enemy's fate in our hands.

— *THE ART OF WAR*, SUN TZU

'Where are we going?' Chase asked as the cab took the side streets to avoid the commuter crush.

'Sascha has something for us to see,' Bella said evasively.

She was such a bad liar that he almost smiled. It didn't help that Chase knew Sascha had moved all of her pieces out of the studio. He glanced at Bella, twisting her hands in her lap and, without thinking, reached across the seats and placed his hand over hers. She glanced back to him, a nervous smile on her lips and went back to looking out of the cab's window.

Maybe this was Bella's attempt to fight Sascha's corner against Zadzisai as the feature artist. Bella had shot him glares throughout the whole meeting after he'd dropped the bombshell. Eight months ago, he'd not have even told the rest of the staff that Zadzisai had been in touch, let alone asked for their opinions. Christ, he'd been out of his depth. He'd kept everything to himself, just like he always had, so that no one would know if he made the right or wrong decision. But Bella had helped him see just how much better the gallery worked when they worked as one.

As an artist, Chase would have told Zadzisai to stick it. But as director he had to make decisions for the gallery. He thought back to when he'd taken Bella to the gallery warehouse, informed her imperiously about gatekeeping. He still felt that way. But he was now part of that, whether he liked it or not.

The cab pulled up to where Sascha was waiting with a grin on her face.

'Sascha,' he greeted with a nod as the tall woman smiled at him, but grinned at Bella. She handed Bella something and then waved goodbye and walked off.

'Where is she going?' Chase asked as Sascha disappeared into the crowded street.

'I don't know,' Bella said, shrugging as she walked into the large building that housed the studio.

'Bella,' he said, tempted to act like a stroppy child and refuse to walk any further. 'What is going on?'

'You'll see,' she said, holding the door to the studio open.

Knowing gnawed his gut. He wasn't going to like this at all.

Chase followed her into the studio space that, last he saw, had been covered in paint spatters and streaks, cast off, wiped-off, dripped and smeared. But now, the entire space was covered in large blank sheets of paper that made him shiver and want to run. Adrenaline dumped in his system, like ice dropped into water, displacing ripples of anger, fear, resentment, longing and so much more.

He cursed. 'What did you do?' He turned to Bella accusingly. He should have known that she'd not leave it alone.

'I wanted to try something,' she offered, twisting her hands.

He went to walk out, but she stood in his way, palm against his racing heart.

'Bella, this isn't something you can fix with pop

psychology and well meaning,' he growled. Hurt flashed in her eyes but was wiped away by a blink. 'I want to leave.'

'You can. But I'd like you to hear me out first.'

He pressed against her hand, testing her determination. She didn't move and he wasn't such a bastard that he'd push right through her. He clenched his teeth together to stop something stupid escaping his mouth like 'please'.

He stepped back and circled the space like a caged animal.

'When was the last time that you created a piece of work that wasn't for sale?' Bella asked, her voice echoing around a room bare of canvas, movement, people, noise.

He bit his lip and shook his head. He couldn't remember. From the moment that he'd been discovered at university, everything had been geared towards a show, selling paintings, meeting buyers, and gallery directors.

'A while.'

'How long?'

'I get your point, Bella,' he informed her curtly.

'Do you? Do you really?' she asked, looking at him in a way that made him think that he didn't. 'Because you picked up a colouring pen without a single thought and helped that little boy see his drawing as something worthy of a gallery. You didn't even think about it.'

'That was different.' And he wouldn't say *entirely* without thought.

'It was different. I know why. But do you?'

'Yes, I get the very heavy-handed, painfully obvious point you're trying to make. That I can't paint because I don't like the pressure of making it financially viable.'

'Oh. Actually, I was going to say that you can't paint because it's not fun any more, but yeah, your suggestion works too,' she said, flippant and furious at the same time.

He bit his tongue, unsure whether she was being sarcastic or not.

'It's the reason it's not fun any more. You don't play with it, the way you used to. You're afraid of wasting it.'

'Because I needed to make money, Bella. We weren't all born with a trust fund—'

'That's not fair,' she whispered.

'It's not fair,' he agreed, 'but it's *true*. It took five years for me to earn enough to pay off the medical bills from my mother's illness. It took another year to be able to pay off my father's mortgage. Those things aren't nothing, Bella.'

'They're incredible achievements, Chase. Admirable and amazing. But what debt are you trying to pay off now?' Grey eyes, wide like orbs, glowing like stars, levelled him where he stood and knocking all the words out of his mouth.

He fisted his hands, fighting an invisible band holding him in place, tension in every line of his body.

'Spit it out, Bella. Stop beating around the bush and say what's on your mind.'

'I think you're spinning out of control, because you achieved everything your mother said you would. And it didn't make you happy. I think you're stuck because you don't know what you want next, because you've never had to ask yourself that.'

'And you have?'

'Yes. Recently, for the first time, yes. Everything I thought I wanted... it was... *passive*. I didn't know *why* I wanted it, I hadn't had to think about why I wanted it, I just did. A marriage, a home, children. The *Hamptons*. They were just things I thought I should want, that I should have. Stages of my life I just assumed would happen. And maybe Olly not turning up on the day of the wedding might actually have been the best thing that happened to me,' Bella said, as if admitting it for the first time, to herself as much as to him.

'And I think you're the same, in a way,' she said with a small shrug. 'You did all this to make your mother happy, but it wasn't because you'd thought about wanting it, or questioned why you wanted it.' Her words were a near-fatal body blow, his heart knowing how true they rang and his soul wanting it to be different. 'I think she'd desperately want you to be happy, because she loved you. And I... want you to be happy,' she said, her words losing steam and confidence for the first time since they'd arrived.

There was something in what she said that he'd missed, but he couldn't quite keep his train of thought, because somehow Bella Carmichael had unlocked the dam that he'd spent years shoving things behind and it was near all that he could do to stay standing.

* * *

Bella gave him a minute to process what she'd said. And if she were being honest, she needed a minute too. She walked over to the table Sascha had prepared for them, fiddling with every single conceivable type of artistic tool, pencils, paintbrushes, glue, paper, scissors, charcoal, erasers, coloured chalks, spray paint even.

She catalogued them in her mind because that was so much easier than facing what she'd nearly blurted at him.

She wanted you to be happy because she loved you. And I...

Fighting the crashing realisation, she focused instead on why she was here. It wasn't about her. It was about Chase. It was about helping him find what was missing. Because she felt it when she was around him – the hole he tried to hide. It didn't stop him from being witty, sharp, devastatingly sexy, which was quite annoying when she thought about it. But it was like a scar he was constantly trying to pull a piece of clothing over. And the more it stayed hidden, the more damage it would do.

She reached into her pocket for the blindfold she'd brought, though it was looking increasingly unlikely that he'd allow her to get through the full extent of her plan. She turned to face him, running the silk through her hands.

'Unless that involves you being naked, I'm not interested,' he said, glaring at the blindfold.

She fought the smile. At least he hadn't left yet. 'Perhaps after we leave here.'

'I can have a cab here in under thirty seconds.'

'*No one* can get a cab in under thirty seconds in New York.'

'Watch me,' he replied, his eyes glowing with determination and just a hint of the humour he always surprised her with.

'Do you trust me?' she asked.

He looked at her, his gaze losing some of that humour. For a moment she thought he might say no.

He nodded, slowly. Carefully. But at least he agreed.

'Will you take your jacket off?' Bella asked, not wanting to get paint all over the rich piece of clothing.

He did as she asked, without taking his eyes from her and threw it over the back of the chair in the corner of the room. He undid the sleeve button and rolled the cotton back over his forearms, and Bella nibbled her top lip to stop herself from giving in to temptation and letting him call the cab.

He smirked at her as if he knew what she was thinking and she let him, because really this could only be incredibly painful for him. And if it didn't work... it could just make things worse. That had to be on his mind as much as it was on hers.

She went to him and pressed a gentle kiss to his lips as she slipped the silk over his eyes and heard him inhale, felt the change of air at her collarbone as she came off her tiptoes from reaching to tie the silk behind his head.

'So what's the plan, I just pick up a brush and start painting with wild abandon?' he snarked defensively.

'No,' she replied simply, reaching for an orange piece of charcoal. She'd decided that she didn't actually want him to pick up anything he didn't want to. She knew that had to come from him and wouldn't force that on him. But that didn't mean he still couldn't *help* create something.

She reached for his hand and wrapped it around hers, pulling him against her back so that they could move together, as one. He could simply let her draw, or, if he wanted to, he could guide her hand. He could also remove his hand any time he wanted to.

But she hoped that he'd give this a chance.

She started off with a wide arc of her arm, heavy with the weight of his hand on hers.

'What are you doing?' he asked, the puff of his words cresting against the sensitive spot just behind

her ear. She hoped he didn't feel the shiver ripple
through her body but the way he stiffened behind
her told her that he had.

'I'm drawing...' She narrowed her gaze at the thick
line of chalk. 'Kind of,' she admitted with a laugh.
And she bisected the arc with a long vertical line
down the centre, the movement catching Chase by
surprise as his hand nearly slipped from hers. Then
he tightened his hold a little and hope flared deep
down inside her.

She wasn't a huge fan of the luminescent colour,
but it didn't matter. She just wanted to mark the paper. To leave something behind. To be seen, or to at
least leave something behind that *could* be seen. Was
that what Chase was missing? The feeling of being
seen and understood. The knowledge that he had
made a literal mark on the world.

'I don't think I like the charcoal much,' she admitted, the flecks of tiny bright orange colouring the
large white paper-covered wall.

'It's not the easiest,' he admitted.

She bit the inside of her cheek. No matter how
much this was for him, she couldn't help but think
that if he saw it, he'd think all this was childish and
silly. Bad. Not good. Certainly not good for him and

she tried to ignore the discomfort of failing, of not doing something perfectly.

'You're thinking again,' he whispered into her ear. 'Know what you *could* be thinking about?' he teased. 'You in that blindfold, stripped bare, while I—'

'Paint! I want to try some paint,' she cried and he laughed gently behind her.

She reached for the cheap acrylic that Sascha had given her. The point was not to have him worry about anything remotely artistic, and she needed to get over herself if she was to help him achieve it. Only Sascha's encouragement with her plan had given her enough confidence to get here. Now she just needed to keep going.

They were beginning to move more easily now; she'd adjusted for the weight of him, and he'd relaxed enough to let her guide him. She didn't bother mixing paint, it wasn't about colour, it was about feel as she loaded a brush and swept it across the page, zigzagging to catch him by surprise, and dotting and stabbing which made him laugh.

She turned, because it was easy, because he was there, and because she couldn't stop herself, and pressed a kiss to his lips, half wrapped in his arms and tucked against his chest. He tried to deepen the kiss, but she leaned back, the smile on his face that matched her own made her heart flutter. She picked a thick marker and drew circles and stars, and coloured them in with splodges of highlighter pens. When Bella returned to the paint though, she began to feel the smallest of guidance from his hand. And she let him pull a little more, loosening her hold as he strengthened his.

The only sound was of the brush against the paper, different streaks and slashes, all in the same colour, because Bella didn't dare break the movement. It was something else entirely feeling the change in his grasp, the turn of his wrist, the movements that were a physical memory for him and nothing to do with sight.

The paint had run out but the brush still mixed what was already on the page. The rhythm of Chase's breathing changed as his gestures became more like movements, and the movements became more determined.

'Do we need more paint?' he whispered into her ear and she nodded, Chase slowly stepping back to allow her to cover the brush. 'Grab a pallet and put some paint on it,' he said, clearing his throat, his tone reluctantly dark.

She did as he said, and he let her lead him over to a new fresh wall of paper. She dipped the brush in a rich green and made the first mark on the paper. She'd expected to have to lead him into it, but he instinctively took over. He swirled the brush into shapes and shades, letting her choose the colours, but creating the patterns and textures.

'Was there spray paint?' he asked as if excited by the prospect.

'Yes, but please remember that I'm not wearing overalls,' she groused as she walked them back to the table. She wouldn't have cared a bit if she got paint everywhere, but he took her words as a challenge.

'Poor Bella, we wouldn't want you to get all dirty now, would we?' he teased into her ear.

Damn this man. Her entire body heated from head to toe, her core throbbing and—

'Bella. The spray paint.'

She jumped and ignored his laugh as she reached for it, shaking the can and returning to a wall covered in crazy patches of paint and streaks, some marks leaving drips and others barely scraping over the colour beneath.

'Ready,' she told him and started spraying as he moved her hand to where he wanted her. The hiss surprised her, but he steadied her with his other hand, moving them at a pace a few feet across the gallery. He held the spray on one point until the paint hissed and spat and dripped, until he called out, 'Next.'

'Next?' she asked.

'Next *thing*,' he said, this time leading her to the table. She picked up a pencil as his hand encased hers. He might not be holding it himself, but he was most definitely now in charge.

It was fascinating seeing him on the brink of losing himself in this, even though he couldn't see what he was doing. Every now and then she'd wrestle him for control, to remind him that it was still fun, that it wasn't one of his artworks, and he'd laugh and let her lead for a while.

It was a dance. And she wanted to tell Astrid about it, knowing that she'd understand, she wanted to tell all the girls about it, knowing they'd find it funny, the image of her leading Chase around blindfolded. And without thinking, she grabbed her phone and snapped a selfie, Chase flinching at the sound.

'What was that?'

'Proof that I got you blindfolded,' she teased as she turned down the volume and snapped a few pictures of the walls. She had planned not to let him see it, but she was pretty sure that he'd want to destroy any and all evidence of the playful, childlike splashes of colour on the walls.

'Does that mean *I* get to take pictures?' he asked, and she knew that he wasn't talking about the walls. He pressed a kiss to her neck and goosebumps rippled out over her skin. 'Call a cab, Bella,' Chase demanded, his voice gently insistent.

'Do you want to see the walls?' she offered, still tucked into the side of his body.

'Right now, all I want to see is you. Naked in my bed, except for the blindfold covering your eyes.'

She knew it was a distraction, from what he feared he'd find, but she'd wanted it to be his choice from the beginning and she would honour that. She tapped across the screen of her phone as Chase slipped the blindfold from his eyes.

'The cab will be here in five minutes.'

'Then I'll show you just what I can do in five minutes,' he said, backing her out of the gallery without taking even a glance at the walls.

Bella locked up as Chase rubbed his hands together in the cold, a little unsettled and hating that she was.

Chase met her at the steps.

'What is it?' he asked, a hand cupping her cheek.

'I... Was that okay? I didn't make a mistake?' she asked hesitantly.

Chase looked deep into Bella's gaze and saw it.

The need in her, the fear. That she might have done something that would make him push her away, or leave. And he hated that she even had to ask.

'It was okay,' he said nodding. 'And if it wasn't, we'd talk about it, or even argue. But it would *still* be okay,' he explained, because he'd learned that from her. 'I'm not going anywhere. And neither are you,' he said, placing a kiss on her forehead, feeling the truth of what he'd said fill him with something he wasn't sure he wanted to look too closely at just yet. But they'd have time for that after the gallery opened. They'd have time for so much more.

23

There is no instance of a country having benefited from prolonged warfare.

— *THE ART OF WAR*, SUN TZU

Chase put down the phone and stared at it for a moment, the feeling of relief coursing through his veins.

'Well?' Bella asked, and he looked up to find the entire staff of Nayak, including Tej, who was leaning against the door frame, hands in pockets, staring at him with the same expectation.

'He's in,' Chase said, nodding slowly, not quite believing it himself.

Cheers filled his office as Maurice hugged Bella before he realised what he was doing and nearly pushed her away again. Ali jumped up and down beside Ye-Joon and Bella's gaze was locked onto his, heat and happiness beautiful on her face. Tej nodded, saluted him with two fingers and left for the date that his mother had arranged for him while he was in New York.

Christ, he was glad it had worked. Zadzisai had just met Sascha who had walked him through the body of work for her exhibition. It had been a conditional part of the agreement, which was absolutely fair enough. Zadzisai had to approve of both the artist *and* the work, before he could 'present' it at the opening of Nayak New York.

This way, everyone came out looking like they'd won, especially if it was presented as having been the plan all along. Zadzisai would provide a few unseen pieces for the gallery that worked with Sascha's debut exhibition.

How better to debut the gallery than with a debut artist? Bella had asked.

Of course, it had all been her suggestion. And that was what he was struggling with. He wasn't jealous, or resentful, but deep down he knew that it *should* have been his idea. That if he was any good at his job, it wouldn't just be relief he was feeling. It should be excitement, right? Pleasure? Pride? Anything but plain and simple relief.

'Everything is ready,' Bella informed them all, cutting into his thoughts. 'The tweaks to the final news blast for the subscribers and the fresh website content. Just say the word.'

'The word,' he said wryly and everyone laughed. Bella did too, but he'd seen the small second's-worth of frown as if she could sense something was wrong.

'Okay, people, we have just four days before the pre-opening. I'm sure we have better things to do than sit round my office, let's get to it,' he commanded. Bella left him a lingering glance, but she was probably the busiest of them all, so she smiled before returning to her desk.

Everything would be better after the pre-opening, Chase decided. It would be easy after that. And maybe he'd stop feeling like such a fraud.

* * *

PRIVATE WHATSAPP GROUP, 3
MEMBERS. 16.42 EST.

SIENNA

So I'm setting this chat up without Bella because, has anyone heard from her recently?

ASTRID

She's pretty busy with the gallery opening.

I still feel bad about the article.

SIENNA

Me too. But she's worked her ass off to undo the damage from it.

PAIGE

She absolutely has.

And, so I had this idea...

ASTRID

?

SIENNA

I just think... what if we went to support her?

ASTRID

Ohhh! I'd love that.

PAIGE

Do you think she'd want me there?
I wouldn't want to spoil the night.

ASTRID

NOOOOO! Not at all. You HAVE to
be there.

SIENNA

Of course you have to be there!

PAIGE

Are you guys sure?

ASTRID

Definitely. Can you get over here in
time?

PAIGE

Yes I think so. Sienna?

SIENNA

It'll be a push, but I can make it
work.

PAIGE

Wait, what happens when Chase
sees Astrid?

ASTRID

Shit.

SIENNA

Wear a disguise.

ASTRID

What, like a trench coat and a hat?

PAIGE

A hat could work. A really
HUGE hat.

SIENNA

ASTRID

I think I actually have one of those.

PAIGE

Of course you do.

SIENNA

Okay. So, you're in? We'll meet in
NY before the opening. For Bella.

ASTRID

For Bella!

PAIGE

For Bella!

* * *

Bella couldn't sleep. She'd left Chase in bed, not wanting to disturb him, and come out to the living room. She walked to the window and looked down on the city that also wasn't sleeping. Slashes of lights down below made it look like the night sky, as if she were peering down on an alternate universe.

I'm not going anywhere. And neither are you.

Would he still feel that way if he found out about the revenge plan? Would he still want to be with her if he found out that she wasn't just Good Bella or Bad Bella, but some crazy combination of both?

Because that's what had happened to Bella since coming to work at Nayak. At first she'd been so hell-bent on destruction, she hadn't worried about being perfect and keeping the peace. And she'd actually enjoyed being bad. Being naughty, being... oh, just *not* worried about making sure Chase didn't leave her like everyone else, because she hadn't cared about him then. Not really.

But now? Now she knew that she'd be devastated

if he walked away from her. Just the thought of it tore her apart in ways that Olly running away hadn't even touched. And as if just thinking about it had conjured it to being, she couldn't shake the feeling that something bad was going to happen. It was as if it was already slipping through her fingers and this time, the future she wanted so badly she could taste it.

'Are you okay?'

She clenched her jaw to stop herself from saying, *No. No, I'm not. I lied to you and I don't think you'll be able to forgive me.*

Chase came to stand behind her, pulling her against his chest and wrapping his arms around her.

'Can't sleep?'

Bella shook her head.

'It'll be okay you know,' he whispered.

She nodded.

'You've done amazing things, Bella Carmichael, I hope you know that,' he said, resting his head on hers.

A part of her rejoiced, and the other twisted in shame.

'We could never have turned things around without you. The team, me. We all came together with you. And it's... special. You should know that.'

His praise meant the world to her. It was special.

They'd become like a family. Like Paige, Astrid and Sienna had become her family. Ones that meant more because they'd chosen to work together, chosen to be together. Not because of blood, but because of friendship. And the thought of either of those two groups, Nayak or the girls, disappearing from her life was so devastating that Bella chose the present. To-morrow would come and would bring what it would bring. But for now, she just wanted as much time with Chase as she could get.

'Take me to bed?' she asked.

'Your wish is my command.'

* * *

Even though it was a pre-opening, everyone was still making an effort to dress in their finest. Ali was putting on her make-up and Bella had offered to do her hair, which had pretty much made Ali's entire year. The boys were getting ready in Chase's office, Maurice pushing both Chase and Tej from making a mess of Ye-Joon's tie.

Bella watched with a smile, the feeling of warmth in her chest spreading. A message pinged from her parents.

Good luck!

They'd offered to come tonight, but she'd assured them that it was better for them to come to the actual opening next week. Tonight, she wanted this to be about the gallery, about Chase. She didn't want to spend the entire evening making sure *they* were okay.

Ali craned her neck, trying to get another glimpse of Ye-Joon and Bella gave up fighting her smile.

'It's like prom, isn't it?' Ali said with an eager smile.

'I guess so,' Bella hedged.

'You guess?'

'We had a family emergency, so I missed mine,' Bella said, remembering how Bea had spiked a fever, and her parents had taken her to the hospital and she'd had to stay at home with her grandmother who had been too upset to leave alone that night.

'I'm so sorry.' Ali's sincerity hit her like a blast, but Bella waved it away, like she always did.

Ye-Joon appeared in the doorway and Ali practically jumped out of her seat, just as Bella was putting the last pin in her hair. Ye-Joon only had eyes for Ali and as she looked over the top of his head to see Maurice, Tej and Chase all standing there looking like proud older brothers, she felt connected to these people in ways she hadn't experienced before. And was suddenly sad at the idea of leaving them. She didn't want to. She didn't want to have to walk away after the gallery opening.

Maybe she could make this work. Maybe, if she told Chase, he might understand. Or maybe she didn't even have to tell Chase. She could just shove it all down and pretend that she hadn't sabotaged him. And they could all just carry on like this.

Oh, she wanted that so badly.

'You look beautiful,' Chase mouthed to her over the heads of the others and she felt herself blush.

'Thank you,' she mouthed back. She didn't have to verbalise her appreciation of Chase dressed in a suit. Her gaze ate him up and, noticing, he raised an eyebrow in mock admonishment.

'Right,' Maurice said, rubbing his hands together. 'Who's ready to kick this off?'

They all cheered and Tej gestured for Chase to lead the way. He cast a glance back over his shoulder at Bella, and that was almost the last she saw of him for the next sixty minutes.

* * *

It was a rush seeing the gallery full of people, mixing, mingling, looking at the art. The walls looked spectacular and the sound of excited voices filled the room. Bella hung back, taking it all in, an adrenaline rush fizzing in her veins at the sight of the gallery's success.

Sascha was beaming, hovering by Zadzisai's side, as he introduced her to some of the journalists invited to the preview, to help whet expectations for the opening next week. Tej was skirting the crowds, hoping to avoid the date his mother had invited for him. Bella wincing as he glared at her, holding her personally responsible. Chase had assured her she'd done the right thing. Tej would forgive her but when they'd spoken on the phone, Bella had quickly realised that Adite Nayak was a formidable woman that few would say no to and survive unscathed.

She continued to scan the guests looking for one person amongst the many faces of an almost packed to the brim gallery, until she felt a tap on her shoulder and turned to stare into familiar eyes, with just a few more wrinkle lines.

'Ms Carmichael?' he asked, holding his hand out for her to shake.

She smiled, relief and happiness exhaled on a

sigh. 'Mr Miller,' she said, taking Chase's father's hand. 'It's very nice to meet you.'

Mr Miller looked around the room, impressed and a little overwhelmed at the noise and the sight of it all.

'My son did all this?'

'He had a little bit of help, but yes. He brought all of this together.'

Mr Miller nodded and took a deep breath, impressed.

'I went to an exhibition of his once. He doesn't know about it,' Mr Miller confessed. 'I...' He shrugged. 'It's hard for me. His mother understood this part of him and I always thought that maybe when he lost her, he'd lost someone who understood him in that way.' Bella watched him swallow and gather himself. He pressed a thumb to the corner of his eye and she looked away, knowing that he'd hate to have that moment of vulnerability witnessed. Over the last week, they'd spoken a number of times, and she already knew that Mr Miller was a man of few words, but deep emotions.

'But this is good,' he said, nodding to himself. 'He's doing for others what was done for him. She definitely taught him that,' he said, his head bobbing again, as if that was the only way he could show his appreciation of what his son had achieved.

'Dad.'

This time, it was Bella who swallowed as she turned to face Chase coming up behind them.

'Hi, son. I hope you don't mind me being here—'

'No,' Chase said, as if surprised himself that he didn't mind. 'Of course not,' he said, his gaze flicking between him and Bella.

'Why don't you show your dad round, and we can catch up later?' Bella suggested as Chase mentally tried to figure out how his father had come to be there tonight.

She excused herself and made her way into the crowd, telling herself that she wasn't running away before Chase could tell her off. She felt his eyes on her back as she slipped through the people and found her way to where Ali and Maurice were standing.

'I think it's going well,' Maurice said nervously. 'It's going well, right?' he asked, turning to Bella, looking for confirmation.

'It's going brilliantly!' Ali beamed and Bella smiled and agreed.

'Well, in that case,' Maurice said, grabbing three glasses of champagne from the passing waiter and sharing them out between them. 'We did it,' he said by way of a toast, and with a broad grin took a mouthful of the sharp bubbles.

Deciding that everything was firmly in control, and that she could breathe a little, Bella took a mouthful just as Ali asked, 'Who is the woman in the hat?'

Turning, Bella caught sight first of the hat, then the two people beside the hat, then the person *under* the hat, and promptly choked on her champagne.

* * *

Chase wasn't quite sure he was happy about Bella and his father going behind his back, but he was really touched that his dad was here. And then because of that, felt ashamed that he hadn't invited his father himself.

But instead of saying 'thank you for coming', Chase said, 'You didn't have to come.'

And instead of saying, 'I wanted to', his father said, 'Bella made it hard to say no.'

Chase huffed out a laugh at the thought of Bella and his father having that conversation.

'I like her,' his father said, looking at a piece on

the wall as if not quite sure why anyone had called it art.

'I do too,' Chase admitted, warmth spreading through his chest and limbs as he said it.

'Daisy would have liked her.'

And Chase nodded, because he knew that too.

They moved from piece to piece and for the first time, Chase didn't feel the need to ask about the garage, didn't feel the need to fill the silence between them because it wasn't uncomfortable. The background noise, so unusual in a gallery, gave them a base colour from which to work and they were picking their paint colours carefully.

His father stopped at one of Sascha's large canvases and considered it carefully.

'This reminds me of one of yours.'

Chase waited for the twist, the anxiety, the rush to hide the block that had all but crippled him for the last eighteen months. 'It's not.'

'No, I know,' his dad said with a conviction that took Chase aback. 'Yours are different,' he said, shrugging. 'I don't know the fancy way of saying why, but I know it's not *yours* but it's *like* yours. The' – he waved his hands in the air, struggling to articulate what he was seeing – 'stuff is different, but...' And his father shrugged again, pulling at the neck of the shirt he'd worn to the gallery.

Chase cleared his throat. 'It *feels* different.'

His father didn't argue with the description which was as much as Chase could have hoped for. They circled the far wall of the gallery until they reached a series that made his father say, 'Oh.'

Interspersed between larger pieces were the drawings by the children from Castledine Elementary, still displayed in their elaborate gilt frames. Bella had pitched it as 'surprising and whimsical, but also pertinent to the gallery's ethos'.

'We have an ethos?' he'd asked.

'You have an ethos,' she'd told him seriously. 'And it's admirable and unique and worth holding on to.'

And he hadn't been able to hide from that in a joke or a kiss and it had sunk into his skin like ink from a tattoo.

'These are great,' his father exclaimed with more enthusiasm than when he'd looked at a painting that would probably fetch somewhere in the region of half a million. That was how his father valued things. 'This she would have *loved*,' he said, looking Chase in the eye and he knew he meant it.

His father might have found it difficult to talk about

feelings and emotions, but his reaction to the thing that brought him joy was just as visceral as Bella's had been to the paintings in the gallery warehouse nearly a month and a half ago. And that was why Chase had wanted to include the piece here. Art should be accessible in whatever form, wherever it comes from, for whoever views it.

And Bella had seen that. Seen that that was how he felt.

He caught Maurice's eye and nodded him over. He needed to find her. He wanted... well, he didn't quite know what he wanted but he wanted to go to her.

Maurice cut through the gallery and Chase introduced him to his father. Two more opposite men you could probably struggle to find, but they immediately fell into a good-natured conversation about the children's pictures as Maurice gestured towards the front of the gallery where Bella was standing with her back to him.

* * *

'Oh my God, what are you guys doing here?' Bella asked as she took in Sienna, Paige and Astrid – wearing the most ridiculous hat she'd ever seen.

And then, shockingly, she felt herself tearing up

as she looked at the gorgeous faces of the women she'd missed as if they'd been scattered pieces of her heart.

'We came to surprise you!' Sienna exclaimed until she saw the tears welling up in Bella's eyes. 'Or not...?' She trailed off with a concern. 'Oh hun, are you okay?'

Bella nodded like a hula girl on a dashboard driving over the Brooklyn Bridge, which only seemed to make the girls more concerned.

Astrid pushed in for a hug, sending the other girls packing as the brim of the oversized dramatic hat got in their way. Paige rescued the glass of champagne she'd been holding as Bella felt Astrid's strong arms around her, squeezing tight to the point of near pain, until Bella tapped her on the arm.

'I'm good, I'm good,' Bella promised, the threat of tears over.

'Okay,' Paige replied, her eyes forecasting that she wasn't convinced. 'You look like you could do with this,' she said, handing the glass back to her.

Bella ignored the glass and grabbed Paige for a hug.

'It's *so* good to see you,' she said truthfully and nearly started crying again. 'I'm so happy for you and Olly. We...' Bella sighed. 'We would have made a terrible mistake if we'd got married that day. I think... I was looking for the full stop on what I thought I should be doing. I think we both were, really. But he was always more of a friend to me than anything else,' Bella confessed.

'Are you sure?' Paige asked, her own eyes glistening.

'Absolutely. I promise. On red velvet cakes,' Bella said, drawing an X over her heart with her fingers. 'And I think you all know how seriously I take my cakes,' she said, looking around the smiling faces of the group, these women her friends. Friends she'd missed more than the family who had never really seen the real her, because she'd never really let them. 'Now tell me, how are you all here?' she asked as her voice broke with emotion.

'I thought it would be nice to be here for you tonight,' Sienna explained.

'And we agreed, but it was going to be tricky because we needed invites and we couldn't just ask because you were the one in charge of that,' Paige explained.

'And I said, who needs invites, when we can simply crash the event?' Astrid inserted. 'But of course, I couldn't just rock up so – ta da! You like my disguise?'

'The hat?' Bella asked, eying the monstrosity that had nearly decapitated one waiter, blinded one of Maurice's friends and drawn more attention than Zadzisai's new artwork. 'The hat?' she repeated, questioning the collective sanity of the group.

'And the glasses,' Astrid insisted. 'Although I may have perhaps overestimated their suitability as a disguise,' Astrid admitted and they all dissolved into giggles.

'But you can't stay,' Bella groaned miserably. 'If Chase finds you here, he'll—'

'He'll what?' demanded a horrifyingly familiar male voice from over her shoulder. 'What will Chase do?' he asked. And when Bella turned to face him, his eyes flickered to the group behind her and then stuck. 'Astrid?'

24

If the enemy is prepared for your coming, and you fail to defeat him, then, return being impossible, disaster will ensue.

— *THE ART OF WAR*, SUN TZU

'Bella? What's going on?' Chase demanded, his teeth ground together so hard he could break a tooth.

What was Astrid doing here? Why was she wearing that ridiculous hat and why the hell was she talking to Bella and looking like they knew each other?

And why were four women, two of whom he knew – *biblically* – all staring at him in different shades of horror? His gut hardened like concrete left out in the sun to dry.

'It's not what it looks like,' the redhead said, while the blonde insisted that 'Bella didn't do anything wrong.'

Finally, Bella took a step towards him, or in between them, he wasn't really sure.

'It *is* what it looks like, and I *did* do something wrong. But,' she said, looking over his shoulder at the people in the gallery, a few he was sure were already looking their way, 'this isn't the time.' She looked at him like she was sorry. Like she felt guilty for something, like it was the end of something and everything in him roared in denial.

'The girls will go, I'll make myself scarce. I'll wait in the office until everyone's gone,' she said, finally dropping her gaze.

The group of women behind her all made noises as if to argue, but he could barely see anything but Bella. She brushed Astrid's arm, who looked at him as if she wanted to say something but she retreated from the gallery with the other women.

Bella moved past him, head bowed as if it were the end of something.

Tej appeared at his shoulder, concern all over his face. 'Is everything okay?' he asked.

'No. I don't think it is,' he said as a buzzing took up residence in his ears.

***

Bella felt sick. Truly nauseously sick. She paced Chase's office, praying that none of the other staff would come. Hopefully Chase would tell them that she'd had to leave.

Because she *would* have to leave.

She'd seen that in his eyes.

There was no way she could continue working here and that devastated her more than she'd expected. The thought of disappointing Maurice, and abandoning Ali and Ye-Joon caved her chest, guilt and loss sharp cuts, stinging every time she took a breath.

She tried to sit on the sofa, but the anxiety flooding her system demanded movement, made her want to run. But not *away* from Chase. To him.

Oh God, it was such a mess. She wiped at the tear falling from her eyes, knowing that she had to stop before Chase came to the office.

She'd heard the vague noises from below as the speeches were made. First by Tej and then Chase. She knew. She'd read the words they were going to say. And then as the sounds from the gallery quietened, and it wouldn't be long before Chase came for her.

And that made her want to cry again. So instead, she set about removing the doctored sugar packets from the coffee tray. One by one, she sorted through nearly one hundred packets of sugar, pulling out the ones she could see the glue on from where she fixed the packet.

'What are you doing?'

She flinched.

Removing every trace of my presence from this place.

'I think some salt packets got mixed up in your sugar.'

She turned to face him and instead of the hugely successful gallery director who should be thrilled with the success of the evening, what she saw made her want to cry all the more. He looked hollow. Empty. As if something in him had just... gone.

'What the fuck is going on?' His defeat was worse than any kind of fury.

She wanted to go to him, to find comfort in him and hated herself for it. But she couldn't hide from this and he deserved the truth.

'I met Astrid, Paige and Sienna a few months ago,' she started and went on to explain how they got snowed in, how they bonded over champagne and cake. 'I felt like for the first time in ages these women understood me. Saw me,' she tried to explain. 'Because we'd all had recent bad experiences with our exes.'

'So, a few glasses of champagne and cake and some shitty life decisions and that leads to me how?'

She knew she deserved his anger, but not his scorn.

'Shitty life decisions? No. It wasn't my life decision to abandon my wedding, and it wasn't Sienna's life decision to be abandoned for something supposedly better, it wasn't Paige's life decision that got her...' Bella swallowed her words, refusing to betray her confidence and parade her violation in front of Chase as justification for her motives. 'It wasn't Astrid's shitty life decision that saw her accused of sleeping with a married man,' Bella pointed out.

Chase stared at her grimly, but she sensed his retreat.

Bella shook her head at him. 'That hurt her.'

'That's between me and her.'

'Maybe so, but you didn't try and stop her from leaving. You didn't try to let her know that Annalise was lying, did you? You let her think that she was a homewrecker. You let her think the worst about herself. That's *your* shitty life decision, Chase.'

He had the grace to look away, leaving her to pick up the threads of the story.

'We realised that we were in a position to take revenge against each other's exes. Paige was travelling to the UK and tracked down Olly.'

'And you got me,' he said, bitterly.

Bella nodded. 'I got you,' she whispered.

Chase let out a bitter laugh. 'Revenge?'

Bella nodded.

'The article?' he demanded.

Bella nodded. 'It was before I knew. Before *we* knew that Annalise had lied.'

Chase shook his head. 'You set up a hit piece in one of the biggest magazines in the art world. It nearly destroyed me.'

'But it didn't. We pulled it back. Tonight was a success,' Bella cried. 'Everything you've done, everything you've achieved... it's all worked.'

'How does that make it okay? How could you do that?' he demanded, struggling to make sense of what she was saying.

'I didn't... know,' she stuttered. 'It was a misunderstanding.'

'You were willing to ruin my life and my career

based on a misunderstanding? Because you all had too much cake?' he said, his voice loud in the silence of the gallery office.

'The moment we realised, we tried to make it right,' she promised, but it came out more like a plea.

'Was there anything else? Other than the article?'

Bella winced.

'What was it?' He needed to know.

She reached behind her and took one of the sugar sachets in her hand.

'You put salt in my sugar? What are you, like twelve?' he asked, shocked.

She bit her lip. 'And the chair.'

He glared at her.

'And you might want to change your computer password.'

'Oh for fuck's sake,' he said, throwing his arms up in the air instead of reaching for her to strangle her. 'Which Bella are you?' he wanted to know. Genuinely. 'The one that is passionate and powerful and soft and silly? The one who wanted...' *what I wanted,* he'd been about to say but couldn't. 'Or the spy that lied, manipulated, schemed and probably laughed with your friends behind my back?'

'Chase.' She came to him, reaching for him, but he stepped away.

'You knew. The moment you discovered that Annalise had lied to Astrid that day, you knew that everything you'd done was wrong. And you chose to lie to me,' he accused.

'Yes,' she said, taking the full force of his ire.

Her surrender nearly undid him.

'I think you should leave,' he forced out through clenched teeth.

'Please don't do this,' she begged, not even raising her face to his.

'Don't do what?'

'Hide,' she whispered.

'What are you talking about?'

'You hide when things go wrong,' she accused, finally raising her gaze to his. 'You put your head in the sand, pretending that everything's fine.'

'Don't you dare talk about my art,' he struck out.

'I'm not,' she said, shaking her head. 'With Annalise, you walked away, to the point where she had to track you down and ruin whatever you had with Astrid. With Astrid, you let her walk out thinking the worst, because it was easier than having to explain how you feel.'

He had no words.

'Because you don't talk about how you feel,' she said as if it were a simple fact. 'You put it into your art.

But you haven't painted for months. So, what's happened to all those feelings?'

'You no longer have any right to talk about my feelings,' he said, shaking his head and turning away because the sight of her was breaking something in him.

'I wasn't expecting you.'

He barked out a cynical laugh. He hadn't been expecting her either.

She shrugged. 'I didn't...'

For someone usually so eloquent, it was nearly hard to see Bella stutter over her words. Her confession.

'You're not what I wanted, Chase,' she said, almost like an accusation.

His brow shot up in shock. He wasn't sure what he thought she'd been about to say, but it wasn't that.

'You're not,' she said, as if she were helpless to do anything about it. 'You say what you think, and you don't care whether it offends or wounds those around you. You keep far too much to yourself and refuse to let people in.'

'Can you blame me?' he asked, offended.

'You actively dislike some of the parts of my life that I enjoy,' she pressed on and he knew she was speaking of the galas and the charity events. 'And you frustrate every expectation I have of you. And despite *all* of that, despite all of that,' she repeated, the tears gathering in her eyes making his heart pound, 'I still fell in love with you.'

'Love me? How can you...?' A part of him wanted to roar in pain, and he couldn't quite understand it. 'I don't even fucking *know* you,' he spat, causing himself as much harm as her.

She nodded, biting into her lip to stop it from trembling. 'I know,' she said sadly. 'I know that's what you think, that's what you *need* to think right now, but actually, I think you might be the person who has known the real me the most,' she said, swallowing.

He turned away from her sadness, because he hated that it matched his own.

She betrayed you. She betrayed you, warred with every single tear he saw in her eyes.

She inhaled, shaky and hurt, defeated in a way he'd never seen her before, and it took everything in him not to go to her. He couldn't. He couldn't trust her.

She got to the door, and turned. He watched her from the corner of his eye, unable to look at her.

'You lied too,' she said softly. 'You said that making mistakes was okay. You said that we'd talk, or even argue, but that it would still be okay. But it's not.'

The sight of her walking out the door was a punch that hit low in the gut and nearly dropped him to the floor. Which was where Tej found him an hour later, bottle of whisky in hand and no judgement.

* * *

Bella stepped into the frigid cold of the Upper West side without her jacket and didn't feel a thing. Until three sets of arms wrapped around her and held her tight. She sank into them and let them hold her up for what felt like an eternity, until she realised that she was shivering.

'Where the heck is your coat?' Sienna demanded. 'Why is this woman never wearing a coat?'

'I don't think she's worried about her coat right now.'

'Let's get her into a cab,' Paige suggested before hailing one from the other side of the street.

An illegal U-turn hardly registered to Bella as she realised that she was completely and utterly numb. She pressed her fingers against her lips and felt nothing. Barely noticed how Astrid and Paige put her into the back of the car.

'Where to?' the cabbie asked.

'The apartment,' Bella whispered, knowing that it would be for the last time.

'Won't Chase be there?' Paige asked concerned.

'He won't come back tonight,' Bella stated.

'Did he say that?' Sienna asked.

Bella shook her head. He hadn't needed to.

Astrid told the cabbie the address and Sienna looked at her worriedly. Bella forced a smile to her lips, and rubbed Sienna's hand, hoping that would ease her concern and then realised what she was doing.

Always trying to make others feel better.

Christ, he was in her head now.

I fell in love with you.

I don't even know you.

Their conversation ran in circles around her head while the girls tried to make conversation to distract her, and shared worried glances over her head that they either didn't think she saw, or didn't care.

They'd get back to the apartment and...

She'd have to pack. She was being told to leave again, leave people she loved like a family, Chase, Tej, Maurice, Ali and Ye-Joon. Her heart ached with a loss she knew she'd barely begun to comprehend.

Where would she go? Who would want her? she thought miserably. She'd done the one thing she'd spent her entire life trying to avoid. She'd made a mistake and ruined everything. There was no smoothing of waters, no making things right. Not this time.

A tear rolled down her cheek and Paige shifted to put her arm around her shoulder and for the first time in what felt like forever, Bella let herself curl into someone's side and let go as someone held her together.

As they drew up to the apartment she asked someone to pass her phone.

Bella dialled a number she should have called a long time ago.

'Daddy,' she said, when the line connected. 'Can I come home?' she asked, her voice breaking on the last word as her father said *yes* and she cried even harder.

* * *

Chase had told the staff that Bella had had a family emergency, but he was pretty sure Maurice didn't believe him. It didn't matter, he decided, locking the gallery's door behind him the following morning. He'd only come to...

What? Stare at her desk. Look for the signs that

he'd missed? Because he'd been pretty damn blind to everything else. But there weren't any signs of betrayal. There weren't any clues to be found for Bella's lies. Because either she was that good, or...

He shook his head, surprised how much he hated the sight of it. Not Bella's desk, but the whole office. The feeling he'd had just before Christmas had come back. Resentment, regret, frustration.

He didn't want to be here. He didn't want to be gallery director. He'd done it for Tej, he'd done it to get himself out of a hole. But his heart wasn't in it. He'd known that the moment that Bella had made that first stroke of chalk beneath his hands.

He walked out into the frigid Saturday morning, hands thrust deep into his long coat, relishing the bite of the winter's cold as it took chunks out of a hangover that barely touched the sides, despite the shocking volume of whisky he and Tej had put away yesterday.

He walked without a destination, ignoring the morning joggers and hum of the city that never slept, even on a weekend morning. And as much as he didn't want it, his brain decided to roll through a greatest hits of his time with Bella. Either he was a sucker for punishment or his subconscious was trying to tell him something. Chase decided it was the latter right around the time he found himself at the door to the studio, his heart pounding, the hangover landing a double tap with anxiety.

He let himself in and braced for what he would find on the walls. The chaotic crazy mess that he and Bella had put on the walls four days ago. His heart thumped painfully in his chest. But when he turned into the studio, the paper that had been up on them when they'd visited was gone. The only sign that they'd been there was the table of art supplies by the far wall.

Loss hit him, hard and fast, rocking him on his feet. He'd never see what they did together. He'd never see what they'd created. The wind was knocked from his lungs, and for one viscerally horrifying moment he thought he might actually cry. Loss. Absence. The knowledge that he'd never see what they made. What he'd painted. Because she'd got him painting.

And it had changed. The way he felt about it now. Ever since she'd brought him here, he'd been more curious than fearful and he'd not wanted to admit it. He'd fought it because fear still had a hold, but the curiosity was strong and getting stronger.

Giving up the fight, he stared at the blank walls, trying to recreate what they'd done, what materials they'd used. But he'd not even touched them. She had. *They* had.

You don't talk about your feelings.

Chase huffed out a bitter laugh. Christ, in comparison to his father he spat an entire encyclopaedia out about his feelings, didn't he? It was one of the things he remembered most after his mother had died. How quiet the house had been. How desperate he'd been to escape. To go to London – just like his mother had predicted.

Old grief returned with new wounds and he wondered if Bella was right. He had left Annalise and Dan to figure things out. He'd wanted none of it, but had he just been running away? And Astrid? Shit. That'd been wrong. He'd been so angry with Annalise and so ashamed, but he hadn't thought about the impact it'd had on her. On what she'd been left to think.

And Bella...

How had all this become so fucked up?

After what felt like a lifetime, he picked up his phone and dialled a number he wasn't sure would accept his call.

'What?' demanded the diamond-cut British accent.

'It's Chase,' he explained.

'I know who it is. What do you want?' Astrid asked, tones clipped and harsh.

Chase rolled his shoulders.

'I wanted to apologise.'

'Then why are you calling me? Bella—'

'Not to Bella. I owe *you* an apology.'

There was silence on the phone. It didn't bode well, but at least she hadn't hung up. He sighed, muffling the microphone. 'I should have explained what happened when Annalise found us in the hotel room. I'm sorry, you deserved not only an explanation, but better from me.'

'Yes, I did,' Astrid said simply.

Chase nodded, even though she couldn't see it. 'I was not... I did not *consider* myself married to Annalise at that point. We were already in the middle of a divorce, but I should have told you that from the very beginning. And at the very least, I should have explained after what happened. I am sorry.'

He heard Astrid's sigh. 'Thank you. For saying that. I... It put me in a not-so-great place for a while.'

'Astrid—'

'But,' she pressed on when he would have apologised again, 'that doesn't excuse the fact that we jumped to conclusions and exacted our revenge without the full story. And we really are – *I* really am

– sorry for the damage that was done by the article. It wasn't right.'

Chase let her words sink in.

'But if you want to be angry with anyone, it should be *me*. Not Bella,' Astrid insisted.

Bella.

Bella who he couldn't stop thinking of, no matter how betrayed he felt by her.

Ask her. Ask her.

He didn't want to know. But he did.

'Is she... okay?'

'No,' Astrid said, with the kind of blunt honesty he deserved.

'Where is she?' he asked, suspicion growing in his gut.

'She's gone, Chase.'

He'd told her to go, hadn't he?

'I just—'

'No,' Astrid said, talking to him like he was five. 'You don't get to say what you said to her and it to all be okay.'

'Hey,' Chase called out. '*I* was the one wronged.'

'No. She didn't wrong you, Chase,' Astrid said. 'She made a mistake. And you punished her for it. So, if you do want to know how she is, where she is, you'd better have a good handle on *why* you want to know.

Because if you hurt her again, what Bella did to you was child's play in comparison to what I'll do to you.'

With that Astrid hung up the phone, leaving Chase open-mouthed and fists clenching.

He got up and paced the studio.

Had he?

She'd wronged *him*. *She'd* betrayed *him*.

She'd made a *mistake*.

The chaos in his mind became too much and he needed it out.

He stalked to the table left with the art supplies and not caring that there was no canvas or paper, he grabbed a brush and some paint and applied it directly onto the walls.

His heartbeat fluctuated as he saw things he disliked and things he loved. Brushstrokes in patterns and colours that weren't planned or created for purchase or a gallery. They were for him.

That was what he'd been railing about when he'd shown Bella the gallery. He wasn't mad at the art world – well, not entirely – for gatekeeping pieces of work. He was mad at himself for prioritising fame and wealth over his creativity. As if the decisions he'd made to pursue what he'd thought was his mother's dreams had taken him one step after another away from the art he'd wanted to make.

You hide when things go wrong. You put your head in the sand, pretending that everything's fine.

She'd known. She'd known and she'd tried to let him see it for himself.

Four hours later, he stood back and looked at the first thing he'd painted in almost eighteen months.

Her. He'd painted her.

25

The skilful leader subdues the enemy's troops without any fighting.

— *THE ART OF WAR*, SUN TZU

Bella drew the covers over her head the moment her phone sounded the message from the Just Desserts WhatsApp Group. She knew the girls were trying to keep her spirits up, making sure she was okay, but she just didn't have the energy to pretend any more.

She'd taken a car home yesterday morning, after the girls had spent what was left of the night before with her. They'd waited on the sidewalk as her bags were loaded into the car, all pretending not to watch the street for any sign of Chase.

She'd even held her breath, hoping that maybe, just maybe, she'd earned a Hollywood happy ever after, where Chase was going to come running, yelling her name, and stopping her from leaving at the very last minute. But he hadn't.

And she'd hated the fact that instead of being thankful her friends were waving her off, worry hidden behind supportive masks, she'd been desperately sad. She'd held it together through the long journey back to her parents' house. She'd held it together as she'd promised them she was fine, before going to her room, locking the door and letting herself fall apart.

That had been eighteen hours ago.

Her phone beeped again and Bella tried not to cry, because she knew that it wasn't Chase. That he'd never want to see her again and her lips wobbled, and her jaw ached and her eyes leaked tears she'd thought she'd exhausted by now. It hurt so damn much. So much, that it ached to take a breath.

A knock sounded on her door and she wanted to ignore that too.

She knew this routine. Her parents would leave her to it. They always did. Because they knew she'd fix it eventually. But she just wasn't sure she could this time.

'Coming in,' her father warned before slowly opening the door.

Shocked, she threw the comforter over her head and did exactly what she'd accused Chase of doing: she hid.

She felt the bed dip from where he sat, just by her knees, and was torn between desperately wanting him to leave and wanting to hurl herself into his arms. But that was what Bea did. Bella wasn't that daughter. She was the daughter who didn't need things like that. And thinking it just made her want to cry again.

'It's a funny thing,' her father said, voice muffled by the covers. 'When you called so late the other night... I was almost happy.'

Bella blinked and risked peeking out from beneath the covers.

'Happy?' she couldn't help but ask, scarcely believing that when she'd been so miserable he'd been *happy*.

'No, not like that,' he quickly corrected. 'But I have waited *so* long for you to want to come home.'

Bella pushed up fully out from under the covers and sat against the headboard. 'I think I'm still missing something,' she confessed, anger beginning to well up from deep within where she'd barely ever looked. 'Because it sounds like you think I always had a choice,' she said, her chest aching from the fact that he didn't see, didn't *know* how hurt she'd been over the years.

It was as if everything that had happened with Chase, not the argument, not the hurt, but *before* then; the way he'd encouraged her not to smooth things over, but to make waves. To stand her ground. To have the arguments. He'd been right. He'd been preparing her for this.

Her father at least had the grace to look ashamed.

'You're talking about when Bea was sick.'

And that was it. Right there. Because in his mind, it wasn't about *her*. Bella. 'I'm talking *me*. About you sending me away.'

Her mother appeared in the hallway, leaning against the frame, watching her and her father.

Bella swallowed. 'And not just when I was younger. But last year too,' she said, the hurt bursting into life like a firework, blooming and mushrooming, and raining down a thousand different hurts over the last twenty years. And this time she couldn't hold back the tears, even if she'd tried.

'Why did you always have to send me away?'

'Oh sweetheart. We didn't want to. Ever. When Bea was sick,' his father tried, 'we didn't want you anywhere near the hospital. We didn't want you to see how scared we were, and we didn't know how to explain to you what was going on. We thought it best that you had some semblance of stability.'

'I thought it was because it was easier for you,' Bella confessed, her throat thick and swollen.

'God no, Bella. It was awful. We wanted you with us all the time. It was horrible without you when all we wanted was to see both our girls, all the time. We didn't want to let you out of our sight for a single second. But... it was a hospital. Bea was so sick. We thought it was best for you. But it wasn't. And we didn't like the way it made you.'

'The way it made me?'

Her mother nodded to her father, as if encouraging him to continue.

'We know how much you took on so that we could focus on Bea,' he said. 'We know you did that out of love, but when that became a habit for you, we worried about you. Worried that you'd lost your voice, your confidence.'

'You used to be so bossy. So determined,' her mother said with a laugh.

'But that was gone when you returned, and it was

our fault that we were just so relieved to have everyone back under one roof that we didn't challenge it, challenge you.'

'And what about after the wedding? Me going to France?'

Her mother looked at her father. 'We didn't want you to go, but we didn't want you to stay with all the press around the wedding.'

'I thought you were worried about the foundation,' Bella confessed.

'Not more than we were worried about you, Bella. God, I'm... so sorry you even thought that,' her father said, the tears in his eyes shocking Bella deeply. 'We love you. So much,' he said, choking on the words as her mother came to also sit on her bed, reaching out an arm to touch her.

'So, so, much,' her mother echoed.

Fissures turned to cracks, emotions flooding from the dam she'd kept them stopped up behind. They poured out of her, the debris of hurt and pain, moments clung to and remembered, released and free-flowing like a river to make space for new emotions, clean ones, not stagnant, but moving and changing and Bella took great gulps from it.

And her parents held her through it all, weathered them with her, as they'd always wanted and she'd always wanted.

She spent the entire day with her parents telling them about meeting the girls, about researching Chase. About starting work and how much she'd loved the people, how she'd pranked Chase and accessed his password. How she'd convinced a journalist to do a hit piece on a man who didn't deserve it, even though her mother was firmly on the side of Bad Bella. She wasn't willing to share about the studio and Chase's art because that was personal to him and she'd betrayed him enough, even though her father insisted that what had happened wasn't *entirely* betrayal.

It felt amazing to have her parents on her side. And she felt desperately sad for the little girl who'd missed that feeling, missed out on that support growing up – not for a single *second* begrudging the care and attention her sister had needed.

'That's a lot to have happened in three short months,' her mother observed.

Bella nodded, but it wasn't the end, because there was one last thing she wanted to ask her parents, still unsure of how far she could push their acceptance of her.

'I don't know what's going to happen with Chase

and the gallery, but... I do know that it's made me re-think what I want. For the future,' she said haltingly.

'You mean the foundation?' her father asked.

Bella nodded. 'I don't... I don't want to work there,' Bella said, realising just how much she didn't want that. She wanted something for herself, like Paige had. Something that made her shine, like Astrid had. Something that she worked hard for, like Sienna did. She couldn't very well go back to Nayak... but perhaps there was something else she could find.

'Of course, Bella. We...' Her mother looked to her father who nodded. 'We only wanted you to be part of it, if that was what you wanted. It was a selfish way of us keeping you, I suppose,' she said with a sad shrug. 'But, you need to find something for you,' her mother assured her, rubbing circles on her back.

Bea and her fiancé arrived just before dinner and Bea promptly stopped upon entering the kitchen.

'Oh my God, what happened?'

'What do you mean?' Bella asked on a hiccupped laugh, eyes puffy and red from crying and her mother wiping her own tears back.

'Did someone die?' Bea demanded.

'Hopefully only *Good Bella*,' her father said laughing and her sister stared at them all like they were mad.

'Here,' Derek, Bea's fiancé said to Bella, as he pressed a signed-for envelope into her hands. Bella frowned, tearing it open as her parents tried to explain to her sister what had happened.

You are invited to the opening of the Nayak New York, a contemporary gallery opening under the directorship of Chase Miller on behalf of Tejvir Nayak.

There must be some mistake, Bella thought, scanning the invitation that shouldn't have come to her. She wasn't on the mailing list. Nor did they send out invitations via signed-for mail. She turned the invitation over and saw, *Please Come,* written in Chase's handwriting.

'What's that?' her father asked.

'An olive branch, I think,' Bella replied and her father's eyes twinkled with a hope that matched what she felt in her heart.

* * *

Chase had never been more nervous in his entire life. Not when he'd first left for London, not his misplaced wedding day, not even his first exhibition.

'Are you okay, man? You look like you're gonna be sick,' Tej asked, genuinely concerned.

Chase nodded and rolled his shoulders. 'Fine.' The word turned into a cough when Tej slapped him on the back a little too hard.

'She's gonna show,' Tej said with a confidence Chase didn't feel.

He smiled and nodded as a smartly dressed couple passed them, the woman wearing nearly half a million in diamonds, and Chase couldn't have cared less. Ali came bounding up to them, her excitement irrepressible, no matter how much Maurice tried to iron it out. Chase was beginning to suspect that most of Maurice's attempts were for show, because they all secretly enjoyed her eternal optimism.

'Sascha just sold three paintings,' she whisper-hissed, as Maurice appeared at her side, with a *shhh* and a, 'Keep your voice down.'

Chase scanned the heads of the rich, famous and just lucky enough to be here at the opening of Nayak New York, and found Sascha staring wide-eyed at a man who seemed to be in the process of telling her about her own work. She caught his gaze and her expression read, WTF? Not about the guy, but about selling her paintings. He could read it because he knew it, that feeling.

Christ, he'd love to be at the beginning of this journey all over again. Would he do things differently? He wouldn't marry Annalise, he thought. He hadn't been right for Annalise and that had made her angry and resentful, not his fault, but not entirely *not* his fault either. He'd buried his head in the sand and ploughed on, ignoring the warning signs, just like Bella had said.

But not any more. He was making changes, starting tonight, whether Bella was here or not. But Christ, he hoped she would be.

Chester C. Carlton swanned past superiorly, ignoring Chase so hard it defeated the man's objective. When he'd found out what Bella had done, he hadn't bothered trying to correct the record. Because, in rereading the article, there was nothing in there that couldn't have been found without a bit of digging. Bella might have pointed him in the right direction, but the man was a gun loaded from four years before, because Chase had been moody, arrogant and dismissive of the way the art scene worked. The only way to change Chester's mind about Nayak was to bring him in, rather than alienate him more, so Chase smiled at the man who promptly squeaked and disappeared into the crowd.

'Making friends and influencing people?' Tej asked with a smirk.

'Always.'

'Your dad not making it tonight?'

'No, he's got a big job on in the morning. He wished us all good luck.'

Chase had gone to see him a few days ago. They'd sat down and finished the heart-to-heart that Bella had started here in the gallery. Chase had wanted to ask about the child he'd been before his mom had been hospitalised. Before he'd taken her dreams and made them his own. He'd been doing it for so long, he couldn't remember what had come before.

'You'd always wanted to paint. You didn't know it was a job, then. But yeah. Paint, pencils, you'd always been covered in some kind of colour. But Chase, she didn't say that to you to put pressure on you.'

'I know,' he'd replied and he did.

'She really struggled with it. How much to say, what to tell you, how much to love you, knowing that she wouldn't...'

His dad had trailed off and looked away until he'd got his feelings back under control. He'd wanted to tell him that he didn't have to do that. He didn't have to hide them from him, but he could see how uncomfortable it made him. Chase just had to make sure that he was different.

'She wanted to write you a letter. You know, open when you get married, open on your fiftieth,' his dad admitted. 'But she got too sick,' his father said with a nod. 'But honestly, the only thing she wanted for you was to be happy.'

And then it was Chase who could only nod.

'Are you ready?' Maurice asked, interrupting his thoughts and checking his watch.

Chase scanned the room, knowing that Bella hadn't entered yet, but secretly hoping that she might have. He looked to Tej, who winced in sympathy, knowing how much this meant to him.

Chase shrugged off the hope that Bella would be here and approached the centre of the gallery. Sascha excused herself from the man still pointing at her paintings and she and Zadzisai joined him. A hush descended over the packed gallery and the lights suddenly felt a lot harsher than they had a few minutes ago.

He wasn't going to miss this part of the job one bit, he thought, which made him smile and the first few people at the front smile back.

'I would like to thank you for coming here tonight and to officially welcome you to the Nayak New

York.' He paused for the applause that seemed requisite. 'I hope that you can now see that we have a special gallery here. One that shows art and joy from established talents, emerging talents and future artists in the making,' he said, speaking of the elementary school art, still in pride of place among household names like Zadzisai. 'Art should be accessible to everyone,' he said passionately. 'Art should be a place and an expression that explores who we are, how we are, how we feel and process the world around us, especially when that world becomes unrecognisable or hard to be in. All of the artists here do exactly that and I am proud and impressed by what the team at Nayak have managed to do,' he said, truly meaning it.

He caught a flash of blonde and tried to ignore the way that goosebumps danced out over his skin and his heart jerked in his chest.

'I consider myself incredibly lucky to have been a part of the first exhibition at Nayak and it will always be something that stays with me. However,' he said, taking a deep breath, 'I think we can all agree that I perhaps haven't been the *best* gallery director the art scene has ever known,' he admitted ruefully, and gentle laughter rippled out across the room. 'And if it hadn't been for the incredible team here, I'm not sure we would have made it.' He grimaced and turned to Tej. 'Sorry.'

Tej shrugged easily and more people laughed.

'But seeing the art world from this vantage has given me a greater understanding of why we do what we do and how important it is to do that with integrity and honesty. So, I'm going to be stepping down after this event and Nayak will be trialling a programme of visiting artists to assume the role of gallery director, with the support of the permanent members of staff, Maurice Bamboux as archivist and registrar, Alison Burberry as gallery assistant, Ye-Joon Yoo as gallery associate and,' he said, looking directly into the wide grey eyes staring up at him as Bella pushed her way to the front of the crowd, 'Bella Carmichael as communications director. Whoever is next, will be in their most capable hands.'

He clapped alongside the guests filling the gallery to the staff that had made this evening happen. The staff that had become the friends he'd not known he'd needed. But his eyes were only for Bella.

* * *

He was stepping down? Oh my God, what had she done?

Everyone was applauding, but panic broke out in

a sweat at the back of her neck as horror filled her chest. Chase must have seen it, because he frowned for a moment and then, with a comment about not wanting to steal the limelight, he handed over to Zadzisai and walked towards her, grasping her by the elbow and leading her away from the crowd, the gallery and out onto the street.

'You can't!' she cried the moment she hit the sidewalk. 'You can't leave. Oh, God, this is all my fault.' She felt wretched. No, she would fix this. 'You can change your mind,' she told him, not quite sure why he was smiling.

'Is that why you wanted me to come here? So that I'd see you quit?' she asked, the thought making her feel sick. *Oh God*. And she'd thought that he had wanted her there.

'Bella—'

'We'll speak to Tej, I'll explain everything,' she said, her hands twisting and barely able to meet his eye.

'Bella,' he tried again and she bit her lip.

He reached up and with his thumb, gently pressed her lip free from her teeth. He lifted her chin and drew her gaze to his.

'Bella. I'm okay. This is the right thing.'

'But if I hadn't tried to sabotage you—'

'Then I quite probably wouldn't have realised that this – gallery director – is absolutely the worst thing that I could possibly do with my life. I wasn't lying. I'm a terrible gallery director,' he admitted. *But why was he so happy about it?*

'I'm really confused, Chase,' she admitted helplessly.

'I'm not. For the first time in ages, I'm not confused at all,' he assured her. 'I know exactly what I want,' he insisted, with a heat that Bella felt flash over her from head to toe.

God, she wished she wasn't imagining things. It was all because she'd had to rush here when the car hit traffic just outside of the city.

Who knew there would be traffic? On a Friday night. Heading into Manhattan.

'I'm so sorry,' she said, feeling the emotions well up from deep within.

'You've said that, and you've said it enough. It's my turn now,' he said, cupping her jaw and she couldn't help but lean into the palm of his hand.

'You were right,' he confessed. 'I've been hiding. For quite a while now. It certainly didn't help my art, or my marriage, and I wasn't lying when I said the only reason there's a gallery opening is because of the team. And I'm happy to be stepping down. Because I'm going to try and start painting again.'

His jaw flickered in the light of the gallery bleeding onto the sidewalk, letting her know that it wasn't an easy decision.

'I... want to take some time,' he explained. 'Just find my feet with it again without the pressure or the weight of having to produce for exhibitions and shows and sales. I want to have *fun* with it. And I would never have seen that without you,' he explained, her heart easing, knowing that she'd done something for him. That she'd helped after hindering him so much.

'You were willing to show me what I'd been hiding from, no matter what it cost you,' he said, reaching for her hands and pulling her against his body. Her hands pressed against his chest, her palm against the racing of his heart.

'You were willing to risk your job, and what we shared, to show me that, and I don't know how to thank you. I'm not saying that my creative block has suddenly lifted and I can magically work again, but I want to try and work through it now. For me. To find what kind of artwork I want to do *now*.'

Pride and happiness shot right through her.

'But you need to come back to the gallery.'

'I'm not sure, Chase. What I did, it was unforgive-able. And Tej—'

'Tej knows. He wants to know how you got my password. I want to know how you did the salt,' he said, leaning in with a smile, as he seemed to breathe her in with a satisfied sigh.

'He knows? And he's okay with that?'

'As long as it doesn't happen to the next gallery director, I think he's going to be fine,' Chase assured her.

'Are you... going back to England?' she asked, fearing that he'd return to his studio there.

'Nope. I'm going to stay right here,' he said, bringing her closer to him. 'Where I can keep an eye on you. I'm going to work at the studio and stay in New York.'

She looked up at him, his lips barely an inch from hers.

'Then—'

'Fuck's sake, Bella, can you stop asking me questions and let me kiss you now?'

She squeaked at his confession and he laughed.

'I'm trying to tell you that I love you. That I made a monumental mistake letting you go. And that I'm devastated that I for one minute made you think that you were unwanted because you made a mistake. So together, perhaps we can make mistakes and learn from them and love each other despite them? Because Bella Carmichael, Good Bella, Bad Bella, whatever way you want to be, I am hopelessly, irrefutably, incontrovertibly in love with you.'

She gasped in shock and Chase took advantage and pulled her into a kiss that was sure to get them arrested for lewd conduct. After a heady two minutes, Chase pulled back, both of them a little breathless and a lot happy.

'Well?'

'Well, what?' Bella asked. 'You want marks out of ten?' she asked with a laugh.

'No, Carmichael, I want to hear that you love me too.'

'Oh, yeah that. Maybe. We'll have to see how that goes,' she said, and pulled him in for the first of many, many millions of kisses to come.

EPILOGUE

THREE MONTHS LATER...

Bella looked down at the message from Chase on her phone as the cabbie turned a corner, his head, and improbably, an arm, half out the window to yell at a cyclist, a pedestrian and a child all in one go.

The summer heat was building hard and fast in New York and as a consequence everyone was out on the streets dressed in as few items of clothing as possible. A part of her yearned to head back Upstate, to feel the cool breeze and shaded trees of the forests by her parents' house, knowing that Chase would love it up there, but work had kept them both in New York for the last few months.

Meet me at the studio?

She reread the message again. Chase had been... not *secretive* about his work, but definitely private and she understood. It was so important that he be allowed to experiment and play with his creativity without the fear of any kind of critical eye. Not that hers would have been critical. But he'd needed to figure out what he liked and wanted from his art before he thought of anyone else. He deserved that.

And if she were honest, she'd been kept so busy by the new gallery director from Sweden, that she'd barely had time herself. The twelve-month placements for visiting artists to step into the lead role at the Nayak had been a great idea – and it still was – but it meant a lot of scrabbling to catch up, to adapt to different personalities and wants and needs. But it had cemented her and Maurice's relationship more than anything else.

'Don't be silly,' Chase had said, laughing whenever she'd complained about it, 'you love every minute of it.'

And he was right.

She'd really found her feet – when she wasn't being distracted by the competing roles of trying to save the gallery and pranking the current director – in a role that incorporated all the things she loved –

art, communication, plans. And perhaps just a little bit of high-level manipulation.

The cab pulled into the alley beside the studio. She paid and got out, checking her phone one more time before she went in to see a picture from Paige on the WhatsApp group of her, Olly and Casper – the dog that had adopted them, rather than the other way round. Hearts and 'aww's had followed from the others and Bella smiled, delighted that Paige had found her happiness with a man who loved her as much as she deserved.

She love bombed the message with more emojis than strictly necessary.

If the girls had been amazing before, they'd been incredible in the last few months. The fast friendship had turned into something more. Ride or die best friends who had turned into a family she couldn't bear to think of living without.

Her parents and sister had been happy for her and Chase, and for her new job, but the girls? They'd been thrilled, they'd championed, screamed and cried their fierce support of her, and it had just made everything incredible.

She and Astrid were meeting up soon – Bella finally agreeing to a yoga class that didn't require losing half her body weight in sweat, on the proviso that they went for cupcakes afterwards. (Red velvet for Bella and fondant fancies for Astrid.)

She'd caught up with Sienna just the other night, meeting her 'sort of' step-daughter, Melanie, over the small phone screen, the young teenager's smiling face shining full of love for Si which was a delight to see. But she ached to see her friends in real life.

Which, of course, she would do because in just a few months' time the entire Karma Club would all be meeting up for what would be, if she and Paige had anything to do with it, the most amazing wedding anyone had ever seen!

Talk of weddings no longer hurt so much. Not now. Olly, Bella truly believed, had always meant to be with Paige. And she... well, she had found a man she'd not have even been able to dream of, but one who was perfect for her in every single way.

After firing off a very quick message to Paige about possible activities for the wedding, Bella slipped her phone into her bag beside the copy of her new book.

First Sun Tzu, and now Machiavelli? You're the only woman I know who'd have political treaties on the same bedside table as erotic romances.

She laughed every time she thought of Chase's reaction to seeing it.

So it was that when he appeared in the doorway, he found her with a smile on her lips full of heat and affection.

'Mr Miller,' she said, a tease in her tone. 'How kind of you to make time for me in your busy schedule.'

'Ms Carmichael, so good of you to come,' he said, his tongue in his cheek. 'If you would?'

She eyed the dark strip of silk in his hands, the blindfold making her blush almost instinctively now, not that she thought that *that* was what she was here for this time.

Turning, she allowed him to tie the silk over her eyes and let him guide her towards the entrance of the studio. She didn't need to ask him questions, or to know what was going on, because she trusted him. She trusted that this was what he needed or wanted and she would happily give that to him if it was within her power to do so because she loved him utterly and completely.

He paused on the threshold of the studio, and she felt him turn to face her. She raised her face to where she imagined him to be and pulse points around her body throbbed in anticipation. His lips claimed hers, gentle, but probing, slow, but carnal just the same, his fingers flexing against her shoulder and throat.

He mmmd against her lips as he gently ended the kiss, and then laughed.

'You taste like red velvet cake,' he teased.

She shrugged a shoulder. 'Maurice thought we needed a bit of a sugar boost to get through the afternoon.'

'Maurice did, huh?'

'Mmm hmm,' she sounded, because if she didn't use her words, it wasn't technically a lie.

The sound of his knowing laughter skimmed over her as he led her into the space where he had spent an enormous amount of time over the last three months. And that time had been more than she could possibly ever have imagined.

She would never have guessed that getting to know Chase would mean getting to know herself too. That was the gift of their love. That it had made her life rich, full, and something joyous as she took the time to get to know *her* likes and dislikes, wants and wishes just as much as his. And together, it was an exciting, thrilling and adventurous journey she never wanted to end.

* * *

Chase brought Bella to stand in what she assumed was the centre of the studio, his heartbeat racing, despite how ludicrous it was to be nervous about this. But she would be the first person to see it. Perhaps the only person, depending on how he felt about it once she had. But still. It was the first piece he'd *completed* in nearly two years. Oh, he'd started hundreds of other projects and pieces, but this was the first one he felt was done. The first one that he was proud of.

'Are you ready?' he asked, not having to tell her what for, or explain himself. She knew him. All of him. The bits that he found hard to talk about and the bits that he was trying to change. And that she loved them was still a little surprising to him.

'Always,' Bella replied and he removed the blindfold and stood to where he could see her, not the painting he had finished yesterday. Because he wanted to see *her*.

Blinking in the light that was filling the space, she focused her attention on the huge canvas in front of her.

'*Oh.*' The word fell from Bella's lips as she walked closer to his painting, taking in the sheer size and magnitude of it.

Months before, he'd wondered what he'd see if she were to look at one of his paintings. And now as he watched a myriad expressions pass across her features, he was glad that it was this one. He was glad that he had waited. Because this piece was one that meant so much to him. More than all of his others combined.

Because this had been *hard*. He'd worked at it, tweaked and teased and pulled it, dragged it kicking and screaming onto the canvas and it had been worth the effort, worth the fight. Because of what he saw in Bella's eyes as she turned to him, the sheen glistening like starlight.

'It's *us*,' she said with a gasp, her fingers pressed to her lips. 'The girls.'

'Yes,' he said, hiding the twist of relief that she'd seen what he'd wanted her to see. It wasn't figurative and not even remotely portraiture. But he'd hoped that it was expressive of the powerful forces that had brought Bella into his life.

The large whirlwind slash of burgundy for Paige, the powerful, eye-catching dark Prussian blue line merging how he felt about Astrid with a representation of her, which he knew that Astrid would understand. The circular weave of Sienna, more cerise than her namesake, but perfect for the woman he'd met several times now since that first fateful encounter at the pre-opening for the gallery.

And at the centre of it all, for him, was Bella, grey brushstrokes melting into gold, melting into white. Her power, her love, her passion, the sense of humour she was beginning to embrace, the strength of her self-acceptance and her acceptance of *him*, he'd poured everything about her into it.

'It's you,' he said. 'And everything that brought you to me.'

There were other paintings, not quite finished, for other things that he still struggled to find the words for. But he'd gone back to where it all started. He'd gone back to painting his feelings, just the way his mother had told him and the way he'd told little Joseph that day in the art gallery. And all his feelings... they were about her. And this was just the beginning, the story of how she had come into his life.

'It's incredible,' she said, her gaze returning back to the painting, searching for and finding new things to see in it.

'Yes. Incredible,' he said, not taking his eyes off her for a single second, seeing all the wonder and fascination that he'd hoped for and more.

She turned back to him, love shimmering in her gaze and he couldn't help himself. He closed the distance between them in short strides and they came together in a clash of tongues and teeth and beating hearts and searching hands.

His desire for her was endless and he backed her up against the table holding his art supplies, her body like fire – twisting and burning – beneath his fingers.

'Christ, you undo me,' he admitted, the confession raw on his throat.

She looked up at him, eyes serious, but bright, intent, passionate and her hands explored his body, pulling the shirt from his jeans, and placing her palms against his stomach, skin to skin.

She pressed forward to kiss him but he leaned back, not yet full enough of her beauty. He loved her flush and wanton. *Bella Tempted*. But that was a different painting, one he hadn't even remotely finished exploring yet.

And as he bit back his smile, Bella whimpered a little.

'Please,' she all but begged.

It was the only time he'd ever let her do such a thing, because outside of this, he'd never let her beg for a single damn thing. He'd give her whatever it was she asked for and more. Oh, the power she had over him, if she only knew it.

'Only,' he said, leaning forward to whisper in her ear, 'if you call me Daddy and tell me to—'

His words were kissed from his lips before he could finish the sentence, and they fell together in a tumble of giddy laughter and frantic touches, melted hearts and hot words, and a deep abiding love that would come to define the rest of their lives together.

* * *

MORE FROM PIPPA ROSCOE

The next book in the Karma Club Series, *The Puck Stops Here*, is available to order now here: www.mybook.to/PuckStopsHereBackAd

ABOUT THE AUTHOR

Pippa Roscoe writes sexy, emotionally driven romances and loves every happy ending in each of her books. After university, Pippa spent four thrilling years working in television. After jumping into publishing and spending five years as an editor, she finally decided to follow her dream of writing and left London to move to Norfolk.

Sign up to Pippa Roscoe's mailing list for news, competitions and updates on future books.

Visit Pippa Roscoe's website: www.pipparoscoe.com

Follow Pippa on social media here:

f facebook.com/PippaRoscoeAuthorPage

◯ instagram.com/pipparoscoeauthor

Boldwood
EVER AFTER
x♡x♡

JOIN BOLDWOOD'S
**ROMANCE
COMMUNITY**
FOR SWEET AND
SPICY BOOK RECS
WITH ALL YOUR
FAVOURITE
TROPES!

SIGN UP TO OUR
NEWSLETTER

HTTPS://BIT.LY/BOLDWOODEVERAFTER

Boldwood

Boldwood Books is an award-winning fiction publishing company seeking out the best stories from around the world.

Find out more at www.boldwoodbooks.com

Join our reader community for brilliant books, competitions and offers!

Follow us
@BoldwoodBooks
@TheBoldBookClub

Sign up to our weekly deals newsletter

https://bit.ly/BoldwoodBNewsletter